Somewhere In Between

Nic Bryan

To Mrs Smith,

Your encouragement gave me purpose. Without it, I would have ended up as an accountant or something. Not that there's anything wrong with that. I just think numbers are hard and words are beautiful.

"What a wee little part of a person's life are his acts and his words! His real life is lead in his head, and is known to none but himself. All day long, and every day, the mill of his brain is grinding, and his thoughts ... not those other things are his history. His acts and his words are merely the visible thin crust of his world..."

- Mark Twain

CHAPTER ONE

The Family Roast

Why is it that something trivial can be burnt into your brain for eternity, but the things that are supposed to matter just slip through your ears like smoke? For example, he could tell you that a person was 14% more likely to die on their birthday, but ask him when his mother's birthday was?

No clue.

It was some time ago now, but Tom could remember sitting at their circular dining table and he knew it must have been a Sunday night because Georgia, his mother, had slow cooked what looked like half a cow, and there was no way she would ever do that any other night. She had set it in front of them all, telling the table that she had marinated it not *once*, but *twice*. The cotton placemat in front of Tom bunched under his plate as if the table felt uncomfortable wearing it, like a teenage boy wearing a suit for the first time.

When Tom looked up, he couldn't help but stare across the table. It was as though he were looking into the gaping maw of some terrible beast, the kind you really only see in low-budget science fiction films. He remembered feeling like the teeth could swallow him whole. They were yellowing, the result of a lifetime of poor dental hygiene and a largely carnivorous diet.

"Do I have something in my teeth?" his father had asked when he noticed his eldest son's stare, stopping mid chew like a feasting lion interrupted.

"Oh, just a small piece of basil or something I think."

Simon, his father, flicked his meaty tongue across his rotting, but otherwise clean, teeth. "Did I get it?"

"Hmm. Nah still something there."

Simon dropped his knife and fork with a clatter and peeled back his lips. "Where is it?"

Tom gave him instructions and Simon proceeded to claw a nail between his canine and front tooth.

"There?"

"No, the other side."

Funny, how he could care so much about having a little piece of salad between his teeth, but he hasn't bothered to brush them since 1985. Just as Georgia sat down to join them, her phone rang and she'd jumped up and scurried from the room.

Almost immediately, their father had slid his plate from the table and slithered to the adjacent lounge, cradling his dinner, looking from one son to the other, as if daring them to stop him.

Tom had watched him until he heard the sound of the TV blaring, and then he picked up his knife and fork and turned to his brother.

"What do you think the best way to dispose of a dead body would be? Like, how do you really do it without getting caught?"

Tom enjoyed these types of conversations — the nonsensical ones. He knew what it would sound like to an outsider. Bizarre. Weird. Even disturbing. But it wasn't like he walked up to people on the street and surveyed them, was it?

'Umm, excuse me ma'am, but if you ever had to, would you hide a dead body in your basement or a forest?'

No, conversations like this, amongst your own people, your brethren, were harmless.

Tom began to dissect his meat, smothering it with gravy and stabbing it with his fork, waiting for Danny's answer.

His brother did not disappoint him. Not that he even considered for a moment he would.

"Well, I guess I'd do it Breaking Bad style," Danny said as if he were contemplating a rather difficult algebraic problem.

"Body in the barrel type deal?" quizzed Tom.

"Yeah, like if there's no body, there's no evidence is there?" Dan said, tapping his temple, his knife point coming dangerously close to Tom's eye socket.

"I don't think you've thought it through, though. How would you know what chemicals to buy or where to buy them? You do a Google search for that information and you're done. The cops are gonna search your computer."

"Well, how would you do it?" Dan asked, waving his fork in the air and flicking little drops of gravy onto the tablecloth.

Tom had his answer ready.

"I think I'd probably just load up the body in the back of my car and speed towards a deserted lake. Wouldn't be a bad way of doing it. If I had a Ute or something, people would look at me suspiciously, but my car would be practically invisible."

"Finally, having a crappy car has paid off for you," Dan winked at him and then looked thoughtful, "Do you think you're going to be able to lift the body into the boot, though?"

Dan raked his eyes over his brother's long, thin limbs.

"Hey! Don't look at me like that! You know what they say: when the adrenaline is pumping through your body, you can do amazing things. Also, it depends: Who died?"

Dan laughed. "A 6 ft 7, 200-kilogram rugby player."

"Oh, I've got no chance then."

"You could burn it instead." Dan offered.

"What? That's the stupidest thing I've ever heard. What are you going to do about the *smell*?" scoffed Tom.

"Put a roast in the oven."

They both looked down at their plates.

"Do you think the smell of a roast would cover the smell of a burning body?" asked Tom.

Dan threw a glance over his shoulder, carefully looking into the kitchen before answering slowly.

"Yes. I do."

"What on earth are you guys talking about?"

Georgia walked into the room and did that thing that mothers do when they pretend that they've got no idea what you're talking about even though they've been eavesdropping on you for the last twenty minutes.

"Nothing. Have we told you how beautiful you look today? Please don't murder us."

"I won't if you stop having inappropriate conversations at the kitchen table."

Tom stood up and she and Danny looked at him in confusion. "Come on, you heard her Danny. We'd better take this to the laundry."

Georgia rolled her eyes and pulled on his arm. "We are eating dinner as a *family*."

Tom's eyes slid to his father. "Are we?"

"Stop it."

"Besides, you were yammering away on the phone to your pal Mel about the latest gossip doing the rounds at Thursday night yoga," said Tom.

"Stop."

The smile that had graced Danny's face moments ago was gone. Did the mood of a room turn like the weather in other houses, or was it just theirs?

Their father had still been within earshot, but unless a corpse was rolled out at his feet, his eyes were not going to leave the TV. It was cricket season, and he had forgotten any other purpose he had in life. Despite his hulking frame, he blended into the furniture of their lives like a beige doily.

Not for the first time, Tom had wondered not *why* his parents were together, but *what* had even brought them together in the first place. It wasn't like their mother was a lively ball of fun, but he thought sometimes he saw a version of her that was different to what she showed them all. Maybe one that was a little rebellious.

It was hard though, to imagine a different version of your parents. Maybe that was the role of all parents, to be eternally fixed in stone in the eyes of their children. But he wanted to know: was there a better version of his father in the 1980s? One that danced to Duran Duran and had a mullet? Surely, he couldn't have always been such an... adult.

Maybe it was their fault. Maybe they'd forced Simon to morph into a parent and he'd never really known what that looked like. In that light, Tom guessed he should feel sorry for his father. But there's a lot of times in life when you know you should feel sorry for someone, but well… you just plain don't.

Particularly when they up and walk out of your lives.

God, that sounded so dramatic, didn't it? But it's the truth. Tom had even less sympathy now for his father than he did six months ago when he'd left them not long after that dinner. Maybe that's why that night was burnt into his brain. Maybe it had been the last meal they ate together as a family—their proverbial Last Supper. And Tom had spent the entire time talking absolute garbage.

Tom really couldn't recall the last time he'd seen his dad. Was it only six months ago? It felt like it had been decades. One minute he was there, the next he'd vanished. Great magic trick—maybe it was actually their father that knew how to commit the perfect crime.

But Tom wasn't really all that surprised. Tom was pretty sure the man was a cardboard cut-out, a mail-order father. He wondered if Simon knew it, too.

It was weird, for sure though. The house had been different ever since. Quieter. But also lighter, like it had been holding its breath. But really, it wasn't a big deal. His father would come back. Or he wouldn't. It's not like he was dead or anything. He just needed a break.

From them.

His family had become too much.

And that was fine. Totally fine.

Tom just wished he could convince Danny. Even now, the kid talked about it incessantly.

"But how do you know if he's ok?" Danny asked him for the millionth time as they sat in the kitchen eating breakfast. "He could be anywhere. Anything could have happened to him."

"Nothing's happened to him," Tom said flatly.

"And how do you know that?"

"Because I just know. He just wanted to get away. Mum says it's a good thing. He's finally doing something for himself."

Tom had no idea what she'd meant by that and saying it had felt strange in his mouth, but Danny seemed somewhat appeased.

"So, he's just… up and left?" Danny whispered as their mother joined them in the kitchen and Tom knew it wasn't really a question.

It was almost as if they were quiet because the kitchen itself was quiet. The fridge had stopped its usual humming. The kettle, which was usually whistling frantically at this time of morning, was off.

Georgia shook her head. "No, no, it's not like that. He didn't just *leave*. I'm sure he just needs some time."

"Hasn't he had enough time already? It's been six months," said Danny.

"I hope the prick never comes back," said Tom.

Georgia looked at him. "You don't mean that."

"Yes, I do. What good was he? What did he ever do for us?"

"He's your dad."

"Only by title." Tom scoffed.

"If it were me, would you be saying such things?" she asked.

Tom shrugged.

"Shut up, Tom," Danny said, with as much vehemence as Danny could ever muster. "I'll just try calling him one more time."

He'd said that a few times before.

Danny pulled his phone out of his pocket and waited expectantly, jiggling his foot against the floor. After it rang out, he took the phone off his ear, pressed the number again, and the routine repeated.

Two, three times.

Danny sniffed. "Not answering."

"Really? No way," said Tom, rolling his eyes.

"Shut up Tom," snapped Georgia.

Tom shrugged and focused his attention on the large framed Australian homestead on the wall. It was painted in a myriad of dark greens, yellows, and a dirty brown. He often stared at it and his verdict was the same it had always been: it was the ugliest picture he'd ever seen. If he owned a house, he would never have such hideous things on display. He'd just have Danny's artworks lining the walls. Danny had never let their parents hang his art. But Tom knew Danny would let him. Danny could never deny him anything.

"Who would have thought it could be this easy to disappear entirely?" said Tom.

Danny ignored him and turned to their mother. "Did you know?"

"Know what?" she asked carefully.

"That he was going to leave?"

She looked between both boys. "I'm... not surprised."

"I'm not surprised either," added Tom. "He's a spineless prick. It was the easiest option, wasn't it? To get up and leave. No questions asked. It makes perfect sense. Why have the fallout, why face the music if there's another option?"

"Oh my God, shut up." Danny threw his hands out. "Why do you have to say every single thing that comes into your head?"

"Well, I'm just being honest, telling it how it is."

"I'm not saying you're not right. But shut up, man." Danny shook his head and walked out of the room. He always did that. Just walked away when he'd had enough. It sounded like healthy thing to do, and in comparison to what Tom did it probably was, but it drove Tom up the wall.

Tom snapped upright. He could have sworn he heard his back crack like a whip. He called out into the hallway after Danny.

"Why? Why do I always have to shut up? We're always shutting up. We can never say *anything*." Tom rounded on Georgia. "I'm sick of it. The old dog has gone, and I'm going to start saying whatever I like!

Crap!

Bumhole!

Shit!"

He lost his nerve on that last one, almost whispering it.

Georgia looked at him sternly. "Tom, look, let's just get through this. Let's keep things normal."

He didn't like how she said it. Like he had no choice in the matter, like he was still a little kid, obligated to follow her rules. There was no point pretending that he wasn't still under her tyranny. He wondered if there would ever be a time when her rule would end.

She followed Danny's lead and walked out of the room. Tom had the distinct feeling it was to avoid hearing his reply. She must have known he'd have one.

He always did.

He whispered it to the kettle. "You mean pretend. Let's *pretend* things are normal."

CHAPTER TWO

A Hacksaw and an Ice Pick

With one deft flick of the wrist, cerulean, cyan, azure smeared across the canvas. Flecks of vermillion and canary yellow began to smudge the canvas, almost carelessly, as if they had been chosen purely on a whim. But Tom soon saw that they added depth to the scene, and suddenly, it became more than some pretty colours. A world was beginning to form; a world seen through the eyes of his brother. How powerful that was, to be able to capture how you see the world. Or even to amplify it, change it—share how you wanted it, dreamed it, to look. Anytime Tom had tried, what he saw ended up looking like a giant mud puddle. How was it that you could add all these beautiful blues and purples and reds and they end up coalescing to form a sludgy mess?

That's how it had always been, though. His brother had always had the way of it. Things came easily for Danny. He had grace coming out the wazoo. It oozed out of his pores; his lithe body and nimble hands moved almost reflexively. He could master a sport in one session. And his brain was just as quick. He could have been a surgeon, a lawyer. Heck, he could have been a movie star. Tom hated to admit it, but his little brother was starting to look like he'd just stepped off a film set. Unlike Tom, Danny had grown into his body and his nose. It was like it had been architecturally designed to fit his face. His own nose... well, it had *character*. His eyebrows were also becoming an issue. They seem to have tripled in thickness in the last few years.

Danny's were light and feathery, like the wings of a baby bird.

It was an absolute tragedy: to be compared to a younger sibling and found wanting.

But you know what topped it off? The thing that really made it truly heartbreaking? Danny was nice. To his very core. The kind of niceness that makes it impossible to hate. His smile was like sunshine peeking through a cloudy day while it rained puppies and lollipops.

But he didn't envy his brother.

Every day, he was thankful he wasn't Danny.

Tom watched him paint in silence. What he liked most, wasn't watching the painting come to life. It was watching Danny as he worked. Straight-backed, a frown knitting his forehead, his eyes not quite seeing his surroundings. If he could bottle that and drink it, he'd be happy for the rest of his days, he was sure of it. Pure, unadulterated creativity. There was nothing else on this Earth as powerful as that.

"Are you a wizard?" Tom asked. "No one is this talented by birth."

Danny rolled his eyes, prodding him softly with the end of the brush. "It's not natural talent. I practise. 10,000 hours. Now can you leave? It's not the same, painting when someone else is around."

"10,000 hours?" asked Tom. He leaned back against the pergola as if Danny hadn't just told him his presence was no longer welcome.

"It's like a proven—but not really proven—rule that it takes 10,000 hours of practise to become good at something. So, really, if you wanted to paint, all you have to do is start putting the time in." Danny said, exchanging his brush for a palette knife.

"Mmm. Nah."

Tom stretched and looked across their backyard. Well, lack of it. Their family home had a great setup for Danny's painting. Like most of their house, the back porch was run down, bits of timber stuck out of the railings and the deck was thirsty for paint. So, it didn't matter if Danny made a mess. No one cared. They were all united by one thing: they just wanted to keep him happy.

"You never stick at anything."

"Ow," said Tom, partly because of the personal attack, and partly because a sliver of wood had dug into his bicep.

"Well, it's true. I wonder what you could do if you put your time and energy into something. I bet you could rule the world if you wanted to."

"Is it a compliment that you just compared me to a dictator?"

"It was a massive compliment." Danny paused. "Based on me pointing out your biggest flaw."

Tom laughed. "You think I'm lazy?"

"You know you are."

Danny was the only person in the world he would let talk to him like this.

"Eh. I guess. I can't really be bothered arguing the point."

"Remember how into music you were? What happened to that?"

Tom picked at the splinter he'd finally managed to dislodge from his arm.

"I just… it's not the right time. I feel like I need some life experience. How do I write love songs if I've never been in love?"

It was a lie. He was pretty sure he was in love, but it was early days. Danny didn't need to know about the girl.

"So, you're saying you need something to happen in your life before you can stop being lazy?"

Danny had not stopped and turned to face him during their entire conversation. Tom winked at him, realising afterwards that there was absolutely no point in the gesture.

"Exactly."

"You realise that if you got up off your arse and started doing stuff, things would be happening in your life."

"Not the kind of things I'm looking for. I want great things. Wild things. Not of this Earth things."

"That's not how life works, Tom."

Tom scoffed. "And you would know. You've had about as much life experience as a moth."

Danny frowned at the painting like it, rather than Tom, had offended him.

"Well, that's not really my fault, is it? I can't help it."

For about the thousandth time in his life, Tom wished he could swallow his words. If Danny was known for his brains and good looks, then Tom was known for his big, fat mouth. Danny got migraines. These were not once-a-year, sleep-it-off headaches. They were invisible battering rams storming his brain every few days, holding him hostage. They'd forced Danny to give up so much, miss out on so many experiences, and Tom just had to be stupid enough to remind him of that. Sometimes, he swore he and his mouth were two different entities.

The migraines had started when Danny was twelve. They were so bad, Tom was terrified that one day he'd come home and find Danny slumped in the bathroom, colder than the tiles, his brains splattered against the wall because his head had actually exploded.

Puberty, the doctors said. *Unlucky, but the most common cause. Normally, kids grow out of it.*

Tom didn't know how normal it was though, to catch your little brother googling lobotomies. He had been dead serious about it, too.

"Tom, it's okay, look—it can actually be done."

It had been a few years ago. Danny had been sitting at his outdated computer, his gangling body hunched over the desk. Tom realised that now, on the cusp of his eighteenth birthday, Danny was probably bigger than him. But Tom remembered him then, still a kid really, his eyes bright like a kid on Christmas morning. Seeing the alarm on Tom's face, Danny had hastened to reassure him.

"Obviously, I'm not going to do it myself, you know. I'm not going to go in there with a hacksaw and an ice pick. But there's got to be a doctor out there that will do it. I just need *something* to release the pressure. But I can't find anyone. I can't find a doctor on the Internet anywhere. I can't tell mum and dad. They won't understand."

They understood better than he thought. No child can imagine what it feels like to be the parent of a sick kid. Tom could, though. Because he saw it all. The strained conversations. The silence. The heads in hands. All they wanted was to make him better. Danny had been prescribed enough medications to fill a pharmacy.

Every single one had failed.

Sometimes, they worked for a little while. That made it worse, though— thinking that things could actually be better. He'd take the new pill when the migraine started and smile when it started to kick in. Tom saw him kiss the carpet once, shaking with relief that *this* time, he could get through it and maybe *next* time would be better too.

But eventually, Danny would become immune to the medication. The migraine would hit and under his sheet of freckles, his face would turn a misty white. Not because of the initial pain, but the realisation that the drugs had stopped working. He would retreat in terror to his room, soon to be strangled by the drum that had begun to beat in his head. He would crumble, but never cry. Crying made the pain worse. Eventually, the doctor gave him Oxycontin. Pretty extreme, especially for a young guy, but they were out of options.

"Danny, I have to tell you—Oxycontin is a powerful drug. You cannot take it more than every ten hours." The doctor's face was pulled tight across his bones, like it would soon give up and gape and sag like dough. Tom and his mother were both there that first time Danny got prescribed the Oxy. His mum sat upright in the consultation chair next to Dan and Tom hung about the door, as if he didn't know whether to stay or go. In the end, he stayed.

Georgia interjected. "Danny will be fine. He is not like that."

Tom could see that the doctor had to consciously stop himself from rolling his eyes. He ignored her and turned back to pressing the magical keys on his medicine computer. Just a few minutes of tap, tap, tap, and presto! The keys to the kingdom of drugs came shooting out the printer.

"I can't fill your prescription any earlier than once a month, so if you don't follow the dosage, you will run out."

Georgina ruffled in her chair and her thoughts were plastered all over her face. *My son comes from a good family and in good families, we don't take drugs. I'd say this is totally unnecessary, but I can't ignore the fact that without trying something drastic my son might DO something drastic.*

Tom didn't really think he would, though. Danny was like the Virgin Mary. He was terrified of that rattling white bottle he carried home from the chemist. He placed it on his bedside table like it was some voodoo token he'd found deep in the Amazon. It was a museum piece—something to look at but never to touch.

Tom sat next to him on his crumpled bed the first time he took it— which was the next day. One whole day without a migraine. Tom was almost angry at him. Seriously? One day. Give yourself a break kid.

Danny's arm was shaking when he lifted the little white pill to his mouth, but it could just have been from the pain.

One pill.

One pill every 10 hours would slowly trickle life back into his broken body: poison to drain away the poison inside his head.

After twenty minutes of watching Danny rock back and forth on his perched legs, Tom saw the tension begin to ease from his body. The Oxy washed over him in a bittersweet shower; he stopped rocking and sat back, his head making a soft thump against the bedroom wall. Danny let out a deep sigh like he'd sunk into a hot bath—like a lifetime of grief and suffering and hurt had been funnelled from his body.

Looking towards the ceiling, Tom felt as though he should be able to see Danny there, up in the air as some sort of ghost, disconnected and utterly free of the skin and blood and veins that had trapped him for so many years.

A heavy breath escaped from Tom's own body. He realised that he too had deflated. Maybe he didn't share Danny's physical pain, but he had some part of it inside him.

Tom wished it ended there. He wished that was Danny's story. "He took some little white pills and everything got better. He started going to school every day, and that was that."

But things never end in a nice, neat little package. Happy endings aren't really a thing.

Pipes screeched from the bathroom as Danny turned the faucet on all the way. It was a few weeks after he'd first taken the Oxy. They had all kind of screwed up a bit, because no one was keeping a close eye on how much he was taking. It would have been pretty hard to do that though, because he was only supposed to take it when he was in pain. How were they supposed to measure his pain when he was always in pain?

"Hey Dan, I'm coming in. I need to piss."

Dan had given a muffled reply, and Tom wrenched open the bathroom door. The violence of his entry shocked Danny and the little pill in his hand jumped like a jellybean into the sink. Fingers scraped the porcelain bowl, and they both watched as it bounced down into the silver grate.

Danny screamed. He actually *screamed*.

"Dan! Calm down!"

Tom grabbed him by the shoulders. Danny swung around snarling, shoving him hard in the chest. Caught by surprise, Tom stumbled backward, and his heel met the top of the stairs. Instinctively, he'd shuffled his feet to try to right his balance, but his toes met only air and he went down, down, down. Pain seared through his shoulder as he took most of the impact on his side and back until his head collided with their dad's golf bag at the bottom of the stairs.

It was hard.

That's what he remembered thinking as pain shot through his skull. *Whatever I've hit is harder than my own head.* And he was right of course. Golf clubs aren't made of soft cheese.

Taking the stairs three at a time, Dan almost toppled down them himself in his effort to reach Tom. He leaped to the bottom of the stairs and prodded Tom all over his body to make sure he wasn't dead, even though he was swearing with more gusto than he ever had in his life. Blood dribbled down his head, pooled into his eye socket, beginning a heavy pattering onto the floorboards.

"Oh my God, oh my God, your head! I've never seen so much blood in my life. It's everywhere, we will never get this clean again. Mum's gonna kill us. Are you hurt bad? Oh God, please don't die!"

"I love how the first thing you say is 'Mum's gonna kill us', not 'are you okay Tom?'"

With a grunt, Tom pulled himself to a sitting position. It seemed important that he did that for some reason. Maybe to show Danny that he wasn't hurt too badly.

"Forget about my head, it's my shoulder."

After the first tidal waves of pain, Tom had grappled to regain control of himself, but lost it as he looked down at his shoulder. Where the dent of muscle used to be, all that remained was bone. Nothing had ever felt more wrong in his life.

"Faaaaaark. Fark. Fark. Fix it. Put it back in. I'm begging you."

"That's what she said." Dan must have been on the edge of hysteria because after he said it, he looked like he'd just sworn at his grandmother.

"I'm not kidding Danny. You've got to put it back in."

Danny crept over, looming over him.

"Just grab it and like hook it back on or something. Like it's a coat hanger. It'll be fine, just do it quickly."

Deep down, Tom knew what he was asking was ridiculous, but the pain had hijacked his mental faculties. The bone was staring at Danny, puckering and shiny through the thin layer of skin. He stared and stared at it.

Tom read his thoughts. "Just don't think about it. It's just a picture that needs to go back on its hook. Just lift it up, and slot it back on." Danny started shaking his head frantically and Tom sighed. "Well, you'd better call an ambulance then."

"What—what should I tell them?"

"The truth—" Tom said through gritted teeth. He did not have the brain power to think of anything else, but the look on Danny's face had him quickly backtracking. "—Which is that I slipped and fell. Clumsy me."

Tom moved gingerly, trying his best to relieve any sort of tension on his shoulder. No position felt good.

"God, I'm good to you."

It was true. If it were anyone else, Tom would rat them out faster than you could blink. But with Danny, everything was different. Tom would move mountains for him.

Of course, Danny couldn't live with the guilt, and he told their parents the truth later that night: he had flipped out because he was terrified of running out of Oxy. Then Tom got in trouble because he had lied to them. Go figure. But that was parenting for you. There's always a favourite, and Tom knew no one was betting on him.

From his room, Tom listened to Danny talking to their parents. He had been sent to his room, by the way. Tom could drive a car, legally buy beer, but somehow, he had been banished to a 3x3 square with a bung shoulder and a stitched eyebrow. He couldn't help but think he was a bit of a hero. At least he had his ego for company.

He heard Danny's soft voice. "Remember what the doctor said? If I run out, he can't give me more. What if I run out and get a migraine? That's why I was so scared to lose the pill."

Even from his bedroom, Tom could hear the shame in his voice. He imagined Danny hanging his head and his parents exchanging an empathetic look. It made a lot of sense. Years of pain had shattered him. But he made it through the month and trotted off to the doctor to get his new prescription.

Without Danny's constant migraines, they all suddenly realised that they had lives outside of Danny's pain. It was so easy to move on. Why wouldn't it be? You don't question your luck when things are going your way. Georgia started taking more shifts at work and Tom moved out, stretching his adult wings. Simon stayed exactly the same, because he couldn't possibly play any more golf than he already was.

About a month later, Tom had come to the house in the middle of the day to get something or do something. He couldn't really remember the reason. He knew Danny was home because, well, he was always home. Danny didn't do much, because he couldn't. He couldn't do anything, but sit around in his room and think about when the next migraine would hit. Hopefully, that would change, now he had medication that was working.

"Hey, Dan!" Tom yelled into the house.

It smelt like darkness and old bedding. Danny didn't reply, so after Tom raided the fridge and opened some windows, he charged up to his room. Danny was lying on his bed, fully clothed.

"Oi dickhead, did you hear me calling?"

As Tom jumped on Danny's bed playfully, he extended his arms to shake his brother but stopped to look at his face. His eyes were glassy and shiny like icing.

Tom laughed. "Hey, you baked cake. Get your head out of that smoking oven. I know it's nice in Candyland but come hang out with your big brother."

Danny turned his head towards Tom, gave him a small smile, and vomited all over his feet. He was grey. He was 10 shades darker than baked. He was charcoal.

"What the—!"

Danny pulled a limp hand to his own mouth, wiping chunks of vomit away.

"Tom it's okay. I just took too much."

He attempted to pull himself up. Breath like sour milk and old grapes washed over Tom and he nearly vomited himself.

"Damn right you did!"

Tom had almost laughed to himself. Just moments before, he'd been thinking about how well it was working, how perfectly Danny had adjusted to it. He should have known. God, he was stupid.

Dan sighed and slumped back down. "The pain was so bad. Needed more."

The little bugger was shitfaced but not as bad as Tom had first thought.

"Please don't tell mum and dad."

Again, he begged Tom. But this time, Tom knew this was something he couldn't hide.

Tom wondered if that was the moment: the moment their family burst into a hundred little pieces. Was it the catalyst they'd all been waiting for? He often thought about that. About what it would take to cause something terrible to happen. World War Three. His family breaking up. Him losing his mind. What would it take? There was always a scenario where it was possible. Thinking about it was enough to drive anyone bonkers. Maybe that was the catalyst. If you think enough about something it will happen.

Give me a million dollars.

Give me a million dollars.

But in reality, he knew things didn't just explode and break into tiny little pieces all at once. Fragments break off and fizzle away gradually until you don't even realise they're not there anymore.

Danny was better now, in the sense that he still had the migraines, but wasn't addicted to painkillers. It was hard to say that word, even in his own head, because he didn't believe it. Danny wasn't an addict. He hadn't been hooked on the pills for years. He hadn't sold their toaster for drug money.

Addiction.

It was nothing like what Tom expected it to be. But it was an addiction because Danny kept what he was doing to himself. He was ashamed. And where there's shame there's guilt. And guilt is to know that what you're doing is wrong. And if you know something is wrong and you do it anyway… well then you have no control. And addiction is all about control.

But by that definition, everyone was an addict. Because we all keep secrets. We all hide things. Every day, we tell lies, and we know it's wrong. Even if we tell them to ourselves. People are hooked on pride.

We'd sell all the toasters in the world to save it.

CHAPTER THREE

Better Man

Georgia knew she'd aged well. In fact, she felt better than ever. Age was a blessing, a liberation. With every year, the numbers grew, but so did her self-confidence. She could run down the street naked now and not really care. When she was younger, she used to have nightmares about doing that.

She also used to have nightmares about marrying a man she didn't love. When she first heard Pearl Jam's 'Better Man' it stuck with her, because it was like she'd written the song herself. Almost as if she'd subconsciously willed it to fruition, she'd married a man that she wasn't sure was really *hers*. She'd rushed into it, wanting it to be everything and it was only something. She'd told herself that love can be a slow burn. Maybe one day it would blossom into the thing she'd always wanted it to be.

She'd always been fascinated, watching the ways other people loved each other. No, not in some creepy peeping through the windows way you're probably thinking. Just little things like looks and touches between a couple. She just wanted to know what their love really felt like. Did everyone's love feel the same? Maybe some people were satisfied with just feeling comfortable every day. Maybe they thought that was love. Some, she knew, could only see the other person. They had no eyes for anyone else. Their family, their friends, ceased to exist. She wondered if that was real love, or if that was something else. She wondered if you were supposed to feel love for that person every day. If you were supposed to never have any doubts.

She didn't know much about love. But she was pretty sure she knew what it was supposed to look like. There'd be a moment, in a group conversation, when someone would say something idiotic, and the two of them would exchange a discreet, sideways glance. One that said exactly what the other was thinking.

Everything would be in that look.

She'd never shared that look with Simon, let alone any lover.

That's how she knew she had never been in love.

There wasn't something broken in her, some part that didn't work, she knew that, because she'd found promising candidates. But they'd only wanted her attention until they knew they had her attention. They told her she was beautiful, and interesting and one-of-a-kind until the compliments turned to let downs. Then she was hard work. The conversation was wanting. That they had priorities that trumped love. How can anything trump love? Isn't that what this whole nonsense was about?

Maybe she should have listened to them years ago and realized that there was more to life than romantic love. Then she could have been a better mother, a more loving mother, if she hadn't tried to save part of her heart for a man. But she wanted it. She couldn't let go. She hungered for a love that would swallow her whole, make her forget her own name, her own children. Was that selfish? Fine, she was selfish. But everyone is selfish. Why should she feel bad for wanting something that everyone else had?

Simon had felt it too, she knew it. The absence of love. Their bedroom had always been cold. She'd tried everything she could think of to bring a little life to it. New bedspread. New curtains. New lingerie. Cold. Cold. Cold. It was him. *He* had made it cold. She was always trying, always expending her energy. She felt like a bloody watermill. But him, well. He'd just slipped further and further away.

She was surprised then, when he'd left, and she'd felt the loss. Like all of a sudden, she wanted to fight for something that she'd never really thought she wanted. But she did and now it was gone. The boys were oblivious, as they should be. Parents were supposed to be armour-plated. They had to polish out their chinks behind closed doors.

Still, she kept the lid on the emails Simon had been sending her. They'd kept in touch, since he'd left. She hadn't told the boys. It seemed worse that way, if they knew that he didn't want to talk to them. But it was a small mercy, for her to know that he was out there, his heart still beating. It was terrible, to feel relief over something like that. She should want him to be happy. She should want to be able to help him. But instead, she settled for alive. She wanted it to, for herself. To feel alive. But it had a whole different meaning to her.

Online dating.

She never thought she would be doing it. But it was like there were invisible hands pushing into her back, propelling her toward something, someone to make her feel alive again.

She matched with a man named Scott. His nose was straight and pert at the end like a gentle ski slope. Stubble lined his diamond-shaped jawline. She wondered what it would feel like to run a finger across the plains of his face. If George Clooney and Ben Affleck had a love child, she was looking at a photo of it.

Days later, as she walked towards him, raising her hand in a casual salute, she studied his face, looking for an obvious flaw. He had sunglasses on. Maybe if he took them off, he'd reveal a thick monobrow.

As if signalled by her thoughts, he raised a hand to his face and pulled them off. Two perfectly curved brows framed deep, chocolate brown eyes. She was close enough to see that he had thick, black lashes. He was smiling down at her with unblemished, disciplined rows of white teeth. He was an Adonis of a man.

Well hello Scott.

"Well, hello Scott," she said warmly, looking up at him. He was tall.

"Hi!"

High. His voice was high. She willed him to speak again, to show her she'd misheard.

"It's great to meet you. Should we go inside and grab a table?" he said.

No. No. No. The sex drive that had crawled out of its burrow and sniffed the air was making a slow retreat to hibernation.

"Yep, sure thing." she looked down at her feet, something Scott should have done as he misstepped and stumbled into the doorway.

Going, going aaaaand gone.

Her mouth automatically pulled into a smirk before she could command herself to keep a straight face. She always did that. Even as an adult, she always laughed at the worst times.

"Oh! You right?"

"Fine, fine." he waved a hand about erratically, smacking the door frame none too softly in the process. This time, as if she were ready for it, her face was set carefully into what she hoped was a polite mask of indifference. And for the remainder of the date, that is how it remained.

She listened incredulously as little white blobs of spittle formed around his plump, perfect mouth. Over his cold cup of coffee, he was explaining to her in great detail the logistics of his work in logistics. As if completely independent of her brain, her eyes kept darting to that cup of coffee, willing him to drink it. It was like he knew she couldn't leave until he had finished it.

"So, road congestion is a major factor in shipping and logistics planning. So, I started thinking, what if we were better at eliminating traffic jams rather than planning *around* them? If we think about re-routing just a small number of drivers, it can potentially eliminate urban congestion."

She stared at his mouth. What would it be like to kiss him right now? Would it feel good? Would it matter how good-looking he was? Would it matter how ridiculous he was? Or would he just be a man, like any other man, once her eyes were closed? It had been so long since she'd kissed a man. She couldn't remember the last time she'd kissed Simon. Maybe she'd forgotten how to do it.

Scott grabbed the salt and pepper shakers, to show her what he meant, because obviously what he was explaining was far too complex for her teeny tiny little brain to comprehend without visual representation.

"Imagine," he shook the salt shaker, "that this a truck."

He looked up at her and she nodded to show she understood that the salt shaker wasn't a salt shaker, it was a truck.

"Right. Now, imagine—" he shook the pepper shaker, "that this—"

"Is a pepper shaker?"

He blinked at her. "No, it's a—"

"Car. I know. I was just joking."

He smiled obligingly. At least he understood that he needed to acknowledge when a joke had been made.

"Uhuh. So, right. The car is a pepper shaker. I mean the pepper shaker is a car."

Good grief.

She could see his nipples through his t-shirt. Loud and clear. His body was taut, there was no doubt about that. If she could just get past his personality, then maybe it could all work out. Over time, she might soften him. It was so hard to judge what he could be, based on the man he was now. Would she look back, five years from now, and think she was crazy to pass up this opportunity? She wasn't too old for love. Love making. Love giving. Love taking. She wanted all of it.

An hour later, they were fumbling keys and goodbyes at their cars.

"Well, it was great to meet you. I had such a good time Georgia. Text me?"

She nodded and raised her hand in valediction. A nice, cyclical ending. As the best ones always are. As she drove away, she felt herself deflate. She could talk herself into it as much as she liked, but she couldn't ignore what her body was telling her.

Run, run, run away.

Tackle life like you'd tackle a jar of olives if you didn't like olives. Eat them all. Seriously. It was the best advice she'd ever gotten. That was what her friend Mel said when Georgia told her about her date that night. What men had to do with olives, she had no idea.

"You cannot go through life hating olives," said Mel.

It was late, and the two of them were sitting on high stools in their local wine bar, straining to hear each other over the noise. Georgia was too old to be sitting on a chair like this. Protests shot from her neck all the way down to her buttocks. She had to stand. She couldn't bear it.

"Well, I have. And I can. And I will continue to do so."

"Blasphemy! You're like Italian or something aren't you?" asked Mel.

"Something like that."

She knew with her olive skin and mass of dark curls that she looked exotic, but in truth, Georgia felt like all she knew was this one little corner of the world. When she was a girl, she remembered travelling through Europe, meeting long-lost relatives, visiting houses and churches, and shopping plazas that her parents treated like old friends. She was amazed at this secret life she never knew she had. But the ties had loosened, the more roots she'd put down here. Simon. He'd leeched her clean.

And the boys—you'd never know they were half European. Their skin was whiter than fresh cream and they put tomato sauce on *everything*. She'd had no choice but to let it go. Her mother chastised her endlessly for it.

"Georgina these boys have no culture! None!" she had held up an eggplant to Tom. "Thomas!" she barked. "What is this?"

Tom had been on the couch playing video games. His eyes widened, and he looked between the two women, staring at Georgia, his eyes pleading for an answer.

"You're on your own." she'd said, turning back to the kitchen.

"It's an emoji. It means…"

"Tom!" Georgia had barked.

He smiled wickedly at the TV. "Just joking. Obviously, Nonna, it's a purple potato."

Georgia didn't know much Italian, but she knew enough to know that the string of mumbled words out of her mother's mouth were curses. God, she'd hate to know how her mother would react if she knew her own daughter hated olives.

"These boys, they don't know how to cook! What kind of men are you raising them to be? I'll tell you, you will have one potato. One big fat potato."

She jerked her head towards Tom. He grabbed the non-existent folds of his stomach.

"I am wasting away Nonna. Feed me. Mum doesn't feed us."

Her mother gave him a soft thwack over the head.

"Don't you talk about your mother like that. She does her best." she pulled him into her bosom for a straggling hug. "You need to help her. You should learn how to cook."

Georgia knew Tom was joking, and she knew her mother was…

well, being her mother, but it had stuck on her. Maybe her mother was right. Maybe she had undercooked these kids. How would they survive in the real world? Tom couldn't even pack a dishwasher.

Mel was still shaking her head at her, strands of honey blonde hair framing her face. Georgia marvelled at that. How her friend could look so young, so vivacious. She hoped she looked just as good.

"You don't know what you're missing out on! How can you travel to Italy, sit in a piazza in Florence, drink a glass of red wine and not eat olives as you watch the crowds? It's inconceivable." Mel said, as she drank deeply from her own glass.

"You do have a point."

"Trust me. All you need to do is eat a whole jar of them. And then I promise you, you'll love them forever."

"And what exactly does this have to do with my dating life?" Georgia asked.

"Men are like olives. You've just got to get through a few, and then you'll end up loving them." she smiled at her. "But seriously. There's no time to waste. Life is short. We've got to make the most of it while we are still young and gorgeous."

She did a little shimmy in her chair and Georgia laughed. Mel was right. There was still time. So much time. But she couldn't shake the feeling that she'd been left standing, while everyone else had found their seat.

CHAPTER FOUR

Space Junk

Danny could not think of a place he'd want to be at less than school. Maybe solitary confinement? Although he always thought he would cope better than others. He liked silence.

Failing.

He'd opened his computer in home room and found the red alert flashing at him, taunting him.

He told himself he didn't care anymore, that it meant nothing. A grade was no indication of what he was capable of, who he was.

Lazy.

Stupid.

Useless.

The words thundered in his head, keeping time with the pounding that had become his constant companion. It wasn't bad this morning though. Only a beating drum, not a jackhammer. Maybe there wouldn't be a migraine today.

Lazy.

Stupid.

Useless.

That's what the teachers thought of him, he knew it. Didn't blame them, really. It wasn't like he did anything to suggest it was any other way. At first, he'd tried to keep up. He'd diligently emailed all his teachers, submitted all his work, like the good little boy he was. But with each grade he dropped, a part of his will went with it, until he just couldn't see the point anymore. It was like walking in on a conversation with a group of strangers and being expected to know all their names.

He didn't care anymore, but he knew Georgia would. She'd pretend it was ok, that they'd find a way to make it better, but by now, he could see through her parent mask: she would be worried. And if he dived a little deeper and opened the locked box she would never acknowledge existed, because she knew it wasn't fair that she felt it, he would look in there and see that she was ashamed. Every parent is ashamed when their child doesn't live up to their expectations. Offspring are supposed to be magical, complete creatures, full of endless potential.

Shivering, feeling like he was sitting on an ice block and not a plastic chair, Danny looked about his home room. They could not have made it any bleaker if they tried. Scrunched up pieces of paper littered the classroom floor and a half-eaten apple rested next to the bin. Even the cleaners had given up. Tattered student posters were haphazardly stuck to the white-washed walls, displaying crude drawings of the 'centrel nerves system'. Christ. How could they pin that up, with spelling like that? He looked at the closest one, a solitary picture hanging off the poster, its corners flapping off the cardboard. Clearly some kid had just printed off the first hit they found when they googled "brain." They hadn't even bothered to at least copy the picture by hand. They just tacked it on, crudely labelling the parts in scratchy handwriting "Frontel Lobe: emotions", "temporel lobe: memory", "cerabelum: balance". Is that what it all boiled down to? Everything he felt, could it be dissected and labelled? If it could, then give the kid an A. But he did think it was ironic, that *he* was the one failing. See? He knew what irony was. He was miles ahead of most of the kids, really.

"Ah, miss, you didn't call my name." he cleared his throat and raised his hand for good measure. He often found that it took a lot for him to get people's attention. How different he was to Tom. All his brother had to do was inhale, and he had heads turning in his direction. Tom was a natural performer. Danny was a born stagehand.

He sighed to himself, trying to rally even a speck of energy. It was like the less he went to school, the less he cared about everything else.

He had to try. He couldn't give up entirely; he couldn't do that to his mother. Tom would, he mused. Tom would make some quippy remark and say something like 'Bill Gates dropped out so I can too' and Georgia would shake her head and sigh and then Tom would know he'd won. But she'd never let Danny. For as long as he could remember, there had been a collar around his throat.

A few of the other students in his home room half-twisted their heads at the sound of his croaky voice, looking at him with disinterest. He'd missed so many days, he doubted anyone in the room would even know his name. He might as well be a statue. No one would know the difference.

Miss Caine looked at him, her face blank. Miss Caine was young, Danny realised, maybe not much older than Tom. Every time she spoke, her voice wobbled like jelly. It was painful to listen to. She was achingly thin, as if her nerves had eaten away at her over time, gnawing at her tissue.

"Oh umm…" Miss Caine looked down in confusion, the tendons in her hands threatening to explode through her skin as she used the trackpad on her mouse. With a smirk, Danny realised she had no idea who he was. There wouldn't be a picture on her computer either: he'd missed photo day. A small part of him wanted to enjoy this, stretch out the awkwardness, see what she would do. No. He wouldn't do that. He wasn't wired that way.

"It's Danny."

She stared blankly at the screen.

"Carter."

"What?"

"Danny Car-ter." he said, with a flicker of annoyance.

He hated that—how irritable he always was. He couldn't help it; it was the monster in his head. The migraines made him a different version of himself. He was always fighting that Danny.

"Sorry, sorry," he mumbled to himself, "that was rude of me. I'm not here very often." he raised his eyes to her, hoping she'd see the regret there, but she was looking at her computer, resolved to track him down, as if accomplishing that could soothe her shaking hands.

The bell rang, and he swept his books off the table, heading to his first class. Kingston Secondary was an ocean. Schools of children darted this way and that way, clustered in loud chattering groups, the noise bouncing off the walls of packed hallways. The cacophony enraged Danny's monster, and he gritted his teeth, lengthening his stride. The grounds were a sprawling reef of smart, double-storey brick buildings and ramshackle portables that looked as if they'd been dropped from the sky like space junk, an eyesore on the otherwise preened lawns. Years ago, there was a population boom, and the school was now bursting at the seams with children. They exploded from the gates, corridors and classrooms. You could barely claim a spot of grass as your own on the oval.

He watched them all, swimming around him, feeling like a sea snail in their midst. It had been too hard to keep friends with the way he was. He knew he couldn't be anything other than a drain on their friendship, and he was nobody's pity party. Better not to have friends. Maybe though, it could have been different. If he could actually hear his own thoughts, instead of tasting them. That's what it felt like, when the headaches were bad: like his brain was rolling in his mouth.

104. He backtracked, looking at his planner. 104, that's where he was supposed to be. Double accounting. He shuddered. 120 minutes of content drier than rice cakes. Mentally, he flicked though the possible teachers that could teach the subject.

Oh, for the love of God, not Mr Doerr, Not Mr Doerr.

Mr Doerr was an ugly old codger, that's for sure. Everyone knew years of drinking had caused his nose to blow up like balloon, and it had only gotten larger with each passing year, each bottle of whiskey he'd consumed. Danny didn't know if it was the drinking, but his skin had gone funny too, kind of see through. As if he'd summoned the devil himself, Mr Doerr came tottering down the corridor.

"Oh, for Christ's sake." Danny muttered to himself, louder than he intended.

A girl lounging on the door frame opposite him sniggered, and he caught her eye.

Sometimes, you meet someone, and you just know they're your person. This girl was his person. Not in like a sexual way, although he had to admit, she was not bad to look at. But it was her eyes that pinned him down. She had one of those faces where her eyes did all the talking. There was a whole story in those eyes, he could see it. She smiled and looked away, flicking her long, raven hair over her shoulder. Little wisps of it had escaped her ponytail, framing her oval-shaped face. Beautiful. Well done on your parents for procreating, bravo.

Taking far longer than any human ought to, Mr Doerr finally managed to get the classroom open, shifting his keys and coffee from one arthritic hand to the other. Danny clicked his tongue, and the girl smiled again. He couldn't help himself. Doerr was a relic from the Stone Age. Danny swore that someone had pointed a remote at him and pressed the rewind button. Everything he did was in slow motion. Even when he spoke, it was slow, as if every word had to be tasted, mulled about in his mouth before it finally dribbled out.

The classroom was set in a wide U shape, and Danny plonked himself on a table near the back left-hand corner. To his surprise, the girl followed him.

"I don't know anyone," she said sheepishly, as if she could sense his thoughts.

He had thrown her a sharp look, one he now realised could have been interpreted as annoyance, rather than surprise.

He smiled widely, trying to correct his mistake. "No, no it's fine. Me either. Are you new?"

"No," she said, her face reddening, "I just don't know anyone in this class."

Fragile little lamb. He was glad no one could read his thoughts. Scanning the room, he realised there weren't too many faces he recognised either. It was a composite class, and most of the students were year 10s. Many of whom he did not like.

"Oh yeah, they're all year 10s." he said, rolling his eyes.

She smiled. "I'm in year 10."

This was going swimmingly. He raised his hands in defeat.

"Ok, ok, I'll shut my mouth. I'm Danny."

"Kyraah." there was a moment of silence." —So how come I haven't seen you before?"

One of the year 10 boys sitting nearby turned his head, his ears pricked. *He* was a prick. Smithy, they called him. He had a mouth like a steam train: always pissing out hot air.

"Because he's a stoner," Smithy called out loudly, his head only half turned in their direction. Danny could see a big, ugly grin on the corner of his big, ugly face.

If Smithy knew what was inside Danny, he surely wouldn't have bothered. Actually, it's likely he would, because people like him don't know anything other than cruelty. One day, Smithy would get his face beaten in. But it wouldn't be by Danny. The jibe bounced off him, his insides left untouched, already wiped clean and sterile from enduring years of the monster. It was kind of a blessing, in a way. It had made him weaker. And that made him stronger.

Danny looked sidelong at Kyraah. "I get migraines." he said mildly, careful not to let any flicker of emotion into his voice. He could tell Smithy was still listening.

"Yeah, and he takes DRUGS." Smithy said, yelling the last word.

Smithy's friends sniggered. Others in the class looked at Danny, their faces carefully neutral. There were no heroes in a high school class. A guy like Smithy could make your life hell.

Mr Doerr looked up from the textbook. "Quiet down now, quiet down."

"Sorry sir. Smithy was just *accounting* for my school absences." Danny said to Doerr, his eyes not wavering from Smithy's face.

Kyraah laughed, the only one to notice his pun. Maybe she wasn't as shy as he thought. This time, Smithy turned around to meet Danny's stare, his eyes darting between the two of them. Danny knew what was coming.

"Be careful hanging around this one darl. He's a bad influence." Smithy said, turning back in his seat.

"He is such an idiot," Kyraah breathed into Danny's ear.

Silently, Danny nodded, his head sending a bolt of pain down his neck. Internally though, he was on his knees kissing Smithy's hands. Because of him, he had a beautiful girl leaning into him, whispering in his ear. Her forearm brushed against his and he shuddered, resisting the urge to look down her dress as she leaned over him. That would be *wrong*, Daniel. So wrong. Instead, he inhaled. She smelt like candy apples.

It was a pattern that continued for the rest of the lesson. For five minutes, they might stare at their textbooks, scribble something down in their book, until one would lean into the other and murmur something, all the while the beat in Danny's head becoming deeper, louder, harder to ignore.

"Hey," said Danny, doing his best to sound breathy and seductive,

"Do you think Doerr is on his last legs?"

Kyraah looked up from reading a paragraph on the Revenue Recognition Principle, and scanned Doerr carefully, the freckles across her nose wrinkling. "To be honest, it looks like he's already dead."

Danny sucked in a breath, pretending to be outraged by her comment. "Ouch! Poor Mr Doerr."

"What! Look at him. He's lucky to have lasted this long."

"To be honest, I'm not sure he'd even notice if he had died," admitted Danny.

They both looked around the room. Smithy, having tired of berating his classmates, was standing up with three other boys, throwing balls of paper into the bin in a winner-takes-all knockout competition. Every now and then, one of them would give a loud cheer, earning a 'quiet down' from Doerr. To their right, a group of girls were sitting in a circle, braiding each other's hair, occasionally picking up a pen to scribble down a note from their books. At the front of the room sat Mr Doerr, sipping from his coffee cup, his eyes about a centimetre from his laptop screen. How, *how* did schools always manage to find and employ teachers like this? Did they do it on purpose so students would appreciate the good teachers more?

Kyraah leaned into him again, drawing him from his reverie. "What do you think is on that computer screen?"

Danny raised an eyebrow suggestively. "Aside from the obvious?" he paused for a moment, thinking. "He's probably trailing the dark web, looking for some sort of life extending elixir."

She giggled. "Like bottled unicorn blood?"

He stared at her. "Oh. My. God. Did you just make a Harry Potter reference?"

"No—" a smile escaped her lips. "Maybe."

Marry me, you beautiful, magical temptress.

By recess, the pounding was reverberating in the cavern of his mouth, pinging from one molar to the other.

"Hey! Danny!"

The familiar voice boomed in his head, but he was glad to hear it. He turned to greet the boy who was bounding away from a group towards him and Kyraah, who had subtly moved back a few paces so she was standing in Danny's shadow. He moved back himself, so they were standing side by side again.

Leeroy was a golden retriever. Sometimes, people irrevocably remind you of a certain animal. With their sharp teeth and pointed noses, some people are sharks. Some people have feathery eyebrows and long necks, just like emus. Danny was sure he himself was a mole rat, or some equally pathetic animal. But with his halo of bouncing blonde curls and oversized grin, Leeroy was a puppy dog. He could charm even the most reluctant adult. He still looked exactly like the fresh-faced boy Danny had met on his first day of high school, years ago, except now he had a little more golden fuzz around the boyish face, and it had been stretched out, losing its childish roundness

"Hey mate," said Danny softly, with less energy than he would have liked. It was leeching from him like a dwindling afternoon sun. Leeroy didn't notice, but he thought he saw Kyraah study him, a frown forming on her head.

"How have you been! Haven't seen you around for ages!"

If Danny were to transcribe Leeroy's idiolect, it would be filled with exclamation marks.

"Yeah, I know." Danny said, looking down at his toes, expecting the silence to hang in the air until Leeroy excused himself and bounded off again.

"Well, it's great to have you back!" Leeroy smiled, gesturing behind him for his friends to come over.

A grey film set around the edges of Danny's vision, like the volume control had suddenly been turned up on the back of his head. Everything started to look like it was two dimensional. *No. No. Not now.*

"These are some of my mates," Leeroy continued, as two boys walked over.

Danny could barely make them out, his vision deteriorating with every passing moment.

"Ali," the taller of the two smiled. "And Grant." the other boy nodded his head. He was athletically built, with a crop of ash brown hair.

Danny smiled tightly, barely able to do even that. He must look like such a rude bastard.

"Nice to meet you. This is Kyraah." she smiled warmly, shuffling her feet.

Danny had to get out, had to leave. He knew he didn't have very long left.

"Sorry guys, but I actually have an appointment with the co-ordinator. Just about my return to school and stuff." Danny waved a hand casually in the air and looked apologetically at Kyraah, seeing the panic in her eyes.

Leeroy only looked slightly surprised. "Oh no worries, man. Will you be back tomorrow?"

Danny had already turned on his heel, but as he walked away, he stopped hesitantly. "I'm... not sure yet."

Leave *now*, the monster snarled at him. He waved, his stomach sinking, despite the fact that it was churning like an unforgiving sea. Down the hall, he half-marched, half-jogged, racing to get to a bathroom or a sickbay or...

Rubbish bin.

Spotting it from the corner of his eye, he lunged for it. He didn't even think twice. It was like a scene from the exorcist.

Huruggggghhhh.

Over the years, Danny had perfected the art of vomiting quietly, but this one snuck up on him. It came out of him like a prized racehorse bursting from the gates. He was scared if he opened his eyes, he'd see some of his vital organs floating around in the bin lining.

Huruuurghhh.

Faintly, he saw a gang of small children skit around him. Fine by him. The last thing he wanted was—

He felt a hand rest on the small of his back.

— an audience.

Shit.

Carefully, he kept his head bowed, shielding the mess. Mercifully, there was nothing left in him. His insides had been stripped clean, and he felt almost light. If it weren't for the vice locked around his skull, he'd almost feel like he could go for a run. He couldn't bring himself to say anything. How to explain it? What could he possibly say to make it better?

"It's okay."

There was silence as his back rose and fell, the small hand stuck firm on the contour of his spine. After hearing that voice in his ear for the past hour, he knew who it belonged to.

Almost as if she was responding to the tightening muscles in his back, she spoke again.

"I don't care. No one cares. It's just vomit. It's just chewed food, really."

He groaned at her to stop and he felt her hand shake with laughter. What a relief it was, to have it out. The vomit and the secret. Someone other than a family member knew what it did to him, and they could look it dead in the face. It didn't scare her.

"Thanks."

He spat expertly into the bin and pulled a tissue from his sleeve, dabbing his face clean.

"So, they're that bad huh?" Kyraah looked sidelong at him as they slowly trekked up the empty hall, the last of the students filtering out into the weak sun for recess.

"They're that bad." he said, deftly popping a mint into his mouth.

"Was that..."

He looked at her, raising his eyebrows. "A mint? Yes."

She paused for a moment. "Do you have anything else you could take?"

He stopped and fished about in his pocket, pulling out some tablets and a bottle of water from his bag. He opened his palm to show her, and she looked at the little white pills, as though he were holding an explosive device.

"Relax," he said, starting to walk again. "It's just paracetamol."

He knew she was thinking about what Smithy had said. It wasn't untrue. It just wasn't true anymore.

"Oh. Isn't there something stronger you could take?"

"Yes, there is." he said mildly.

"How often do you... vomit from it?"

It was like they were discussing the weather.

He paused, trying to come up with an answer. "Well, it depends. Medication usually helps. If I take it before the pain gets really bad, then I don't usually vomit."

"You didn't take it today?"

"Forgive me, I was a little *distracted*."

34

She smiled and Danny had the pleasure of watching a flush of red creep up her neck. He looked at her, studying her face, trying to get her to look at him. She was determinedly staring ahead, her face giving nothing away. Two could play that game.

"Too bad about the vomit. I mean, I was planning on kissing you." he said it playfully, so she knew he didn't really mean it. He realised that no sentence with the word 'vomit' in it was remotely sexy, but he tried to keep his face blank just like she had before. His traitorous mouth was twitching. He'd never been so bold in his life. What was this girl doing to him?

She wrinkled her nose playfully. "What an absolute shame."

"Ah well, another time then."

They'd reached the school reception, and Kyraah looked around, as if she were only now registering where they were.

"I'm going to go home." Danny said softly, sensing her confusion.

"Oh."

She looked down. He wished he could take chin and make her look at him so he could study what was in those molten green eyes.

"Will you be back tomorrow? I mean, not that it really bothers me either way, I do have many other friends, as you can see." she gestured around the empty reception area.

"Do you know what, I reckon you should try hanging out with Leeroy and his friends. He's a really nice guy."

She looked at him, her eyes narrowing. "So, is that you telling me that you won't be here tomorrow?"

He laughed and then sighed. "I don't know. I hope so."

She nodded, and he smiled and waved goodbye to her before walking up to the desk, manned by a very large woman with curly black hair. Her name was Jodie. She probably had a last name, but she was just one of those adults at the school that never got called by it. She was always just Jodie.

"Oh Mr Carter! It's been a while since we've seen you here."

"Hi Jodie."

"I basically have nothing else to do if I'm not cleaning up your vomit from sickbay."

"I'm glad I play such an important role in your life."

She rolled her eyes and gestured with her head for him to come around. It was like a home away from home. A few years ago, they'd put a little bed in there just for him. It was more like a cot, but it was enough for him to curl up in, cradle his head, and wait the migraine out. He did exactly that, and Jodie shook her head indulgently, throwing an icepack at him.

"Oomph." he said dramatically, catching it in his guts. "Do you actually want me to vomit all over your nice clean floor?"

"Well, I figured you were going to anyway, might as we get it out now."

His smirk faltered. "I kinda... already did."

She didn't gasp with sympathy or call him a *poor little lamb*. You could just tell Jodie was one of those people that knew what pain was. Some people know it, some people don't. The ones that know it are quiet, because they know words can't do a thing.

"Have you taken anything?"

"Yeah. Paracetamol."

She scoffed. "Yeah, that'll fix it. Got anything stronger?"

He paused. "Yeah. Doesn't usually do much though."

"Take it anyway."

"Are you allowed to tell me that?"

She huffed. "Frankly Danny, I don't give a shit. I'll say that in court if I have to. There's no shame in making yourself feel better when you're this sick." she levelled him a look. "You're a masochist sometimes Danny."

Sick. That's what he was, according to the school nurse. He was a sick masochist. Thanks for the character profile, Jodie. God, he must really be in here a lot. He bent over his bag and pulled out his meds. He stared at them.

It wasn't Oxy. But it sure as hell wasn't Panadol.

Furtively, so Jodie wouldn't see, he slipped them back into his bag. He didn't know why. Maybe it was because he was too scared to take anything more than Panadol these days. Or maybe Jodie was right. The monster was the company he deserved.

He felt like it was only minutes later when the door burst open. He'd fallen into a light slumber.

"Bloody hell Jodie, just when I thought you were alright."

He unfolded from his foetal position and turned around, looking at the door grumpily.

"Shut up."

It wasn't Jodie.

It was Smithy, and it looked like someone had finally made good on Danny's prediction: his face looked like a hot jam doughnut. Blood was pouring out of his nose. Plonking himself on a chair, Smithy crossed his arms and tilted his head towards the ceiling.

"What happened to you?" Danny asked gleefully, a big stupid grin spread across his face.

"I said, shut up." Smithy pinched his nose, looking steadfastly at the ceiling.

"You know, if you were just a bit nicer to people—"

"What part of *shut the fuck up* don't you understand?"

Danny almost laughed then, almost tsked to himself and turned away, but he saw something in Smithy's eyes then that made him stop. He knew that look. It wasn't anger. It was a feeling he knew well.

Pain.

And he didn't think the cause was his bloody nose.

He wished he could make it better. Say something so profound that Smithy remembered it for years to come. But words don't work like that. Pain doesn't work like that. Relief is only ever temporary. As he sat up, his head resting against the wall, his monster began to beat away, drumming its assent.

CHAPTER FIVE

A Naked Cat

Oh, it hurt.

It was like eating a bad curry. Like liquid biryani just sitting in your guts, gurgling and rolling about. You kind of want to vomit, but the nausea isn't quite bad enough. You feel like you have to hold onto your insides so they don't drop to the floor.

Tom had just been dumped. He was trying to explain the torrent of emotions raging within him. He was finding his housemate to be a less than sympathetic pair of ears. He shared the apartment an old school friend; Mickey, a girl he'd always had a perfectly platonic relationship with.

"So just dry crackers for you then?" Mickey said dryly.

"No see, here's the thing. In a few days, you start to feel a bit better. Your nose starts to twitch a little at the smell of food. After a week, you don't feel sick anymore. Just weak. And after a while, all that's left is a food aversion. Love is...." Tom gestured grandly, jumping up onto his knees spilling corn chips across the sofa. "Curry. Love is a messy, delicious curry."

Mickey eyed the empty wrappers and dirty dishes surrounding the sofa. "You seem to have gotten over your food aversion pretty quickly."

"Well, I know that in a week I'll feel better. And that knowledge brings me comfort now." he said, winking at her.

In the 24 hours following his spectacular dumping, Tom had

consumed:

- 7 KitKats
- 3 glazed donuts
- 1 large bowl of cereal
- 12 chicken wings
- 1 chicken burger
- 1 medium fries
- 1 litre of Coke

He was basically weaned on Coke. He remembered the time he stayed at his cousin's house for a week when he was thirteen and all they were allowed to drink was water. He nearly went insane. Every time someone spoke to him at the dinner table, he wanted to drown them in a bucket. Surprisingly, he was a pretty skinny guy. *She* said she liked skinny guys.

No, stop it.

Any time he thought of her, the previous night's conversation played back. Again and again, he relived it, knowing he could do nothing to change it now.

It had been a particularly intense moment of Neighbours and the drama had caught his attention. Tom was sprawled across the couch dressed in his work clothes and an old singlet. She was perched on one of the hard wooden kitchen chairs.

"Are you watching this? Half the town is about to die." he glanced over at her and saw that her head was bowed. Idly, he looked at her scalp, thinking that her head looked like a naked cat. Not enough hair to quite cover everything up.

"Hey, your scalp kind of looks like—"

"Tom."

There was something about her tone then. About the way she almost spelled out his name. He peered into her face and his stomach clenched.

Just a little. Just enough.

"What's wrong?"

"I need to tell you—" she paused, looking away from him. "I'm trying to tell you—" a little tear blobbed from her eye. "I'm having doubts."

She wouldn't look at him. She was all folded up in her seat. Legs tucked under her. Hands tucked into her lap. Head tucked into her neck.

"Ok so doubts to me is like you're not sure if you can handle my mustard-coloured sweater which is fine, because I just wouldn't wear it and I don't like it that much, anyway. I only wear it all the time because I don't have many sweaters. I'll get rid of it. But it sounds like… it's not the sweater you want to throw out." he placed his hands on his hips and raised his eyebrows at her.

"Why do you always have to do that?" she said.

"Do what?"

"Be so dramatic and… strange. I'm trying to tell you something serious and you don't even care."

It felt like a military coup. She came at him out of nowhere, rounding him up, forcing him to stand trial for his sins against her.

"I know that. I do care. I'm asking you if this is something I can fix."

She didn't look up. Nothing.

"But I don't think it is." he said carefully.

She raised her eyes.

"Oh, don't look at me like that. Don't look at me like I'm some pathetic loser."

He jumped up from the sofa and strode into the kitchen, busying himself with the kettle.

"So, what. You don't like me anymore."

He mockingly clutched his hand to his chest.

Silence.

That meant no. Sand was pouring through his fingers. Every word seemed to drain it away faster than the next.

"Well, when did it stop?"

He was talking like he was discussing that night's dinner options. Well, he knew what she was having for dinner. Black pudding. To match her black heart. Oh God everything hurts.

"A while ago." she said.

It was bad enough that she was breaking up with him, but it was even worse that she'd wanted to do it for a while. How long had she been keeping this in? That was what really got him. That she'd kept it secret for so long.

They stared at each other awkwardly. They were strangers now.

"Well, thank you for your candour. Now that our relationship has come to a cessation, I will kindly ask you to see yourself out. How was that for serious? Pretty good huh?" he was walking away, talking like a madman until he reached the bathroom. He turned the faucet on, leaving the door open a crack, hoping that she might follow him, beg him to forget it all and then they would have lovely naked shower sex. But she didn't. She just left.

Afterward, he did loops of the apartment. He looked in the pantry and then the bathtub and then out the window. He saw a dog try to jump up some stairs and fall backwards, its rump little body twisting quickly to right itself. Ordinarily, he would have found it amusing, but he couldn't even lift a smile. What was wrong with him? Danny had endured years of pain, and he was torn up over a three month break up? *Get a grip Tom. You're better than this Tom.*

None of her stuff was there. Not a toothbrush or a renegade sock. Nothing. How can it all be wiped away so quickly? How can people do that? He closed his eyes, willing himself to get over it. That's how he liked to operate. Just pack up and move on. If you could do that, then it was like there was never really a problem to begin with.

Lara. No. Please. No. I can't eat anymore. Please.

You will. You'll do it if you love me.

She mashed another cookie into my mouth. And another and another. Dough was congealing in my throat, spilling out of my nostrils like spaghetti. I tried to shout, to scream, to even retch.

This was not an acceptable way to die.

"You've really got to stop doing this. You haven't moved since this morning."

Tom emerged from an icy sleep to find Mickey sitting on the end of the sofa. She was picking cookie crumbs off the couch, unaware of the terror gripping Tom. It had seemed *so* real. God, dreams were terrifying.

"I'm assuming this is what you nearly choked on." she said, looking at a cookie crumb as if it had personally offended her.

"Mmm thanks."

He snatched it from her hand and threw it into his mouth. He then detached a particularly large and unwilling corn chip from the fibres of his cotton singlet and popped that into his mouth too. It achieved its intended effect of irritating Mickey, because he saw a slight shadow fall over her face, pulling at the corner of mouth.

"Planning on cleaning up or showering any time soon?"

"I did."

He gestured to a pile of dishes he had stacked neatly by the couch. She said nothing, simply bending over and scooping them up. If he didn't know that it was a silent protest against his existence, he almost would have felt bad.

"Here, let me help you." Tom stretched out a foot and poked a long-nailed toe into the spongy flesh of her thigh.

"Oh God. You're disgusting. Keep your toe jam away from me."

"Toe jam?" he sat up, intrigued.

"Yeah, that's what you call all the stuff that collects underneath toenails."

"Ok, if you stop explaining this to me, I'll get up and help you clean." he said, pretending to vomit into a cushion.

She ignored him and pressed on. "Like, think about it. No one ever cleans under their toenails, do they?"

"I certainly haven't. But then I don't exactly think I'm a model of exemplary hygiene practices."

Tom looked down at his body. It really wasn't an attractive sight. No pants. No deodorant. No sex appeal. He really had to get it together.

"Yeah, so all that dirt and—", she gestured to the chip crumbs on the floor, "food scraps—", she gave him another frown for good measure, "—collect under there. Stays there for months, just decomposing, simmering into this thick soup that just gathers and gathers and then—"

"Okay, okay you win. I'm up."

He got up to help her with the dishes, still in his underwear. Mickey was the type of woman you didn't want to wear pants for. Not in a sexual way, he didn't want to, *you know*. It's just that he knew that he didn't have to make an effort for her. They were friends, despite their differences. She was mature beyond her years, and he was... well he wasn't *as* mature. He could admit that. But it worked. He was lovable and charming, and he knew that counted for something. They were the odd couple, without the couple part. Maybe that's how it should be with women from now on, he thought to himself. Keep the relationship part out of it. He really didn't need all that drama.

Even though the cleaning was a nightmare, he was eternally grateful the apartment, because now that he had moved out, he could not contemplate ever going back again. Moving back in with your parents, or parent, he should say now, is like signing your own death warrant. You're voluntarily giving up your sex and social life. You can't have people over if you live with your parents. They're always there, in the background, slinking around. Parents were like FBI agents. Interrogating your life choices. Assigning you to house arrest if you did the wrong thing. And always, *always* listening to your conversations.

Tom used to dread what would come out of his friend's mouths. They had no idea what it was like playing out your adolescence in his house. Saying 'shit' in front of their parents made you interesting. Saying it in front of his got you blacklisted. He was always on edge. You know those families that scream at each other and then get along fine the next? Well, his was the opposite. Have you seen the movie The Quiet Place? That was their world. They ran the house without a sound and in the background, there were monsters. No one ever yelled. It was terrifying. The anger would just simmer away, hovering beneath the floorboards. It was better now that Simon was gone, but it was still there. Years of habits don't exactly change overnight.

He had to get out of the apartment and clear his head. His thoughts, limited as they may be, were sending him around the twist. It was 2 o'clock in the afternoon and he'd done nothing but watch TV for two days straight. His body needed sunlight. He dragged himself out and sighed as he took up a steady pace. But his thoughts did not slow. If anything, they sped up, keeping in time with his quick steps. The phrase overthinking is funny. It suggests that thought is measurable. Like there's some standard to how much a person should think. But the whole idea of thought is that it is abstract, that it flows this way and that way and then back again and oh look! A leaf. Isn't it too late in the year for falling leaves? That's thought. Random, complex. Whirling. He'd recently heard that some people didn't have an internal narrative. That they didn't think words. He tried to think if he really did or not. He always thought he'd had thoughts, but now that he thought about it, he realised he saw everything. It was like a movie was playing constantly in his head. Everything he thought, he *saw*. Was he special? Some sort of brilliant human anomaly? He always knew he was different.

The sight of the Yarra River blessedly brushed aside the yammering voice in his head; its gentle water wind sprayed into his mind. His body deflated, its silent thanks that the view had managed to shut his brain up. God, it was exhausting having a brain and a mouth that talked as much as his did. Maybe that's why he was always tired. And skinny. His brain and mouth just ate up all his energy.

He shook his head, keeping his eyes on the river. It wasn't a spectacular sight, but it was strong and sure. The water on this side of the bridge was always the colour of dry dirt, the colour of the bush. Like it knew where it came from. It didn't try to be some sort of fancy city river.

On the other side of the bridge, it was different. A haphazard huddle of skyscrapers cast the river a stormy blue; a deep blue when the sun could bounce off the glass of the buildings. There weren't any banks. The river licked at the concrete foundations of the city, like it could one day be a threat.

This city was the whole world. Nothing was bigger or more important than Melbourne. It was the sporting capital of the world. Want to debate on that one? Tell me another city in the world that has not one but TWO public holidays for a sporting event. It was nuts. Brilliant, but nuts. His heart bulged with pride any time a foreigner mentioned how much they loved this place, how cool they thought the laneways were, how good the coffee was. *Melbourne coffee is the best in the world*, he'd tell any tourist he met. He liked a double shot caramel latte himself.

Birrarung Marr was bustling with people. Families picnicking, runners huffing along the track, lovers stretched out across blankets. He hated that. When you expected a place to be quiet and instead there were *people*. He settled himself on top of a particularly hard and smooth area of packed dirt and watched the couples, wishing he'd thought to bring his own blanket.

He stretched out on the hard earth and stared into the glittering gums above. He'd never known any other tree to do that. When the wind blew the leaves off a gum tree they actually sparkled. Number one thing to do in Australia as recommended by Trip Advisor should be:

"Lie down and watch gum trees glitter in the sun. And then drift into a lazy sleep as the wind and sun speckles warmth into your face..."

Cool fact for you: Apparently, Birrarung Marr is more dangerous than New York's Central Park. A young cop told Tom that with enthusiasm. She and her partner had been on patrol in the area when Tom's wallet and phone had been stolen. He wouldn't have bothered to report it, because it would be so much effort, but when he saw them, he figured it was the right thing to do.

"Ok so what were the circumstances of the crime?" she took out a pen to scribble his account. He was already regretting this.

"I fell asleep in the park at about 2:30 today."

The pen waited.

"And my stuff got stolen."

"Uh-huh. What was stolen?"

"Phone and wallet."

He cringed at his stupidity. Yes, great idea. Fall asleep in the middle of a park with your wallet and phone next to you. He might as well have just put a bow on them.

"Estimated value?"

"$650. I had some McDonald's coupons in my wallet that I'm pretty sad to have lost as well. Can I claim those?"

She raised her eyebrows without raising her eyes to him. "Not unless the summative value of the coupons is over $20."

A small smile glinted at the corner of her mouth. With her head still down, he was allowed to look at her with fresh appreciation. Her short-sleeved shirt fitted snugly into her belted navy pants and her hair was sleek, knotted neatly at the base of her neck. Her chin was squarish, but in an attractive woman-in-power kind of way.

"Drats."

"Okay." she looked over her notes, her tone becoming businesslike once again. "Did you get a look at the person who robbed you? Obviously, we get a lot of reports from this area, so we will have more chance of finding this person if you can give us any sort of detail..." her voice trailed off, waiting for him to try to colour a vision of his robber.

"It was a guy. He spoke to me. Woke me up."

"He woke you up! What did he say?"

"Sorry matey."

"Sorry matey?" she stretched out the e-y almost mockingly.

"Yep. And then he took off."

"You didn't chase after him?"

Tom narrowed his eyes. "By the time I realised what had happened, he'd disappeared up river."

"What? He had a boat?"

"No, I mean he was running away from the city." his cheeks were starting to heat up.

"Didn't see what he looked like?"

Tom sighed. "Just the back of him. Greyish hair. Loose pants. Dark jacket."

She scribbled these details down. He could see she was getting bored with the story. He was sick of telling it himself. He knew he wouldn't get his stuff back. She knew it. Time to move on.

"Are we done?"

He was hoping to catch her off guard with his abruptness, but she surprised him again.

"Pretty much. You're very unlikely to see your things again. Sorry."

She tacked the last word onto the end. She flipped the paper over her pad, readying a new sheet for the next crime and turned to dismiss him. In another world, she would be his next girlfriend.

"Think of it this way — it could have been a lot worse." she smiled sympathetically and joined her partner standing a few feet away.

Was that what the world was to cops? Life or death, no middle ground? Nothing in between? Guess it had to be. He wondered what she had already seen. She could hardly have been any older than him, but he felt like she had seen the world. Maybe she had broken up a drunken brawl on Swanton Street. Like she had just been there when violence exploded from mid-level insults and vicious shoves. She was a cop. There was no choice but to rush in and do the job expected of her, knowing that she would be battered against the might of full-grown men. Maybe she'd seen a seen a suicide. Maybe on the train tracks. With wide eyes, Danny had once recounted to Tom the story of a local boy who'd killed himself on the tracks. That story haunted Tom. He knew his own pathetic, pink-skinned little body hadn't lived a day. He really knew nothing about the darkness of the world. He hoped it stayed that way, but he knew it couldn't.

He was terrified of the day he would finally see it.

CHAPTER SIX

Meatloaf

Tom swiped away the empty chip packets and dirty laundry that littered the couch and pushed her down so she was laid out before him. There was a pouch of fat about her stomach. It seemed immovable, like an ancient stone wall. Her breasts were round, smaller than he would have thought. She moaned like an animal in heat when he touched her. It surprised him that he could do that. That his fingers had such great power.

How did we get here? It was just a few days ago that he swore to himself that he could never see her in this light. How quickly things can change.

He locked eyes with her and gave a devilish smile.

"This is better than I imagined," Mickey said.

"What, have you been imagining this have you?" His fingers continued to run over the length of her thigh.

"I've been thinking about it for so long."

He stopped and looked up to find her watching him, her eyes heavy with lust.

"I knew that one day we would end up like this." she said.

A small explosion of laughter erupted from his mouth.

"Oh yeah baby, we were destined to be together," he said, chortling until he saw the look on her face. She couldn't possibly be serious.

She sat up. "Are you being sarcastic?"

"Are you?" he asked slowly.

"No."

"Me either." And just like that, Tom was married. As Mickey slowly lay back down, Tom thought of a hundred different ways to leave and never come back.

I have diarrhoea.

I just remembered my mother is in the hospital.

I have a third nipple.

The air between them was thick, and he knew that she knew that he knew she was in love with him. Tom was frozen. He could not will his fingers back to action.

"Mickey—I can't. I can't do this."

He sat up and turned away from her so she could fix herself up.

"What's wrong?" she said as she got up, oblivious of her breasts wobbling like jelly moulds. He tried not to look at them.

"I don't want there to be any… miscommunications."

God, he fancied himself a good guy. Maybe the best guy. He had more self-control than 100 monks. Maybe even Jesus himself.

"Clearly there's already been a miscommunication."

Her eyes were rock hard lumps as her hand began wildly searching for her clothes. She found her bra and latched it on, quicker than he'd ever been able to take one off. She began to wriggle back into her jeans.

"How?" he asked carefully.

"Well, I would have thought, you would never be so stupid, to think of me as someone you could just do *that* with."

Those poor pants. She was going to rip them soon if she didn't get them on.

"That if we were ever in *that* situation, you would have thought about the consequences."

"I'm thinking about them now." he said. He hoped his impish smile would be enough to quell her anger. Apparently, it was not. Was he not as cute as he thought he was?

"How could you possibly think you could sleep with me and that would be it?"

He stood up and put his own shirt on, starting to feel like a rat trapped in a hot bucket. How to explain the brain of a man? We are opportunistic creatures. We are jungle animals. We live for the chase, the fight, the moment. We are not lions. We are lame zebras that could be struck down and eaten at any moment. We must take any opportunity that comes our way, because there may never be another. Today could be our last. We must feast or be feasted upon.

"You've seen the Discovery Channel, right?"

She shook her head furiously. "No, no. I'm not going to let you attempt to diffuse this by listening to you unravel some stupid analogy."

She'd finally managed to dress herself, although he decided against telling her that her shirt was on backwards.

"It wasn't a stupid analogy. It was quite good actually."

"Shut up Tom."

He agreed and shut his mouth. There was no way he could get out of this. That was clear now.

"Now that I am properly dressed, I think I'm going to go out for a while."

She flounced away and swiped her keys from the table and was about to snap the door shut when she rounded on him again. Almost. He was so close.

"And just so you know, I'm not—like I don't have *feelings* for you. It's just because we're friends. I thought you'd have more respect."

She spat out that last word like it was dirt. A thick hot wave seeped into his stomach, but he couldn't help but hear the jazzy blare of R-E-S-P-E-C-T in his head. It's almost like an autoimmune response when someone says that word. Respect. Cue Aretha Franklin.

The thing was, he'd decided that he didn't really want someone again unless what he found in them was love. It was different for other people. They thought what they had found was love, but really, deep down, they knew what they had found was contentment. They were okay with it. Most people are happy with being content. But he didn't want to look at his life and think yeah, this is okay.

He wanted greatness. He wanted to be a photographer and a famous musician and a philanthropist and a millionaire. He wanted to be a teacher and a skydiving instructor and build houses for children in Africa. He wanted to defend the accused in court. He wanted to write the great Australian novel. There was no way he could wake up every day to the same life, the same old routine, because he knew that if he did that, there would come a day where he would fall into a pit and maybe he wouldn't ever crawl out of it. And he couldn't drag someone else down with him. If he was going to do it, if he was ever going to have that life, he knew there could not be a shred of doubt in his body about how he felt about them. It had to be show stopping, fall-to-your-knees love. A kind of love that would be able to save him. It was unfair—unfair to any future girl that would ever have the displeasure of dating him. They didn't deserve someone that felt that way about love. But that's how it was going to be. Love or nothing. Greatness or nothing.

It cost him.

Dearly.

Mickey asked him to move out. He was hardly surprised, but as he sat at the all too familiar family dining table, with its sad old placemats and a thousand scars across its face, he couldn't help but wonder if his near dalliance with Mickey was worth it. Worth being back inside this old house. Not beautiful, antique old with classic arches and magic nooks. Not even retro. Just old. Ugly old. Forever dark old. Sad old. Fake laminate covered the bench tops and floor of the kitchen as if it were a cheaply made film set. The walls were the colour of off milk and there was a chance that with every opening and closing of a door, the handle would fall off. It happened to Danny when he was in the bathroom once. He was trapped inside for three hours. It's not like his parents didn't have money. They had been sitting on a nest egg. When you have no hobbies and no friends, he guessed it built up pretty quickly. But maybe the separation had cleaned them both out. It was the first time he'd thought about it, actually. How was his mum coping financially now she had the house by herself? Was their dad still paying the mortgage? See, this is why he was glad he'd moved out. They weren't his problems when he wasn't near them, when he wasn't looking at them.

His mother was looking at him.

"So, what's your plan?"

Danny stared resolutely at his plate as their mother placed her knife and fork with a soft chink onto her plate and folded her hands together, her eyes fixed on Tom's face. The interrogation had begun, and he knew he'd be facing it alone. He loved Danny, but the kid couldn't even flag down a waiter, let alone stand up to their mother.

"Plan?" Tom asked innocently, as if he had no idea what she was talking about.

He knew exactly what she was going to say. In fact, he didn't even need her here to have the conversation. He could recite all of her parts by himself now.

"Yes. What are you going to do with yourself? Now that you're back home?"

He didn't know what the connection was, but apparently being back home meant he had to *do* something.

"Well, I sent through my application and I should be accepted into the priesthood any day now." he said, tucking into his dinner with forced gusto. "That's what you meant right?"

She fiddled with her fork. "I'm just asking. What are your plans for the future?"

"I don't know. Why do we always have to plan to do something with our lives? Why can't I do what I'm doing and be happy?"

"I would be happy for you. If that's what you really wanted."

She had this look on her face like she was a cat that had just learned how to use the toilet.

"You would be happy for me if I spent the rest of my life working at a chicken shop?"

Since the age of 16, Tom had been working at Cliff's Chicken, a little grease box in the centre of one of the busiest streets in Melbourne. He liked Cliff. He'd never met a person who better suited their own name. He was easy going and tougher than an old sponge.

"Sure. If that's what you really want."

That's some serious metaphysical shit right there. She could not possibly pin her happiness so completely to a state of existence that didn't exist.

"You're not happy with me working there now, so why would you be happy for me if I worked there in the future?"

"I'm only unhappy because you're unhappy."

"But if my happiness changed, you'd be happy."

"That's right."

He frowned at her. "But how could you distinguish the two states? How could you be so completely unhappy now and so happy then?"

"I'm a mother. That's what we do."

Sitting straight-backed in her chair with her lips pursed and eyes glinting, she looked like Queen Elizabeth atop a throne made of self-righteousness and cheap pine.

"It concerns me that your emotions are so adaptable." he said.

She smiled and so did Tom.

Victory: Thomas.

He liked bringing out this side of his mother. There was a shadow of fire in her. Again, he couldn't help but wonder what she was like before she met his father. He bet she wasn't hunkering down and studying when she was his age. She would have been head banging all night to punk rock. He heard her sometimes, singing in her room when she thought they were all out.

"Tell me. Just tell me one thing."

God, she was unrelenting.

"I don't know. Accounting?" he honestly could not think of anything worse to do with his time. He'd rather lick dog poo off the sidewalks.

She scoffed. "If you're going to become an accountant then I'm going to become a stripper."

Tom nearly choked on a mouthful of potato mash. He heard Dan splutter next to him as well.

"Excuse me?"

It was the wildest thing he'd ever heard her say. Things like that weren't said in their house. She didn't even look abashed. She just shrugged, stood up and then danced, shimmying and sashaying as she took the dishes to the sink.

"What is happening in here? God, my eyes. *Stop.*"

Later that night, Danny and Tom were sitting in the lounge room. It was dark, lit only by the small flat screen in the corner and the occasional glow of headlights from the street. Danny was on the sofa, his long legs stretched across half the room, a teacup balancing on his thigh. They were always drinking tea. He didn't know where that had come from. They weren't English. They weren't anything. Just tea drinkers.

Danny's eyes were focused on the TV. Suddenly, he turned his eyes to Tom.

"Mum's right."

"What?"

"You need to do something with your life."

Tom couldn't believe Danny was taking her side. He would never back anyone over Danny.

"You want me to be an accountant so I can do your taxes?"

"No. I want you to get your life together."

Tom reeled back. Where was this coming from? It was so *un*-Danny like. Tom could have said so many things back to him. Here was a guy, barely an adult, recovering from an addiction to painkillers, telling him to get *his* shit together. But he couldn't say that to Danny. It would be a low blow, even for him.

"What would you like me to do your Majesty?" Tom said instead, folding his hands in his lap obediently.

Danny shrugged, his face set as it usually was—like a sheet of blank paper. It never gave away his secrets. People were always telling Tom his own face was so *expressive*. He could be an actor, they said. He'd usually then do a famous line from a movie like '*You can't handle the truth!*' and then they'd give him a strange look and say, '*Maybe not*'.

"It doesn't matter. Just do something. You're throwing it all away."

"Jesus Christ. Why does everyone act like I should be a supreme court judge?"

"Because you could be one. You could do whatever you wanted. You're the smartest person I know."

"Tha—"

"But you won't."

"Don't hold back or anything."

Tom didn't really mind Danny insulting him, because it was Danny, but he didn't like it. He might be the only person in the world Tom took seriously. And he really didn't want to have to think seriously about the things Danny was saying.

"Well, I'm pissed off. You're healthy and you're wasting it. The last few years I feel like I've just been watching you waste away."

"Funny. Could have said the same thing about you." Tom said coolly.

Turns out he wasn't below insulting Danny after all. They stared each other down until Danny's eyes flicked back to rest on the TV screen and he was a marble effigy again.

Really, Tom saw now that it had made perfect sense that Danny had become an addict. Danny knew that he'd never be able to do any of the things that are supposed to define you in this life. In a way, his addiction probably gave him some sort of identity. Strange, how much we need that. A job title. A name. A problem. Was it the more titles we had, the better we knew ourselves? Is that really why people got PhDs?

Tom's mind trailed back to Mickey, and he saw the image of her naked body stretched out in front of him, her face filled with regret and embarrassment. It was the same problem with girls. He didn't believe anyone, no matter how close they got—girlfriend, brother or mother—would ever really know who he was, see him how he saw himself. He wasn't even really sure how he did see himself. There was a part of him that was completely untouchable. He kind of knew that if he didn't find it, one day it would drive him mad.

Tom had no love for Al, an old friend of the family's. So, when his mother broke the news to him and Danny the next day that the old bastard had passed away, he didn't have much of a reaction. It was clear though, that Danny didn't feel the same way. Tom couldn't understand why. Danny could hardly remember Al. They didn't see him or his wife and daughter anymore.

"How?" Danny asked, his voice soft, his hands grasping at his jaw.

Georgia looked between the boys before answering. "I guess there's no point hiding it. Al was having some... personal troubles."

Tom waited for her to elaborate and when it became clear that she wouldn't, he smirked to himself. Classic. That was her idea of transparency. *Personal issues.*

He really tried to think of when he first realised that he hated Al. He knew he was pretty young, because he couldn't remember a time when he didn't hate him. The meatloaf incident was probably the earliest memory he had of hating him. He also hated his daughter. A lot. Peet. They were always crashing his family gatherings. She was always stealing kisses from his grandmother.

It was at one such gathering Tom was sat at the kitchen countertop next to Peet and a few of the smaller cousins. Or younger ones he should say. Peet was a large girl; her bottom gathered in little bunches over the edges of her chair. Her face was smudgy, almost as if someone had tried to erase it. There was nothing sharp about her features, except her piggy little currant eyes.

"Hey Peet, do you want my meatloaf?" Tom had picked the slimy square up with his knife.

"Umm, no thanks. I have mine."

Her eyes were focused on her meatloaf. She was pushing it around her plate, her mouth turned down.

From behind them, hands shot out to grab both their shoulders.

"Having fun kids?" said Al.

The scrub of Al's beard penetrated Tom's ear canal. Neither of them answered. Instead, Peet slammed her cutlery on the table.

"Do I really have to eat this?"

Tom had felt a bit sorry for his mum. She really didn't like cooking. If she had heard Peet say that, it might have been the thing to stop her from ever cooking again. Al's grip on Peet's shoulder tightened. Tom was surprised by her tenacity. Or stupidity, it was hard to tell. Al was a fearsome thing to behold. With his wild eyes, beard and bald head, he looked like a wild beast. Al lowered his voice, but somehow it was more terrifying that way, and whispered in their ears.

"You will eat your food and I will not hear anything more."

Peet looked around hoping to see another adult watching them, but everyone was outside sitting at the big table, chatting over pyramids of meat. Al turned on his heel to join the adults and Peet scarfed down her meatloaf. She might have even snorted it up her nose it was gone that quickly.

One of the younger cousins pulled on Peet's sleeve, demanding her attention. They seemed drawn to her as they never had to Tom.

Tom quickly slid his meatloaf onto her plate. He guffawed at his brilliance, sending out brain signals urging Peet to turn around. But it was not him that made her turn.

"Are you joking?" Al pressed his face into Peet's and her piggy little eyes were lit with fear.

"What?" she said, still with that attitude in her tone.

Be scared. Be sorry. Be anything that might make this man take pity on you.

"Your still haven't eaten your meatloaf!"

His voice went up a decibel with each syllable, mirroring the rising dread that was washing down Tom's body. Peet looked at her plate and her face contorted in confusion and fear.

"But... I did."

Just say you did it.

Looking at the heavy frown on her face, Tom wasn't sure she had pieced it together. Simple logic just kicked in and she concluded that if she had eaten her meatloaf, then this meatloaf must belong to someone else.

"This isn't mine! I ate mine! I did!" she protested as if she were on trial at the Supreme Court.

Just say you did it.

Something in her tone shot through the icy layers of Al's heart because he paused for a moment and looked at Tom.

"Thomas, did you see anything happen here?"

Just say you did it.

If his tone had been threatening like it had been to Peet, he probably would have confessed. But it was considerably softer and Tom knew that he did not suspect him in the slightest. He was the older one, more trustworthy and too mature for foolish pranks.

"No."

Peet began to cry. Big heaving sobs that made strings of saliva spin about her lips. Tom kept his eyes on his empty plate and his head bowed as his uncle dragged his cousin from the table and away from the party so he could punish her without watching eyes. That sounded quite sinister, but to a child it *is* sinister. As an adult now, Tom knew that he probably lectured her and at worse, maybe spanked her (as his own father had done to him on a few occasions growing up).

But still, it was the worst thing Tom had ever done. It wasn't *that* bad. But it was inexcusably mean. Under bright unforgiveable lights, it showcased the worst of him. Every time he looked into that memory, he felt like Dorian Gray. A little uglier, a little more exposed. He never told Peet the truth.

Tom hadn't seen Peet in a decade. Her mum left Al not long after that day. Idly, Tom wondered if it was because of the meatloaf incident. Had that been the moment that had splintered their marriage beyond repair? Had Peet told her mum all about Al's threats?

"Hey Dickbag." she said, sidling up to Tom. "You look like shit."

Peet had purple hair and a bosom the size of Mount Rushmore. She had paired a very short, pleated skirt with laced up boots and even Tom could see that it was completely inappropriate for the daytime, let alone her stepdad's funeral. She had some nerve, telling him *he* looked like shit.

"Oh, hey there Marilyn Manson."

"Original."

With one particular finger directed towards Tom, she strode past to stand by the coffin with her mother. The back of her cellulite dashed legs gleamed in the unforgiving sunlight streaming through the high, slanted windows of the room.

He wished he could say something snide behind her back, but he didn't have an audience. Danny hadn't come. He'd given no explanation, just shook his head ferociously and said 'he couldn't'. Even their mother hadn't come. She'd said she felt too uncomfortable: everyone would ask her questions about their dad. It was true, but why did Tom still have to be here? How did that work? How did Danny get out of it, but Tom had to wear a stupid suit and pretend to be sad for a man that he had hated?

He'd never been to a funeral, but the outdated wood-panelled walls and long uncomfortable benches were exactly as he imagined the interior of an old church to look like. There were bouquets of flowers scattered about the room and piled upon the closed casket, but they didn't quite mask the old room smell that lingered about.

Tom stared at the casket. He had never seen a dead body before. Did Al still look just as he did in real life? Perhaps a little pale, like a waxen doll, or was the old bastard just a hunk of meatloaf now? Soft and squishy, his flaccid face swimming in decomposing juices. Inwardly Tom shuddered, and not just from the image his brain had conjured. Tom was scared that one day he'd wake up and be in total darkness. Just like Al, the chemicals in his brain will re-align overnight and suddenly he wouldn't be able to make sense of waking up every day and eating, working, sleeping, shitting. Was that how it worked? One day you were okay with your stupid boring life and the next you couldn't get out of bed?

"Hits men differently I reckon."

Peet had sidled up next to him again. The funeral procession was about to begin.

"What?" Tom snapped.

She stared into the casket. "I just don't know if he really knew, you know? What was happening to him."

"Do you know what Peet? Screw the meatloaf. I wish I could go back in time and take a big sloppy dump on your plate instead."

He saw the confused look on her face as he twirled, snarling to himself, her words were ringing in his ears. Lately he had felt like he'd been hurdling from one calamity to another, grasping at straws. What if Peet was right, and he had no idea what was coming for him? What if he couldn't turn it around?

CHAPTER SEVEN

Very Painful, Mostly Usless Superpowers

It was a week before Danny went back to school. Maybe that sounds like a long time, but for Danny, it was practically honour roll worthy. Quite often, a bad migraine is followed by more bad migraines. Like a whole 'it's got to get worse before it gets better' scenario. Except it never did.

So, Danny writhed, rocked and whimpered for five days in his bedroom, praying to Baby Jesus to end it all, one way or another. You would think, after years of pain, you'd eventually grow accustomed to it. But pain isn't like that. Each cut bleeds new blood. And that's what each migraine did to him. It cut into the walls of his brain and bled him out, until he could take no more until finally, the pain would subside, and the grey matter would weakly stretch and stitch together in a clumsy knit, only to be ripped open once more.

But, despite the crippling pain, he felt strangely... *light*. He couldn't believe it, but he actually *wanted* to go back. He'd been absent for so long, a mere floating head in the sea, that he'd never known what it could be like to be a part of a community, for people to notice that he existed, and to question when he was gone. Leeroy had been texting him, asking him if he was okay and when he was coming back. Why? He didn't know. He couldn't fathom how all of a sudden, he mattered.

"So, you're going back to school tomorrow?"

Tom stirred a freshly made cup of tea, as per their usual after dinner routine, looking questioningly at the lunch ingredients Danny was taking out of the fridge and Danny himself.

"Yep." Danny said.

His head was buried deep into the vegetable crisper. He could feel Tom's eyes burning into his back. Re-emerging with a tomato and wilted spinach in his hand, Danny was annoyed to find Tom still looking at him. He raised his eyebrows as if to say *'Well? Is that okay with you?'*

Maddeningly, Tom stirred his tea, the spoon chinking against the porcelain. Chink. Chink. Chink. Danny closed his eyes, praying for patience.

"Yeah, sure, I mean, I can't stop you."

Danny slammed a chopping board on the table and roughly started to slice the tomato.

"So, then I guess it's *not* okay with you then."

"Can you make my lunch too?"

Danny just glared at him. Surely Tom knew he'd be getting no lunch, and no easy way out of the prickly argument he'd started. He was always stirring, always looking for a reaction he never actually wanted. Tom couldn't stop himself.

"Look, I just... I wonder if you going to school is actually the best idea."

Danny resolutely stared at the tomato.

"You cut a whole tomato up. What are you going to do with all that?" Tom asked.

Ignoring him, Danny started pilfering through the cupboards.

Tom sighed. "It puts you in a bad position."

Danny scoffed, holding an onion and a loaf of ciabatta. He could tell Tom was wondering what the hell was he making.

"The position of having an education so I can set myself up for life? Yeah, terrible right?" Danny cut the bread, turned the grill on and began to dice the tomatoes.

"Can you stop being such a sarcastic little b—" Tom collected himself, taking a sip of tea, "you can't tell when the migraines are going to happen. You can't take medication that will really do anything. You're setting yourself up to fail."

"What am I supposed to do?" Danny asked, throwing his hands up, nearly losing the plate of tomatoes to the floor.

"I think you should leave." Tom said blandly. "Surely you can't be doing very well anyway."

The little red notification flashed into Danny's head again. *'Due to low attendance, you are at risk of not successfully completing year 11...'* The school's roundabout way of telling him he was failing. He was failing because his head was faulty. He felt like a used car, thrown in the junkyard because he was barely putting along, breaking down at every corner. Throw it away. Raid it for parts.

"No one would think less of you for leaving." Tom said, like he knew what Danny was thinking. But he had no idea.

"I am so proud, that I wake up every morning. Nobody thinks about that. Nobody pats me on the back. I think I deserve some congratulations. Do you know how goddamn hard that is? To get out of bed knowing you're going to be in pain? Have you thought about that?"

Danny was waving the knife around, and Tom eyed it cautiously. Tom put a hand to his heart, setting his tea on the kitchen counter.

"Mate, I am *so* proud of you. I cannot believe what you go through. If it were me, I would have—" he stopped himself, for once thinking about what he was about to say. "No one would think less of you for leaving." he repeated, more firmly this time. "It just makes sense. Take some time off, wait puberty out, the headaches will get better, and then go to TAFE or something and finish later."

Tom's face lit up. "Hey, you could take the year to travel and paint! How amazing would that be? I mean, I haven't seen you paint much lately. This would finally give you the time."

Tom was looking at him so eagerly that Danny didn't have the heart to tell him the truth. It wasn't time that had stopped him painting. Really, he had all the time in the world. It was something else. Something that filled his body with lethargy. Something that moaned and groaned in protest whenever he even thought of doing something productive. He'd packed up his paints and stuffed them in his wardrobe.

"Mum would think less of me." Danny said instead.

It was true. Even though he had tried so hard not to disappoint her. His whole teenage life, Danny felt like he had been running on the spot, his arms spinning like pinwheels, his legs jarring and cranking each time they hit the ground. The harder he tried, the more he wanted something, the further it seemed to drift away. Who would think that he'd be missing so much? No school meant so many other nos. Tom made it seem like it was a simple choice.

"She wouldn't." Tom said, but the words sounded flat.

Even though it was a logical decision, they both knew that Georgia would never support it. Danny didn't know how he knew it, but it's just what happens when you spend most of your life around a person. Especially a parent. They rarely surprise you.

Danny began to delicately pick basil from the herbs lining the kitchen sill.

"Bruschetta!" Tom yelled, causing Danny to jump and drop his pickings in the sink. "You're making bruschetta!"

Danny eyed him like he'd lost his marbles.

"Sorry, I've just been trying to figure it out this whole time—what you were making." Tom looked thoughtful for a moment. "Are you planning on taking bruschetta to school for lunch?"

"Well, there aren't a whole lot of options are there. Seeing as neither you nor mum have been shopping."

Tom mimed playing a little violin. "Oh, the poor little rich boy doesn't have a packed lunch for school."

"We are not rich."

"We aren't poor."

Danny gave Tom a levelling look. "I'm going to school."

Turning his head, Danny slowly scanned the crowded corridor. He felt like he was an immovable statue. Definitely not one of the buzzing little creatures flitting from one locker to next. Get it all out now, he thought. Because by the end of the day, you'll be sick of the sight of each other.

He kept his head above the crowd, still searching. How ironic would it be, if on the day he actually showed up to school, she was away? That would be his luck. If God kept this up, then he was sure to die celibate. If he kept craning his neck like this though, he'd also die a virgin because all the girls at the school would realise he was a desperate loser, and then they'd tell all the other girls on the planet and he'd be done for.

So, as he set off down the corridor, he looked at his shoes instead.

The bell had rung, and it was starting to clear out, leaving only a few late comers. Some pulled books slowly from their bags like they were still half asleep, barely registering that classes had started. Others, namely the younger ones, dived headfirst into their lockers, their hands zipping through the neat collection of papers and textbooks, desperate to find the equipment they needed. He remembered that feeling. Wanting to be on time to class, eager to do the right thing. He was starting to see now that it didn't matter. Things were going to happen, one way or another.

So, he meandered down the hallways, taking in the unnatural quietness of students' learning, breathing it in, remembering it, because he knew that in a quick beat, he'd be done with it. He'd finish school, *one way or another* and then he'd never have a reason to come back. Strange, how a place could be such a cornerstone in your life one day and then the moment you leave you never see it again.

"Danny!"

He whirled around. Leeroy, Kyraah, Ali and Grant were standing in a huddle behind him, completely oblivious to the fact that they were all supposed to be in classes.

"Hey." Danny said simply as his eyes darted over the group.

The two boys, Ali and Grant, were standing slightly apart from the other two, as if there was an invisible barrier between them.

Ah.

With that one gesture, it all clicked into place. It had only been a week. But in high school time, a week is like six months. Kids move fast. It's as if they don't realise their lives don't end after high school.

He understood then, why Leeroy had been messaging him. It wasn't about Danny. It was about the girl. It made sense. Leeroy was funny and charming and *uncomplicated*. Danny was a mess. Kyraah met Danny's eyes, and he knew she could see that he had seen it—seen their intimacy.

"Why aren't you in class?" Danny asked the group, collecting himself.

Ali grinned at him. "Why aren't *you* in class?"

Danny shrugged. "Everyone knows I don't have to be. You lot will get in trouble though."

As if summoned, their head of senior school, Mr D'Angelos, rounded the corridor and blinked at them all. He was a portly man, and always looked stressed—which he probably was. He paused, looking at Danny for a moment before he turned and rounded on the others. Danny smiled widely at them behind Mr D's back. Being chronically ill was almost like having a superpower. A very painful, mostly useless superpower.

"What are we doing out of class?"

"We were helping Danny sir."

Ali's eyes flicked towards him and Danny frowned at the easiness in his voice. He hardly knew Ali.

"He came late to school. We just wanted to make sure he was okay."

Danny couldn't tell if it was a lie or not. His face was cool as glass. It was clear that Mr D was also facing the same struggle as he ran his eyes over them, his face turning redder. He threw a final glance at Danny and dropped his voice.

"Are you okay Mr Carter?"

Danny saw Kyraah shuffle her feet and Danny felt himself reddening, mumbling in the affirmative.

He knew Mr D was inwardly cursing himself. He'd broken the teenage code. Rule number one: Getting sympathy from adults in front of your friends makes you look weak and uncool. Mr D knew that. He'd been in schools long enough.

"Well, that's… very good of you. Mr Carter, you are lucky to have such good friends."

Danny nodded obediently.

"Off to class then."

The group obeyed, and Danny could feel Mr D's eyes burning into their backs. Speaking of superpowers, that was one only teachers really had: the ability to produce laser beams from their eyeballs. Well, teachers and Superman.

Kyraah tugged on Danny's elbow as the group headed back towards the locker bay, teachers eyeing them suspiciously from their classrooms as they walked past, the group's voices floating into the rooms, disturbing the quiet they had fought so hard for.

"It's good to see you again." Kyraah said quietly, casting a sidelong look at him.

Was it? She looked like she meant it. But Danny couldn't shake what he saw. Or more what he *felt* between her and Leeroy. The intimacy. The closeness. He wouldn't get in the way of that. He was good at staying in the shadows.

Danny wrapped his arms around himself, and her hand dropped to her side. "Likewise."

She accepted his curtness with a small smile. It only made him feel worse. But it didn't matter, he told himself. It was one girl, one fleeting moment in his life that would eventually be lost to time. It was a speck, and he would brush it off as easily as he ever had.

She would be forgotten.

CHAPTER EIGHT

Black and Navy

Tom didn't know why, but something inside Danny had shifted. He was a little quieter, his eyes a little duller. He was slower to laughter, quicker to retreat from conversation. Maybe he was just a teenager. Tom didn't think he'd ever acted that way himself, but then he and Danny were different people. Tom had always thought they were like black and navy, but he was beginning to notice the different streaks within them. Danny had a kind of silence about him that Tom did not understand, because Tom voiced every thought he'd ever had.

What goes on in that broken brain of yours, brother?

Tom knew that Danny's brain was always ticking and he had a sneaking suspicion that his younger brother was much, much smarter than he was. He was definitely more talented, that's for sure. Tom marvelled at what the boy could do with a paintbrush. Like how could all of that imagination just slip out of his hands? The only thing Tom's hand was good for was… well, you don't need much imagination to finish that sentence.

He watched as Danny skewered olive after olive on a small fork, sometimes throwing a cracker into his mouth, swilling it all down with a tall glass of water. The boy's palette was questionable, that's for sure. He didn't even stop to slather it in tomato sauce. Danny paused for a moment as his eyelids fluttered, a tell-tale sign that a migraine was brewing. Maybe it was the cost of Danny's beauty, of his talent. Maybe God had let Tom off scot-free because he felt bad for how ugly and stupid he'd made him in comparison. Or maybe Tom's turn was coming. Lately it felt like the numbers were stacking against him: the robbery, the breakup, his dalliance with Mickey—he felt like it was all leading somewhere.

Danny was the only one he told about it. In usual Danny style, he listened in silence, his face as empty as Tom's bank account. Danny rubbed his temples, and Tom wished he could have shut himself up. Danny didn't need Tom adding to the weight pressing on his skull.

"So, you think—" Danny paused to take a slow breath, exhaling softly though his nostrils, "you think that something bad is going to happen to you?"

"I just can't shake the feeling that something terrible is right around the corner. Like… I've got a feeling."

Danny nodded his head wisely bringing the pads of his fingertips together as if he was some all-seeing, all-knowing God.

Tom narrowed his eyes. "You think I'm crazy."

Danny held up his hands. "No, no, I just think—"

"Stop smiling."

"I'm not smiling," Danny laughed. "You're just being paranoid. You're always paranoid."

"Gee, thanks. But don't you ever get that feeling? Like things are about to change forever?"

Danny looked Tom in the eyes.

"That's how life is. There's *always* something bad around the corner, because we're human and every day we get closer to death."

Silence echoed about the kitchen. Why did they always seem to have these talks in the kitchen?

"Well shit. That was a mood killer. Thank you very much for that." Tom said.

Danny smiled. "No worries. Any time you want some cheering up, I'm here for you."

"You mean any time I want some motivation to blow my own brains out? Yeah, I'll come running to you."

Danny shrugged. "Just telling you how it is."

Tom wanted to argue with him, tell him he was being a pessimistic little shit, but he couldn't bring the words to his lips. How *very* unlike Danny. Tom told himself the kid was just grumpy after going back to school. Tom didn't know what happened, but something must have. Maybe it was good for Danny, to experience some teenage dramas. You haven't really had the full teenage experience until you've cried in your bedroom all night, listening to music that shakes the very foundations of the house. Tom was thankful he was old enough now, to have put that kind of self-loathing behind him.

"So, have you sorted things out with Mickey?" Danny asked, changing the subject.

Tom hated that he'd told Danny what had happened. But he couldn't help himself.

"Not… exactly." Tom said, fiddling with a hole in the white doily covering their table.

Not for the first time, he wondered at the interior design choices his mother had made when furnishing the house. She wasn't the most stylish of women, but the place looked like a nun's bedroom.

"I don't know how to fix it." he added.

"Have you tried saying 'sorry'?" asked Danny.

Tom dropped his voice to a whisper. He didn't want his mother hearing them talk about s-e-x.

"Hi Mickey. So sorry for trying to *boink* you the other day." Tom paused, looking thoughtful. "Is that how you use boink in a sentence?"

"I think it's a noun, not a verb. Oh, hang on, let me trying a few sentences. 'I enjoy a good bonking.' Hmm noun. 'Let's boink tonight.' Verb, definitely a verb there. I don't know, I'm confused. Do you know what's more confusing than women? The English language."

Tom sighed. "Aren't you supposed to be giving me advice?"

"Look, just… invite her out or something. Make the first move." Danny looked brightly at the olive he was eating. "Extend the olive branch."

Tom frowned at him and his olive. He'd never really had a taste for them.

"Clever. I never understood that saying. Why olives? Is there something particularly peaceful about them?"

"They are a very non-threatening fruit."

"I'm not sure that they're a fruit."

Danny rolled his eyes. "Well anyway, invite her out. It's a Saturday night. Surely there's a party on."

Tom's stomach gave a painful twitch, like it was trying to hurl itself off a sharp cliff.

"You're friends. You've been friends for a long time. She won't throw that away so quickly." Danny gave him a pat on the back as he stood up, still rubbing his temples as he left the kitchen.

Tom didn't share Danny's confidence. Mickey's words were ringing in his ears.

We're friends. I thought you'd have more respect.

Clearly, he had been prepared to throw it all away. Why would she honour it now, after what he had done?

CHAPTER NINE

Big Personality

What was she doing here?

This was a party Tom had brought him to. He shouldn't really be here, let alone a girl that was a year younger than him. All the people here were clearly Tom's age. Some sat in a huddled groups around a fire, and others milled about a makeshift dance floor. Danny had sworn to forget her. He could hardly do that if she started popping up everywhere he went.

"Who's that?" Tom hissed, following Danny's gaze as they stepped into the dimly lit back yard.

"No one."

"She's pretty."

Danny didn't like the way Tom's eyes raked her body. He knew Tom was taking in the skirt, the top, the hair. He never seemed to make any effort, but women were drawn to Tom. They were never like that with him.

Thankfully, Kyraah hadn't seen them. Danny turned his back on her before she could. But he knew he couldn't hide. He just needed a moment.

"Well, she's taken, so don't get any ideas. Besides. You're far too old."

Tom looked affronted. "I'm not that old."

"Don't be creepy."

Tom rolled his eyes. "She's off limits, I get it. She's yours. You don't have to spell it out."

"She's not—" but Tom had already walked away, beckoning for him to follow.

Danny watched him for a moment as he stopped at the drinks table, grabbing a beer. He looked at Danny from the corner of his eye and then slowly put the beer back.

"It's fine, you can have a beer."

"Oh, I know—I just thought—I didn't want to make you uncomfortable... I'm driving anyway." Tom floundered.

Danny rolled his eyes. "A whiff of beer isn't going to turn me into a pill popping monster. Seen Mickey yet?" Danny asked, sending Tom floundering again.

"No. I—I don't think she's here."

Danny patted his back. "Funny how people don't show up to parties you don't invite them to. Don't worry about it. She'll get over it...eventually."

Danny knew he sounded reassuring, but really, he wasn't so sure. He really had expected her to come. Maybe this was something she couldn't get over. He sighed to himself. *Our ties to one another are so damn fragile. Any relationship could be broken. The only question was, what would it take, to make a clean cut?* For Mickey the answer was clear enough.

It took 20 minutes for Kyraah to spot Danny and then another 20 for her to approach him. He wondered, if their situations were reversed, if he would do the same. He didn't think he would.

"Hey, what are you doing here?" she said brightly, as if she'd only just spotted him.

"Hey." Danny was surprised at how evenly his voice came out. He nodded towards Tom who had started to dance, the only one moving on the dancefloor. He had to admit, he was quite good. "I came with my brother."

"That's your brother?" her voice was louder than he remembered.

He took in the glassy sheen to her eyes, the slight slur of her words. She'd been drinking.

"You two don't seem very similar."

"Don't we look alike?"

She took the opportunity to look Danny up and down. It made him shiver. He didn't like that she could do that to him. He was glad he was leaning against a pole so he could still look cool and aloof. He was sure he looked cool and aloof.

"I guess you do. But he has a big personality."

So, by comparison, did that mean his personality was small? He'd never gotten that saying. Why did being a loud attention seeker mean that you had more personality? Not that he thought Tom was those things. Well, he was, but he was more than just those things.

Danny nodded slowly, looking away from her. He didn't want to make this easy. Something held him back from her and he wasn't quite sure what it was. She stepped closer to him and he stood up a little straighter. Smiling, she grabbed his arm and led him away from the dancefloor. Was he dreaming? As they rounded the corner of the house, Danny locked eyes with Tom and saw him whoop mutely and pump his fist into the air.

Kyraah stopped as soon as they rounded the corner. It was amazing, how much quieter it was on this side of the house. It was almost as if they were the only two people at the party.

She looked up at him and her eyes seemed even bigger. He hadn't really noticed just how much taller he was than her. It wasn't until he looked at those eyes and thought about kissing her that he realised what a feat that would actually be.

"Danny—"

She was fighting the same thing he was. He could see it. It was a betrayal. It was wrong. It was all in her eyes. But he was so *sick* of feeling everything, feeling pain all the time. For once, he just wanted to feel good. He deserved that didn't he? To live for once?

He wanted to grab her arms and pull her body against his. He wanted to feel her lips on his and marvel that they were even softer than he had imagined. He wanted to taste the booze on her breath, because even that couldn't ruin the moment he had stolen. For that is what it would be. Something that wasn't his. He was so used to things being taken from him; he didn't know how to reclaim them. And he didn't know how to begin to explain that. So, he just shook his head, refusing to look at her until he felt her step away from him.

"Danny?"

He shook his head again, wondering where his words had gone. It would be easier, less painful, if he could explain it to her. Explain that he didn't deserve it, the moment she was offering him. Instead, he turned from her and stared resolutely at the sky until he knew he was standing alone. He was thankful she had left him, hadn't pushed him. Not that she would have gotten anything out of him. He almost marvelled at how he could shut down, clam up like a criminal under interrogation.

He was broken, he knew it. Completely broken.

CHAPTER TEN

Biggie Smalls is the Master of Everything

Moonlight was hitting the road dead on. It was one of those nights where the road looked like a silver finger of sand. It seemed to stretch on into the horizon, like a mystic portal had opened from the sky. The trees zipped past in a silent shimmer.

Tom would have had the music pumping, ('90s rap of course—Biggie Smalls is the master of everything) but Danny was sprawled in the back seat, his head lolling against the window, his breath escaping in rhythmic huffs. He did that often: curled up in the backseat. Tom didn't know how he didn't get car sick. He looked over at his sleeping form. The kid had been quiet after the party. Tom wondered what had happened behind the house. Maybe Danny was worried about his kissing prowess? Surely, he hadn't had much practise. But what if... he'd never had *any*? The thought almost made Tom cry out in frustration. Was God determined to completely suck all the life from the kid? To never let him experience all the wonderful things it had to offer? At least Danny had gotten to experience it tonight— even if maybe he'd used too much tongue.

Tom gripped the steering wheel, racing through the trees as the road cut through the scrub. It's funny in Melbourne, how quickly suburbia can turn to bushland. Or bushland turned into suburbia. They seemed to be in the middle of nowhere, sweeping down this smooth, unforgiving road, when civilisation was no more than 20 minutes away.

Tom felt like the only creature alive on planet Earth. Maybe it was the moon, but he felt very connected to all the aliens on the other planets. Like maybe he was an alien. The only one on Earth. He felt like they'd chosen tonight to reach out to him:

Tom

Tom

We can hear you. We are listening.

And they'd just be sitting there, in their spaceships in the sky, all straight backed and relaxed, knowing that they held all the answers to all the questions the tiny puny humans have because they'd discovered the fourth dimension and spoken to God himself.

How many more of us are there?

Why do I exist?

Why did God invent smooth peanut butter when crunchy makes it obsolete?

Sure, they were *listening*. But they weren't *answering*.

He looked back at Danny in the rear-view mirror as a shadow crossed his face. Tom's stomach dropped with a sharp, uneasy pang— Danny looked like a corpse; darkness hung in the hollows of his cheeks and eyes. His skin was a ghoulish reflection of the pale night.

A flicker of movement to Tom's left suddenly caught his attention. He backed off the accelerator and turned his head to see two glowing orbs shining from the darkness of the trees.

Aliens?

His brain was working too slowly.

The bushes parted, and a kangaroo hopped onto the road. They were common in these parts. His body kicked into action. He hit the brakes hard and heard the *pup-pup-pup* of the ABS kick in as the car squealed closer and closer to the roo. With every fibre in his body, he willed the car to stop, to slow. But apparently, human will means very little to the laws of physics.

He never knew how loud a car crash was.

He felt his whole body tense, and he gasped—maybe to suck a final, last breath of air in as Danny made a horrible noise, something between a curse and a rattling scream.

Tom had always heard about the dangers of swerving, so he kept the steering wheel true, hoping to squeeze the car around it. But the animal stepped further into their path and Tom got to look it dead in the eyes as its head smashed into the windscreen. The glass shattered and its body slammed into the bonnet. The car skidded before it came to a final, jolting stop. At the last second, he must have turned the wheel because they had ended up sideways, on the wrong side of the road, on a blind corner.

"No, no, no, no." Tom felt sick. He knew this wasn't a good spot to have ended up.

"You have blood coming down your face," Danny said shakily.

Tom looked at Danny, his pale, unmarked face once again illuminated by light. The light grew brighter.

A car rounded the corner.

It was so unfair. They hadn't seen a car the whole drive back from the party.

This time, there was barely a sound before the impact. There was no way the driver could have known they were there. He had no warning. There was an explosive thump as the car hit.

Blackness.

Blackness.

Tom was expecting it, expecting to pass out in the impact, and maybe he did for a moment, but he saw it all. The first hit, then the impact of the car against the trees, the airbag deploying; it all happened in one shot, like he'd forgotten to close his eyes.

Then he blinked.

A whimpering moan came from the back seat and Tom snapped his head up, paining shooting down the length of his spine. He ignored it, whipping around and straining against the seatbelt digging into his chest.

Tremors of terror rolled over him as he took Dan in. He was ravaged. His head was swelling and his eyes were beginning to bulge under his forehead. Tom didn't dare take his eyes off Danny's face as he fumbled for his seatbelt buckle, not only because he was scared to look properly at his body, but because he felt that the second he turned away, he would lose him.

Reluctantly, Tom ripped his eyes away from Dan and grasped for the door handle. The door swung open, and he lumbered to the back door; somehow the back of the car had remained relatively intact. His stomach dropped out of his body as he saw the damage done to the other car. It was a mess. Even from a distance he could see the driver was slumped over the steering wheel.

Movies never show what really happens after a crash. Paramedics didn't come sweeping in with their sirens wailing. Tom called them, his phone battery dying seconds after. He got back into the car and sat next to Danny, stroking as much of his face as he dared to touch. The idea of doing first aid crossed his mind, but he looked so beaten that Tom thought he might crumble under him. At some point he must have fallen asleep, because it was torn from him as quickly as it had come.

"Tom? It's Tom isn't it. You're the one that called us, aren't you?"

Tom was sentient enough to realise he was no longer in the car.

"I'm Tom," he croaked and then pointed to a stretcher that was being wheeled past him. "And that's Dan! DAN! DAN!"

Tom didn't know how many times he screamed at Danny, terror taking over the reins of his mind, pulling on his vocal cords.

Gentle, but forceful hands gripped his shoulders.

"It's okay mate, it's okay. He's still alive. Just let us do our job."

The hands pushed Tom, and he lay down, his brain trying to make sense over the words. *Still alive. As if his status of living had yet to be decided.* How could he be so close to death now, when just an hour ago the kid had been filled with life? How could the lips that had kissed a girl now be covered in blood? The image of Danny caked in blood haunted Tom, even when he found out later that most of the blood had been his own, courtesy of a broken nose from the force of the airbag.

As he recalled, without consulting medical reports, he had the following injuries:

Broken nose.

Several lacerations to the face and head.

Dan's injuries were far more extensive. It probably went on for pages and pages, but there was really only one that Tom could recall.

Traumatic brain injury

CHAPTER ELEVEN

When the Dam Walls Come Down

Dan was staring into a bowl of cornflakes. They were soggy, slowly drowning in a heavy dowsing of milk. He prodded them with his spoon, barely submerging them with his touch.

"Well done! Keep going."

Poke. Poke, poke.

"Come on, scoop them up."

A woman in her twenties, although her thin, meatless frame aged her a decade more, made a scooping motion with an invisible spoon.

Tom watched them, ignoring the doctor that stood by his side. It had not taken long for Tom to realise that doctors were a special breed of person. They were always in a rush, always glancing at their watches whenever they reluctantly stopped to speak to any of their patients' families. They were immune to tears. Never reacted to them, never shed them. They didn't care, not like the nurses did.

Tom motioned for the nurse and the doctor stiffened at the slight.

"I feel like he's close, like he could almost do it."

The nurse spoke quickly, launching her words at Tom before he could even speak. Tom was already shaking his head.

"I saw him scratch his arse earlier. He can pick up a spoon properly."

The nurse hesitated. "You think he doesn't want to feed himself?"

Tom made an affirmative grunt.

"He's only been here a little while—it's pretty hard to tell with traumatic brain injuries."

The doctor's bald head snapped up and Tom knew he thought she was overstepping the mark, but Tom liked her honesty. He liked honesty in all people, especially when they shouldn't be giving it.

The doctor cleared his throat. "His most recent brain scan shows little swelling. The contusions appear to be reducing. *Atomically*, he should be regaining normal functions."

Tom recognized the implications in the doctor's words and thought back to what the doctor told them when Danny was first brought into the rehabilitation unit. The doctor's words had been burnt into his brain. It felt like a lifetime ago, but in reality, it hadn't been long at all. Tom's own injuries were still far from healing. His nose felt like a hunk of beef slapped on his face.

"In car accidents, the brain is often severely injured because the inertia will cause the brain to hit the skull and in 20-30% of cases, this causes contusions—brain bruises." The doctor had said.

Georgia had nodded a little too quickly. Tom thought she might vomit all over herself. She'd barely spoken since the accident. Like a house of cards, she'd folded in on herself.

"Somewhere in this process, the brain chemistry can change. We don't exactly know why. It could be because of the damage done to the frontal lobe, or it could be due to a tearing of nerve fibres—something MRIs and CT scans can't pick up. It's almost ironic: the brain is arguably the most important organ in our bodies and we know so little about it. But Danny's brain, right now, is probably overwhelmed by too many chemicals."

The doctor leaned toward them and used his hands to mime his next analogy—a little too enthusiastically in Tom's opinion. He guessed it was interesting, but when it's your own brother, it kind of dampens it a bit.

"It's like everything is kept safely in a dam and only a river is supposed to get through... but imagine if the dam walls came down... the brain is hit with a tonne of dopamine, serotonin, norepinephrine..."

The doctor threw his hands in the air and leaned back in his chair once more.

"The brain is a delicate organ—even small changes can drastically affect it."

Tom thought Georgia might never be able to speak again. She kept opening and closing her mouth. The doctor's words had hit *her* like a broken dam. Instead, Tom spoke and felt his own words tremor in his mouth. But if he concentrated on what was here, what was now, then he wouldn't have to think about what had *been*. Wouldn't have to think about the little brother he was supposed to have protected. The little brother he'd failed. If he focused on what was here, the boy in the back seat became a blur—dregs his consciousness could barely swill about. The last thing he wanted to do, was to peer down that tunnel and see Danny limp and colourless and—no. *Don't look there. Don't look.*

He was just a kid. He didn't deserve this.

The hospital had pressed counselling sessions on Tom, telling him they were *free* and that it would *help* him process everything and he really should *go*, but he just couldn't see the point. Either he would be asked to look at what had happened—examine it, dissect it, or he would be told to bury it. Well, he didn't want to think about it and he was already not thinking about it, so in his eyes, he'd already counselled himself.

He knew clear as day that he could not change what had happened. He could only change what was happening now. He would do everything he could to make sure Danny became everything he had been. That was his future: to reunite this version of Danny with the Danny of a few weeks ago. A fraction of time, but the two were just that: fractions. Tom could mesh them together again.

"What will all those chemicals do to his brain, I mean… to him?" Tom had asked.

The doctor had spread his hands and shrugged his shoulders, as if he was being asked to predict the weather for next July.

"There's really no telling. So many factors can affect what could happen…" he trailed off, perhaps sensing they thought his answer was—well, that it sucked. He started to reel off the possibilities. "He could have memory loss, issues paying attention, dissociative disorders, depression, he could develop substance abuse—"

Tom and Georgia had looked at each other then. At least there was no chance of Danny *developing* substance abuse issues.

Tom sighed, trying to focus on what he could see now. He looked at the nurse watching Danny with a forlorn expression. They didn't like the young ones that came here. It was etched into their downturn mouths, the little bit of distance they put between themselves and Danny. The way they turned backs to him and their hearts away from him. To watch their bodies, break and wither—it was wrong. You knew they still had years left on the clock. They told Tom that Danny was a 'cutie' a 'real looker', even if he did need a few square meals. Danny certainly was thin and reedy, but his eyes looked bigger than ever, like the bay windows of a house for sale.

But no one really had any idea what was going on inside his brother's body. Tom felt like shaking him, banging his head against a wall a few times to see if he might be able to sift the lumps out of him and strip him back to what he was. As he watched, he saw that Danny's chin was tucked into his chest and he was flexing his freckled fingers in his lap. The spoon lay neglected on the thin wooden table of the recreation room. For all its canary yellow walls and bright posters tacked onto the walls, it still felt dark. It didn't fool Tom.

"Go and talk to your brother and see if he says anything. See if there is a reason he's not eating," Georgia said, nodding towards Dan. Ordinarily, he'd balk at taking orders from her, but he was relieved to even hear her speak.

Tentatively, Tom walked up to Dan and awkwardly pulled up chair, taking a seat next to him. The nurse walked off to help another patient, giving them some privacy.

"Given up on them, ey?" Tom nodded towards Dan's half-drowned cornflakes.

There weren't too many others about in the room and the table afforded them an intimacy that wasn't often available at the busy rehab centre. He leaned in and sighed, his blue eyes looking into their twins as he met Danny's. Tom shivered. The shutters were open but there was no furniture inside.

"What's going on Danny?"

Tom looked into Danny's face to see if his words had taken effect, but Danny only averted his eyes to look at the table again.

"Why are you punishing yourself? You need to eat. You can't live off an IV forever."

Danny's brow furrowed. He raised his eyes to Tom. Somehow, he'd gotten through.

"I..." his voice failed him, rusty from disuse. He coughed and tried again, but it was as raspy as ever. It would have been almost comical if the words that followed didn't come out of his mouth.

"I don't need to eat."

Tom waited, but Danny just looked at him.

"Because of the IV?"

"No."

Again, Tom waited, but Danny seemed content to sit in silence. He gave up.

"So then... why don't you need to eat?"

"Because I don't." Danny said.

"Is there any way I can phrase that question and get a different response than 'because'?"

Danny cocked his head and then got up and walked out of the room.

Something inside Tom told him not to follow, to let Danny just have the rest he obviously needed. He was tired. He was allowed to not make sense. Maybe there was something Tom was missing, some piece of vital information that would make their conversation clear. But he couldn't shake the voice inside his head that told him it wasn't *him* that was missing something.

"What happened?" Georgia asked, her eyes following Danny as he loped out of the room.

"That," said Tom, "is an excellent question."

CHAPTER TWELVE

The Boy in Room 14

Even after all these weeks, Georgia still felt sick to her belly. There was an angry, churning pool inside her, bubbling and hissing after every meal she ate. Maybe she had actually eaten something bad, and a parasite was growing fat and happy inside her. All she knew was that she couldn't stomach the thought of feeding it. Eating was becoming a laborious affair, and she approached it with as much trepidation as she did when she cleaned the boys' toilet. Besides, she felt a grim sort of satisfaction in watching her belly shrink and then disappear entirely. She was a magician, turning fat to skin and bones. She'd been taught her whole life that food was pleasure, and pleasure was a reward for the happy, the healthy, the good. How could she indulge, as if there was something to celebrate?

It was terrible. Horrific. She couldn't look at it, couldn't think about it except it kept coming to her: the sound of tires and teenagers screaming battered into her brain, again and again, as if she had been a passenger in the car herself. Tom didn't talk about what had happened, but she knew it must be inside him somewhere. He kept it to himself. Not that she was asking. Something warned her away. She didn't know if it came from her, or if it came from Tom, but it was a barrier she could not breach.

She felt like a child again.

She wished she could bury her head in her own mother's arms and let it all pass by. But that was a pipe dream. There was no one but her to protect her own. She had no idea if Simon knew what had happened. She had to believe that if he did know, he would have come storming through the hospital doors. No father could ignore something like this. But the truth was, she hadn't told him. But she hadn't told anyone. She just couldn't fathom picking up the phone and telling people. Why did that have to be her job? In the end, word had got out. She knew eventually someone in their circle would contact him, she was sure of it. Really, it was the least of her problems.

She needed to be there for Danny. It was difficult to do that though, when she had to leave him every day. The hospital closed to visitors in the evening, and every night guilt met her like an old friend as she passed under the lit-up exit sign that adorned the front entrance. *Tomorrow, I'll be back tomorrow.* It was only 12 hours, really, and he'd be asleep for most of that. He wouldn't even miss her. Not that she was entirely sure that he even registered her existence when she was there. He still wasn't communicating much. The hospital wasn't good for him. He needed to feel the comfort of his own space.

It was time he came home.

She squared her shoulders as she stepped from the car, her hands juggling her keys and the takeaway she'd picked up for Dan. The smell had made her stomach growl in protest, but she was trying to entice Danny to eat something. He hadn't eaten any of the hospital food. Just another reason why he should come home—not that her home cooking could work any miracles, but she'd try.

She'd come ready to fight today. As she walked down the corridors to Danny's room, she scrolled through the arguments she was going to make. She'd given up her work, taken a leave of absence so he'd always have someone around to look after him. He'd be more comfortable in his own room, having his family around him all the time. If they denied her, she swore to God she'd pick the boy up and march him through the doors anyway.

Taking a deep breath, she rounded the corner and stepped into Danny's room. She expected to see him as he usually was: propped up in bed, staring mindlessly at the TV or picking at his nails. But he lay flat on his back, his hands pressed into his chest, his face like cool marble. Bouquets of flowers were arranged around his upper body, wisps of baby's breath tickling his nose. It took her a moment to realise the flowers were the ones friends and family had sent him after the accident. A few of the bouquets still had cards tucked into their heads.

"Who... did this to you?" she breathed.

A slight tilt of his head told Georgia he'd heard her, even though he remained silent. She stormed out of the room and found a nurse looking at a computer screen. The smile the nurse gifted Georgia as she looked up quickly died.

"What's wrong?"

The nurse's tone was instantly business-like as she maneuvered her generous hips around the reception desk. Georgia was glad the woman was quick to action, because she didn't think she could summon her voice to her lips. She'd always found anger to act like a vice, compressing her, squashing every part of her. Georgia followed the woman to Danny's room, turning the corner to see her standing at the door, just as she had.

"What... on earth?" she muttered, before looking back at Georgia. "You... didn't do this did you?"

Georgia scoffed, nearly choking on her own saliva. The nurse nodded and turned to Danny.

"Daniel." she said sternly. "What's going on here? Why are there flowers all over your bed?"

He sighed, slowly opening his eyes and pulling himself up. "Well, I *was* enjoying being surrounded by this beauty." he brushed some rose petals from his blanket.

"Well, that's—nice," the nurse said, coming over to his bed to run a practiced eye over him. "But why were the flowers all around your head dear?"

"Because I was thinking about how nice it would be to lie with them around me. What it would feel like to lie like that *forever.*"

The nurse looked at Georgia from the corner of her eye.

"And you haven't... fallen out of bed or anything? Can you remember hitting your head at all?"

She asked the questions with genuine concern, running her fingers delicately over his buzzed scalp. Georgia knew she was checking for new bruises and bumps. All she could see herself was the fresh scar curved above his left ear.

"No." he said, looking up at the nurse expectantly.

The nurse's frown deepened, and Georgia cursed herself. Why did she have to go running for the nurse? If she had of just waited a moment, she could have thought this through. It was obvious from the beginning that Danny had arranged the flowers himself. There was no reason why anyone else would do it. There was no reason why he should do it either, for that matter. But now it was clear to her and soon it would be to the entire medical staff, that the boy in room 14 wasn't quite right. And if something was wrong, well, she could kiss her chances goodbye of getting Danny back home anytime soon.

Georgia forced a laugh from her belly and the nurse looked at her like she had lost her marbles.

"I just remembered— Danny's brother is coming soon."

The nurse looked at Georgia, her eyebrows like great arched bridges etched into her face.

"The two of them are always playing pranks on each other. They try to freak each other out by doing weird things. They used to have this creepy doll head, and they would put it all around the house to try and scare each other. Once it turned up in Tom's bed sheets."

Whenever she started blabbering like this, she would suddenly lose control of her arms and they would begin to wave about like ribbons. She nearly knocked over a vase of flowers.

"Right. Sounds very funny." the nurse said, in a tone that was anything but amused.

Georgia waved another hand out. "It's just silly teenage pranks. But it explains this." she said, remembering herself as she pointed to the flowers scattered around Danny.

The nurse gave a less than convinced grunt and turned to Danny. "So, have you got your sense of humour back young man?"

His body hardly turned as his neck swivelled in the nurse's direction. Georgia shuddered inwardly. She remembered being fifteen, watching Chucky for the first time. Did she just compare her child to a murderous doll?

He blinked at the nurse a few times before answering. "Is that something I can lose?"

The nurse laughed, turning to face Georgia. Looking over the woman's shoulder, Georgia could see Danny looked genuinely concerned.

"Maybe you're right. It's not really my type of humour—pranks and sarcasm."

She began to bustle about the room, opening the blinds and scooping up the cards that had fallen over on the dresser. Georgia guessed Danny knocked them down when he was collecting all the flowers.

"I don't really get all that. Too hard to know when someone's joking and when they're just being mean." she smiled at mother and son before walking to the doorway. Georgia scooted out of her way, sidling up beside Danny's bed.

"Just yell out if you need anything. I hope your little joke works Danny." the nurse said, winking at him.

Georgia listened to the sound of her shoes clapping on the linoleum fade before she exhaled. She didn't realise she'd even been holding her breath. Looking at Danny, she realised he still wore the same worried expression on his face.

"How do I find it?"

"What?"

"My sense of humour. How do I get it back?"

He turned to the window, as she could see the light and shadows of the sky reflected in his eyes.

"I've lost so much lately." he murmured.

She knew she should say something comforting, perhaps reach out and soothe his hair, but she couldn't force herself into the actions—actions that should come easily to a mother. She didn't want to touch him, afraid that if she did, he wouldn't feel like hers anymore. She felt like the cord between them had been cut again. The worm in her belly rolled and roiled, feasting on her insides as she began to collect the bouquets and scoop up the stray petals that littered Danny's bed.

CHAPTER THIRTEEN

Ice, Ice Baby

The road was long and straight; the small restaurants that jostled the pavement seemed to continue forever. It was busy, yet quiet. Cars streamed down the road in both directions, their wheels squelching and squeaking as they lost friction on the metal tram tracks.

There were people on the streets, but not as many as there should be. Melbourne, the city with the winning smile, had a problem with methamphetamine. Tom supposed most cities did, but this area was a renowned hot spot. Amongst the graffitied brick walls and shop front canopies, ice addicts convened in scattered groups.

Tom couldn't remember the last time he'd showered or ran a comb through his hair. Could he pass as hipster tramp? Wasn't it kind of cool these days to be smelly and unkempt? Mickey's face as he met her at the restaurant confirmed that it was not, although she kept quiet, electing instead to use her mouth as her main source of air intake.

At least one good thing had come from the accident. No, two good things:

One: He could be as stinky as he liked and no one would tell him off.

Two: No one could be angry with him. Mickey had all but forgiven him. In fact, she'd been bending over backwards to try and make things normal for him again.

"Danny's not even out of hospital," he'd replied every time she'd called to invite him out. He'd never been so popular in his life. His phone was filled with text messages and missed calls. Hers was the only one he answered.

"I know. I just thought a distraction could be good."

Did she know what was going through his head? Did she know that every time there was silence, he could hear the brakes, hear Danny's scream over and over again?

"Are you buying?"

He could basically hear her eyes rolling over the phone. "Sure. Limit is twenty dollars." she'd said.

What she hadn't told him though, was who *else* she'd invited. Why do people do that? Just assume that you like their friends, just because they like them. Seems pretty narcissistic really.

"It'll do you good," said Mickey as she waved to her two friends over Tom's shoulder.

"I thought it would be more fun with a few of us."

Tom nodded, thinking that at least he could sit back and let the conversation wash over him. He really didn't have the energy for much else.

Eddie had a thick beard and a full head of hair. There wasn't much face to look at after all that hair, but when you studied his deep-set eyes, you could see they were almost black. He had two interests: his job and his dating life. He liked to talk about them both equally and exclusively.

"Hey," Eddie said when he reached them, but his eyes were somewhere else.

Lucinda smiled by way of greeting. Her eyes were large and dewy, making it easy to overlook the stupid things she often said. Inwardly, Tom shook his head, marvelling at how Mickey could be friends with people like them. Maybe it was because she was so nice. Nice people tend to be surrounded by assholes. All good people love to torture themselves.

They were seated outside a small, non-descript Vietnamese café in rickety metal chairs. Tom felt unsafe on many accounts. Tom turned his head to see a man in his 30s —he could have been much younger— striding towards them. A checked shirt was wrapped around his waist and he wore nothing but stained cargo shorts. His exposed chest was meatless and sinewy.

"Can you spare a smoke man?" his voice was grating as he stood close to Eddie.

"Sure mate." Eddie's tone was personable as he offered a cigarette to the man.

"Can I have a light too?"

Eddie wordlessly lit his cigarette, avoiding eye contact.

"Thanks mate."

"No worries."

The man charged off and Eddie rounded on them. "God this place has gone to the dogs." Eddie sniffed. "It never used to be this bad."

"It's 1pm and I don't feel safe walking down the street," added Luc.

"Don't be stupid, they're not going to do anything to you." Tom snapped.

Tom's blood had risen so quickly it surprised even him. Only Mickey seemed to notice though, resting her hand on his forearm as if it would give him the patience he needed to put up with their idiocy.

"You don't know that." said Eddie staring after the man, "don't you see all the shit that's on the news? Half the shit that happens these days are caused by these people."

Mickey sucked in a breath. "Eddie."

Tom wanted to slap him, like a good hard hit might bring a layer of compassion to the surface of his being. Danny wasn't like *them* now, but what was the difference anyway? A bit of an addict, a lot of an addict. There wasn't a spectrum was there? It was like just because you let something foreign into your bloodstream, and it didn't matter how much, you were something less than human. Was there a name for that? Some sort of cultural disassociation? Us and *them*. History described monsters. Human beings that had become something else in warfare. They were inhuman. No one could believe that people could be that evil. But guess what? In the grand scheme of things, those history books weren't written all that long ago. And the truth is, you have no idea what you would do if the situation demanded it. Everything is situational. Add a little desperation, a little bad luck, and you wouldn't recognise the version of yourself you'd become.

Tom wondered where the addicts' families were. He tried to imagine what they were like. Was there a mother and father at home, on the couch, sitting with their bodies locked tight, waiting for their son to come home? Living in commission housing with no curtains and no hope? Or were their families nestled in the big houses with the big gates in the next suburb over? Maybe they didn't even notice when someone didn't come home.

His heart panged. For them, for Danny, for himself—he didn't know.

With a gargantuan effort, Tom turned his stiffened body to the menu and squinted at the imperfect English translations.

"Mick, what are you having? The pho looks good," he said.

Tom could feel Mickey's eyes on him. He knew why. She was expecting him to blow up, to hit her stupid friend with every limb on his body and every insult in his vocabulary. If he were telling the truth, he was surprised as well. It wasn't like Tom to show restraint. Maybe he really was growing up. He was however, vividly imagining what it would be like to drown Eddie in a bowl of beef pho.

It wouldn't be the worst death imaginable. Pho is magic in a bowl. It was invented by the Vietnamese to give humans one of the only pure and complete sensual experiences available on this planet. Yes, that does sound very sexual, but that's what pho is. Sex for the stomach. It engages all the senses. You smell it before you see it. Lemongrass and sizzling beef wafts to your nostrils, tickling them in a playful foreplay. Then it's a vision to behold. The bowl is the size of a trough and it's not like a bag of chips when you look inside and its only filled halfway. Oh no. This thing is piled high with tender beef and bean sprouts. Tom had a philosophy about life, one that just sort of sprung to mind when he was thinking about pho: the best things in life are simple things, the small moments. The best foods are simple foods.

Tom's stomach was cramped in hunger, despite having eaten most of the group's appetizers.

He stabbed a chopstick into the last dumpling. "Do you know," he twirled it around, "I think I could easily eat 25 of these."

"Well, you can't just say that." said Eddie through a cloud of smoke.

Tom couldn't decide if his smoking annoyed him or not. He wanted to be more annoyed than what he actually was.

"Ah, I think I can. I'm pretty sure I could eat 25 dumplings no worries." Tom stabbed his skewered dumpling in Eddie's direction, aggressively waving it in his face.

"I reckon he could," said Lucinda.

"No. 25 dumplings is a lot of dumplings."

"Have you seen how small they are?"

"It doesn't matter anyway. You can't say something like that unless you can eat 25 dumplings." Eddie spoke slowly and surely, like every word he was saying was a neatly packaged gift from God and on it read: 'To Eddie. From God.'

"But I don't want to eat 25 dumplings." Tom said, like Eddie was a child who'd just declared he was going to walk to the moon.

This was fast becoming one of the stupidest conversations Tom had ever had, and he was the King, no—*Supreme Ruler*—of ridiculous conversations.

"Well, then it's an opinion and not a fact. Expect that someone is going to challenge you unless it's a fact." Eddie's face was perfectly calm.

Tom wanted to wring his neck. Why was he having to defend his opinion on pork dumplings like it was the last bastion of value and pride in his being?

"Is that what they teach you in law school? How to use logic to argue pointlessly?" Tom quipped.

"I'm not being funny. I'm just saying. You can't say you can do something unless you've done it. Unless you can actually eat that many dumplings, then you can't."

"I legitimately think I could eat 25 dumplings."

"Then prove it!"

"But I don't want to eat 25 dumplings!"

"Oh my god. You two. Shut up. You're talking about *dumplings*." said Mickey, rolling her eyes and beginning to arrange her cutlery. Their food had finally arrived. Tom hated her maybe more than he hated Eddie in that moment. She was supposed to have his back. She was supposed to know that Eddie was a worthless wart on the flesh of the world.

"Shut up yourself."

And just then, as Tom went to reposition himself, the universe decided that he didn't look like enough of a dick already, that he hadn't had enough bad things happen to him lately, and pulled his chair from underneath him. He landed on his ass. The group broke out in laughter. You know how sometimes laughter diffuses a situation?

Well, this was enemy gunfire. Tom looked into Eddie's face and saw his eyes remained unchanged and a hardness to the corners of his smile.

So, Tom did something he wasn't proud of. That's not said lightly. He was a stubborn ass, so it was hard for him to look at his actions with any admissions of fault. But this one... was definitely questionable.

He picked up his bowl of pho and poured it over Eddie's head. Bits of noodle clung to Eddie's hair and broth trickled in little rivers down his face. It would have been hot too.

After a second of silence the girls gasped and muttered. Tom revelled in the fact that finally, he'd lost his damn mind. In all honesty, it had been a long time coming. A string of guttural words launched from Eddie's mouth—his vernacular of swear words was much more impressive than Tom's.

"My jeans! Do you know how much these cost you little runt?"

Ok so he didn't say runt, but you get the idea.

Eddie sprung up from his chair, knocking glasses from the table with a sprinkling crash. The girls screamed, but Tom knew there was no stopping him. He could see the predatory look in Eddie's eye. Tom was off—off like a rabbit at a racetrack. He had no qualms about doing that; he was not waiting around to get his face bashed in. He had never been in a fight and knew he'd never win. His feet pumped the pavement. Was he flying? He almost trampled a homeless man and his dog as they were curled up outside a bakery a few shops up. He was Muhammed Ali, ducking and weaving through streetlamps and under the arms of unassuming passers-by.

Eddie's heavy steps thudded behind him. There was no way he was going to catch him. *Give up Eddie, you cannot beat me.* An insane smile sprung to Tom's lips, just as a hand yanked the back of his top. That was enough to upset his balance. Tom lurched forward. Some common sense must have kicked in because he didn't fling his arms out to break the fall—breaking the fall meant breaking his wrists. So, he took the brunt of the impact on his left shoulder.

He hit the pavement. Hard.

The skin on Tom's face became finely grated cheese as it sliced against the ground. It hurt like hell. He thought maybe even for a moment that's where he was because he couldn't feel a thing. Like someone had cut the cord between his brain and his body.

"I think I'm dead," he whispered to Eddie's shoes.

Eddie was standing over Tom, panting, his eyes scanning Tom's body for signs of life. Eddie dug his foot into Tom's ribs and Tom looked up into his face. Eddie's eyes were still flashing and his foot reeled back as if he was winding up for a kick.

"Oh God! Don't. Please don't kick me."

People were staring, but Tom continued to cradle his face into the pavement. If he didn't see the kick coming, then maybe it wouldn't hurt so much.

It wasn't as much mercy as it was an unwillingness to cause a scene, but Eddie retracted his extended leg, muttered something under his breath and then sharply turned and walked away. Tom rolled onto his back and lay there, in the middle of the pavement, like he was some sun drunk teenage girl hoping to get a tan. Gingerly, he prodded his own face, assessing the damage. He could already tell that his left eye had started to swell. He saw Mickey jogging up the street and he looked at her, a maniacal grin spreading across his face.

"Does anyone have some ice? I think I need some ice over here!"

A gaggle of people gaped at him as they walked past.

Yep, he'd definitely lost his damn mind.

Spitting and hissing like a wild cat, the oil sprung from the fryer, catching Tom's wrist. He gave a little hiss himself. Scars slashed and dotted the soft canvas of his skin, making his forearms looked like abstract paintings—a testament to all the oil burns he'd received over the years. It was unavoidable, when you were bent over a deep fryer for hours on end. It was the sacrifice you had to make in order to cook good chicken. Nay, *great* chicken. That oil had to be bubbling hotter than the fires of hell. If you wanted to tear your teeth into a coating that was somehow crispy and buttery at the same time, then the oil had to be raging. If he was going to leave any sort of legacy on this Earth, this would be it. If he were to die tomorrow, God forbid, people would remember him and say: '*That Tom Carter: dumb as a wooden post, but boy, could he cook a good bird.*'

"Would you stop staring into the fryer and actually do some work?"

Old Cliff didn't really mean it. He was all bark and no bite. Tom could spend his whole shift dancing in the store, and Cliff would just shrug his bony old shoulders, mumble under his breath, and leave Tom to it. He loved Tom, and if he had to admit it, Tom loved old Cliff.

Cliff looked older than his years, his grey hair cropped close to his scalp, his wrinkles running deep into his flesh, carving cruel lines into his forehead. A naked lady lounged across his bicep, and Tom had spent many of his hours at the chicken shop staring at her plump lips and breasts, forever immortalised in the blue ink.

Maybe real women had found the tattoo off putting, because Cliff had never married. Well, at least there was no wife Tom ever knew about. But Tom was pretty sure Cliff was single. Some people just have the stench of solitary about them, and it wafted from old Cliff like garbage. The only thing close to Cliff's heart was a carton of Peter Jackson Blues, tucked neatly into the breast pocket of his shirt. He always wore a shirt, usually a short sleeve one. Maybe to show off the naked lady. He wasn't an ugly man, really. He just looked like he'd lived a life.

Although how he'd ended up owning and running a chicken store, Tom had no idea. Why Tom was still working there, he also had no idea. He definitely hadn't expected to return to work so early after the accident. But nothing stopped. The banks didn't hold their bills, his stomach kept demanding food. He wished he could say the same about his mother's. He'd noticed she'd started losing weight. Another good reason to return to work. He needed to get away from her. The house was starting to feel very small. He felt like she was everywhere, floating from room to room, staring at the walls like they lived in a high-end art gallery, as if Remembrandts and Monets hung from the walls instead of cobwebs and family portraits.

Tom yawned and stretched, twisting and turning, his red apron hanging like a stiff tent from his neck. It was late on a Saturday, and like most food stores on the strip, their little shop was lit up, open for business—that business solely being the alcohol-fuelled revellers that poured from the clubs and bars at this hour. He both hated and loved working this shift. Hated it, because having to deal with drunk people was not fun, although he didn't work the register anymore. Cliff had hired a few young kids for that, and a pimply wispy girl called Saraya was there now, taking orders. Working the graveyard shift was kind of great though, for a study of the human psyche. Why go to university when you could learn everything you ever wanted to know about the human condition by working at a chicken shop? There were always crazy people and crazy stories.

Loud voices trailed into the store, heralding the entry of their owners long before they crossed the threshold. The first girl who entered tripped on the step leading into the store and fell onto her knees. Laughter exploded from her friends, far louder than the incident really warranted. Tom exchanged glances with Cliff.

"I'm too old for this shit," Cliff said and turned on his heel, thumbing a smoke from his pocket.

"Ok Murtaugh."

Bastard, Tom thought, although he made no move to enter the front of the store himself. He would stand where he was, half exposed in the shadows of the kitchen, still visible to the customers if they cared to make a scene, although in his red apron and matching cap, he didn't exactly cut a threatening figure. He could be dressed in a leather jacket and pants and people still wouldn't find him intimidating. Was that an intimidating outfit? He was thinking of Arnie: *Terminator* but maybe it was more Halle Berry: *Catwoman*.

The girl had been picked up by two of her friends, her dress barely clinging to her upper thighs, her legs fluid and loose like strings of overcooked spaghetti. Three boys made up the tail end of the group and while the girls were silly and sloppy, the boys were sullen and slow. Tom glanced at the group furtively, seeing they were about his age and dipped his head, so it was sheltered by his body. For some reason, when people his age came into the shop, they always goaded him, throwing him jeers and snide comments. They looked at him too much, the boys and the girls, as if he were some kind of late night special. He'd gotten good at hanging in the tombs of the store—listening, watching, but never seen. He was a ghost. Just like the Phantom of the Opera. Phantom of the Chicken Store.

"I'll have a cheeseburger thanks." one of the boys said, leaning in close to Saraya.

Christ. That voice cut clear to the back of the shop, as if it was coming from a speaker next to his ear. Tom knew that reedy voice, so thick with its own confidence it was strangely solid. To be sure, he looked over his shoulder from the corner of his eye. Sure enough, there was Eddie, his thick beard unmistakable, his eyes black and cold even from a distance. He was wearing a short-sleeved party shirt, and Tom noticed with pleasure that the pits were stained with sweat, even though the night was unseasonably chilly. Tom's stomach gave an uneasy flip, and he ran his eyes over the group once more. Glassy eyed, every single one of them. Maybe they'd had more than just alcohol tonight.

He groaned to himself. The last thing he wanted was another run in with Eddie. He didn't have it in him. Couldn't the universe see that he was already beaten down?

"We don't... we don't sell cheeseburgers." stuttered Saraya.

Eddie blinked silently at her, as if he'd been told that breathing had now been made illegal.

"Yes, you do," he said stoutly, burping into his collar and pointing at the menu above Saraya. "Below the salads it has a burger option."

"Yes sir," she said to a man no more than four years her senior, "but that's for a chicken burger. If you read the first ingredient, it says chicken."

"Is she taking the piss?" he announced loudly, turning to his group.

The girls shushed him and the boys tittered. Tom didn't recognise any of the others, thank God. The last thing he needed was for a bunch of people he knew to know where he worked. Not that he was ashamed. He just didn't want them to make him feel like he was ashamed. There was a difference.

"Yeah, I think so." the boys laughed, and Tom saw Eddie bristle.

His tone had changed, clearly trying to pass for nonchalant with his next words.

"Well, whatever then, just whip me up a beef burger."

Saraya glanced to the back of the store. *No, no, no. You've got this. You don't need me. Grow a backbone girl.*

"We don't have beef on the premises sir. It is a *chicken* store."

Tom swore there wasn't even a drop of disdain in her voice, but the boys howled with laughter and even the girls began to snicker. Tom almost felt sorry for Eddie. Almost. He was proud of Saraya, but he felt uneasy. He had no idea where this was going to go, where Eddie would take it.

"So just make some beef then! Jesus CHRIST."

Eddie yelled the last word, sending some lingering customers skittering to the door. Ordinarily, his friends might try to calm him down, but Tom could see they were too far gone themselves to do anything, even if they wanted to—which they didn't, because they were laughing hysterically. It would have been funny, if you weren't on the receiving end of it. The difference between victims and monsters. Perspective.

Tom had had enough.

"Tell you what," Tom said loudly, rounding the corner from the back of the store and appearing to stand next to Saraya, before she melted into the background.

"You bring us the cow, and I'll chop it up for you. How does that sound?"

Eddie's mouth opened and then he snapped it shut like a crocodile. "Well, well, this is where you work."

He pretended to take in the surroundings, his eyes lingering on the cracks in the walls, and coming to rest on Tom's apron and cap.

"I'm not surprised."

Tom wished, he wished with all his heart that he didn't care. That Eddie meant nothing to him and his taunts even less. But he prickled, like a cat, no, like *Wolverine* and he would unsheathe his claws for all to see. He was ready to fight. Should he rip his shirt off in a throe of uncontrollable rage? On Hugh Jackman maybe that looked great, but on his skinny frame he doubted it would have the same effect. No. He wouldn't fight Eddie. He would destroy him with his words instead.

"And I'm not surprised that you can't read a menu. How are you getting through your Uni course?" Tom lowered his voice to a dramatic whisper. "Do you pay someone to write your essays for you?"

Before Tom even had time to savour the impact of his words, he felt the impact of a fist hitting him square in the face. Saraya let out a strangled cry and dimly, Tom registered a few of Eddie's friends gasping as they watched on, their eyes as big as wagon wheels. Tom reeled back and clutched his nose in shock, checking that it hadn't been pushed off the edge of his face. It hurt like hell, but it was still there.

"What the—" Tom looked into those cold, dark eyes, and he registered for a second that they were still burning with rage. The hit hadn't sated his anger. Eddie's arm reeled back. *Move,* his slow, dumb brain told him, but maybe his rubber heels were glued to the floor with chicken fat, because he couldn't. Not one bit.

And again.

This time, there could be no doubt that something shifted, because he *heard* it. The sound of his nose splintering and buckling echoed through the chambers of his skull. Tom was surprised there was even a bone to break since it had hardly had time to heal from the accident.

As if a dam had been waiting to break, blood oozed in great thick gloops from his nostrils. Panic rose from his toes, and Tom felt like he would die right there and then, drowned by his own fear and blood. What a way to go. He finally understood how all Shakespeare's tragic heroes felt, dying in pools of their own blood. Scared shitless.

It was over as quickly as it had begun. Brought back to reality by the shouts and cries of his friends, Eddie must have realised the gravity of what he'd done. He legged it, all thoughts of cheeseburgers falling from his mind. His mates quickly followed suit. The girls seemed confused, half torn between staying and running away. But in the end, they'd looked at Tom with pity and stumbled out the front door, yelling after the boys. A good job too, because moments later Cliff had come back from his smoko.

Cliff took one look at the scene, at the blood not so much dripping but dribbling onto the white tiles, and he shouted a string of curse words.

"What in God's name happened here?"

Cliff spotted Saraya in the corner near the drinks fridge, frozen, her hands cupped around her mouth. Wordlessly, she lifted her wide eyes from Tom's face to Cliff, and his hard features softened.

"It's okay sweetie. You're okay."

Cliff strode over to her and pulled her into a hug, his big coarse hands surprisingly gentle as they smoothed her wiry hair. Her cap must have slipped off during the fight. No, fight wasn't the right word. Fight infers there was something of a match, a battle. During the *beating.* Her cap must have slipped off during the *beating.*

"Umb. Excu- me. Lil helb?"

Talking was excruciating. Tom's nose felt every wiggle, every twitch.

Cliff threw him a look before ignoring him. "Don't worry sweetie, I'll take you home. Nothing to worry about."

She nodded, fat tears sliding down her greasy face as Cliff led her to the back of the store. He reappeared a few minutes later, rounding on Tom who had taken a seat on the counter in the semi-darkness. At least Cliff had the good sense to close the front door and turn the outside lights off.

"What the hell happened?" Cliff demanded.

"Why ah you so angwee?"

"Because I was gone two minutes, and I return to find my store covered in blood!"

"It wasen my fauld."

Cliff gave him a levelled look. "Bullshit. I know you."

Tom looked him in the eye for a long moment and saw, despite himself, Cliff roll his eyes.

"Why do I piss ebewwone off?" Tom said, really struggling to get the word 'everyone' out through the traffic jam between his nose and mouth.

Cliff sighed. "You can't do that, Tom. Rile people up. You don't know what they're capable of."

In a move he regretted, Tom opened his mouth to retort, and a glob of blood fell into it. He spluttered and spat on the floor.

"Jesus." Cliff said in disgust.

"Has an-y-one tol- you -dadt you sound egg-cac-lee like my mum-b?"

"Even with your face punched in, you still don't shut up."

"Id's truly a talen-d of mine."

Cliff shook his head. "No, you know what's actually a talent? Staying silent. Listening to what people are *really* telling you. The more you talk, the more you miss."

Tom just couldn't help himself. "Look oud! Ol Cliff handin-g down some li-b lessons."

In a move that Tom read as a surrender, Cliff pulled out a mop from a cupboard behind the counter and began to spread the blood across the floor.

"If I don't try to wisen you up, who will?"

CHAPTER FOURTEEN

Adult Disneyland

To say that Georgia had not been pleased to pick him up and drive him to the doctors was an understatement. Tom had pleaded with Cliff to take him to the doctors himself, but the old man wouldn't budge.

"What, and not tell your mum? No way. What kind of responsible adult would I be?"

If Cliff was the poster boy for responsibility, then Tom was an orange.

Tom was saved from a reply by a fierce knocking—a fine feat really, as the panes of the shop door were made from Perspex.

His mother.

If blood dripped from Tom's nose, then fire spouted from hers. Thankfully, Cliff had tried to vouch for him on the phone. From his position on the counter, Tom could only hear snippets. "A scuffle with someone he knew", "he didn't start it", "nose broken". He also could have sworn he heard the word "hero" in there.

Like Zeus himself, she'd stormed into the shop, her hair whipping about her face in a sudden breeze.

"Dear god," breathed Cliff, his eyes widening.

Tom threw his elbow into the old man's ribs.

"Sorry, sorry." Cliff muttered.

Her eyes scanned the room swiftly, settling on Tom. The Terminator had found her target.

"You."

Before she got to him, he tried to wiggle off the counter, thinking he could make a run for the back door. Calling her was a terrible mistake. He should have just showed up at home hours later with a new nose. Just as his feet touched the ground, a high-heeled foot stepped on his left foot, and long fingernails dug into his upper arm.

"Oh no, no, no. You're not going anywhere."

"Cand talc. Nose bwoken."

She smiled at him prettily. "Well, that's fine then. I'll do the talking."

All car ride he heard it. She paused only for an intermission at the all hours clinic, and once his nose was packed with gauze, he heard it all the way home.

"I just don't get it," she said for about the 100th time, shaking her head as she stared ahead at the road, the click click of her indicator reverberating in the quiet dark.

"Well, if you jus- le-d me explain—"

"Oh, I get it, don't you worry. *You didn't start it. It wasn't your fault.* Blah blah blah. Just like the other day. Same story. You didn't start it. But you come home and your eye looks like a spoiled piece of fruit."

He really didn't like her right now. It amazed him, how many versions of his mother there could be. Angry mum. Sad mum. Sarcastic mum. Silent mum. He wondered if caring mum would ever make an appearance.

"But you tell me, just tell me if you didn't do something, or say something to provoke that guy again."

He remained silent.

"Well?"

"You said no-d to say any-ding!"

She growled. "I know you're going through that whole 'teenage angst' thing—" she used little air quotes as she said 'teenage angst'.

"No, I'm no-d! I'm no-d even a d-eenager!"

She barrelled on. "But you can't do that. You just don't know what other people are thinking, what they are capable of Tom."

"Well clearly d-ad guy's a psycho." he said.

"No, this is precisely my point. You have no idea." she hit her palm against the steering wheel. "You have no idea what that kid might be going through. And—"

He looked down into his lap, then shot his head up again in a move that made his nose pulse painfully. "Look I geddid ok? I stuffed ub. I'm sowwy."

She held a hand up to silence him. It dawned on him where he might have gotten the whole talking too much thing from.

"One last thing: you also need to consider how your actions impact others. I don't need this right now. And Danny doesn't need to see you like this, with what's gone on."

She just had to hammer that final nail in, didn't she?

It amazed him, how quickly he'd become accustomed to everything. Say what you will about the human race, but there is no denying that we are remarkably adaptable. Within days, Tom had gotten used to the look of his new nose. He looked like a young Owen Wilson. Strangely, he was okay with it. It made him interesting.

As much as he didn't want to admit it, he'd also gotten used to seeing Danny in a hospital bed. He almost couldn't imagine what it would be like now to have his younger brother at home, painting on the deck, singing in the shower. He didn't want to grow accustomed to that—to this version of his brother. Since the last time Tom visited, Danny had found his voice, but it still wasn't the same. He sounded like Danny, he looked like Danny, but he wasn't the Danny he knew. He shuddered to remember their last conversation, and the strange look that had settled on Danny's face when he had said he didn't need to eat.

Before he turned the corner and entered his hospital room, Tom said a silent prayer, hoping that this time, a little more of his brother had returned.

"Hey Da—"

"What's in a soul?" Danny asked, turning to him and cutting him off.

Not a great start.

Initially, Tom thought he had misheard him. "A soul?"

"Yes, that's what I asked."

"Like in here?" Tom jabbed a finger softly to his own heart.

"Is it part of the heart?"

"This conversation is weird, even for our standards." Tom said, taking a seat and trying to lighten the mood, but Danny simply blinked and waited.

Tom sighed, knowing he would have to give him an answer. If he were being honest, he wanted to give one. Conversations about stuff like this was his bread and butter. He was the master in philosophical nonsense. All he needed was an excuse to unleash. If Danny wanted an explanation, he could give it, certainly. But it felt strange to talk about something like that in a place like this, where souls were coming and going so often.

"Well, if you believe it exists, then I'd say it is definitely tied to the heart."

"Why?"

Tom shrugged, "Because they're both so similar. Surely you couldn't have both a heart and a soul. I reckon the soul sits deep in there." he pointed to Danny's heart. "Like it's stitched into the very walls."

Tom couldn't tell if even he believed his own words. Sometimes he thought sarcasm was stitched seamlessly into the walls of his very own heart, and there was no way he could rip one out without destroying the other.

Danny ploughed on. "But what does it do?"

"Hmm. Well, I guess it doesn't really *do* anything. But you couldn't exist without it. You'd just be like, an empty shell. You're still alive, but you're nothing. All your bits are working properly, but the thing that was deep inside you got sucked up like a whorl of dust, and the heart just becomes—a heart. There's no deep magic in there anymore. No hidden secrets. It's like when you were a kid and you went to Disneyland and you thought it was so magical, and there's all sorts of incredible creatures lurking about, but then you go there as an adult and you're like 'Oh. This is just a place.' It's still the same, it still works, but there's no magic. Humans without their souls are like adults at Disneyland."

Danny was quiet, digesting Tom's monologue. Why was he taking this so seriously? It was the first real conversation they'd had since the accident. Tom was just happy he was interested in talking to him, but for possibly the first time in his life, he wished their conversation was a little more... *pedestrian.*

"But like that's just me making stuff up. I'm only joking around."

"How do humans lose their souls?" Danny asked.

Fleetingly, it crossed Tom's mind that he would make a brilliant parent one day. He would be able to answer any question his kid threw at him.

"Why are you asking me this?"

Danny's eyes darkened. "I just want to know."

"Okay. Okay." Tom didn't like seeing that look on his face. He just wanted to keep Danny happy.

"How does a human lose their soul? Hmm well, you can lose your soul by committing acts of evil—case in point being Lord Voldemort, who, as we all know, shattered his soul by committing murder. However, I think we can extend this to other evil acts. Anytime we do anything that is evil, even a little bit evil, our souls split a little."

Into his mind floated the memory of the meatloaf and what he'd done to Peet. It was a small thing, but in his eyes it was evil. Did that split his soul, even though he was a child? And if it did, then what had the crash done to him? It would have imploded his soul into smithereens. Sure, it was an accident. But it was still his fault. He was the reason Danny was in this bed. He hoped Danny didn't remember it. He hadn't showed any sign that he knew about the accident, and Tom hoped he never would.

Tom shuddered to himself. *Don't look there, Tom. Don't look.*

Danny looked like he was expecting more. Tom didn't even think about the words that came out of his mouth.

"And, I think our souls are hurt when bad things happen to us. There's nothing we can do about that. Each terrible thing just takes a bit away from us."

Fear gleamed in Danny's eyes. "Tom, I think I've lost my soul."

"What? Why are you saying that?" Tom asked mildly but his eyes lowered to the floor.

He'd said too much. But he couldn't help it. He didn't know that's what he was going to say. Sometimes the truth just spills out of you.

"Because I can't feel it anymore."

Danny was almost clawing at his heart, like when someone drops their glasses in the dark and have to pat the ground to find them again. Tom shuffled over to his brother's bed, half sitting, half standing by his side. He tried to pat his shoulder.

"No one can feel it, Danny. Not really. I can't feel mine."

"Well, maybe you've lost yours too."

"Don't be silly. C'mon." there was a heavy pause. "Time for you to get some sleep I reckon."

Tom left the room soon after, mumbling something about finding a vending machine, but in truth, he needed to put some distance between him and Danny. He felt oddly shaken by their conversation. As Tom rounded the corner and stood in the empty hallway, he raised a palm and subtly patted his heart. Maybe he was just being paranoid, but he could have sworn he couldn't feel a heartbeat.

Like an irate hummingbird, Tom watched as his mother buzzed from one room to the other, huffing little sighs and snorts as she exchanged piles of clean clothes for dirty ones. She'd finally gotten what she wanted. Danny was coming home tomorrow. She was determined that the house, and his room in particular, was as clean and fresh as possible—a concept that was completely foreign to the place. It wasn't that they were filthy pigs or anything. It was just hard to keep a house in order. Particularly when two teenage boys lived in said house. But Tom knew it hurt his mother to have a messy house. For every pair of dirty socks she found on the floor, another frown line would etch into her forehead. It was starting to look like a washboard dirt road.

Standing at the threshold of Danny's room, Tom tried to make his mouth move. He desperately wanted to talk to his mum, to tell her that something didn't feel right about Danny coming home, but she looked so purposeful that he didn't know if he could do it. He wanted to say happy, she looked so *happy,* but the word didn't fit. Her mouth, her shoulders seemed to be permanently sagging these days.

As if she sensed his attention, she looked at him and gave him a brief smile. Before he knew he was doing it, the words spilled from his mouth.

"Do you think Danny is ready to come home?" he said it with as much care as he could; he was careful to make his tone conversational. Her movements slowed, and she looked at him sharply. Those clever eyes scanned his face, and he knew he needed to watch himself. The last thing he wanted was a fight. He was too tired to fight her.

"What makes you say that?" she said, sitting on the end of Danny's bed.

He squirmed uncomfortably, picking at a piece of wood that was splintering from the door jamb. Jesus, you could tidy the house, but there was no denying it needed a serious face lift.

"He just doesn't seem like… himself."

She looked away from him and busied herself with Dan's clothes again and Tom didn't know if she was trying to hide her concern, or if she thought his admission too stupid to pay it any thought.

"Mum?"

Georgia gave another one of her irritated huffs. "The doctor said that was normal. He said there would be some changes."

"Yeah but… he's been acting a bit *weird*."

You knew things were bad when you used the word weird as a euphemism.

She sighed. "I don't really want to hear about it to be honest."

She shook her head, standing up abruptly. After years of living together, he knew perfectly what that gesture meant:

Well, it was nice talking to you, but our session has concluded. Should you wish to pursue the subject further, I suggest that you do not.

She left the room. As much as he wanted to follow her and shake her shoulders, he knew better than to push—it would not get her to see what was happening. He wasn't sure himself what truth he wanted her to acknowledge. But something in him didn't feel right, and he knew she felt it too. Maybe he just wanted her to acknowledge that she had that feeling. That she, like him, felt sick inside, like her stomach felt empty and heavy at the same time. He didn't know why it was so important that they share their digestive problems, but he wanted to know. He was sick of a lifetime of *not* knowing.

The room was surprisingly cheery despite the hospital décor of cheap carpet and peeling walls. Tom guessed that the doctor's wife had spent some time wondering about IKEA, picking out sleek shelving units and chic, industrialised lamp shades, perhaps with the thought in mind that if she brightened up his office, some personality might leak into the miserable bastard himself. Tom didn't know him well, had only had a few conversations with him, but that was all he needed to make up his mind. Tom was a great judge of character. With a good look, he could tell if someone was worth his time.

Georgia's nails delicately hammered into the doctor's desk as the doctor went through the patient discharge forms.

"So, it's really important that when—"

Tom saw the doctor's eyes subtly float to the outpatient information.

"—When *Daniel* comes home, you monitor his behaviour for, firstly, any significant changes. Is he acting in a way that is out of the ordinary?"

Tom threw a glance at his mother. The doctor continued, oblivious.

"Is he experiencing mood swings, irritability, anger, dissociative or delusional disorders?"

She stopped tapping her nails. Tom's voice broke the doctor's monologue.

"Sorry, just hang on a second there—delusional disorders?"

The doctor nodded. "In rare cases, brain trauma can manifest all sorts of dissociative and delusional disorders: Anything from schizophrenia to depression to obsessive compulsive disorders," he caught the look on their faces and gave a little chuckle, "Oh don't worry, you and I would both know if your brother was exhibiting any of those symptoms."

Tom leaned forwards, trying to wipe his face clear of any emotion. "So, *hypothetically, if* we—" he gestured to all three of them, "Did end up noticing that he had one of these mood disorders, what would be the course of action?"

A ghost of a smile appeared on Georgia's lips before she looked mortified, realising what she was really laughing at. It hurt Tom that she felt that way, like it wasn't okay to laugh anymore.

The doctor didn't notice. "Well, it really depends on what type and how severe the mood disorder is."

Tom spread his hands on the desk. "Give me worst case scenario for like a disillusional mood disorder thingy."

Answering questions is a part of the job. Tom imagined the doctor repeating the mantra to himself. He could see it written all over his face.

"It really depends."

That had to be his favourite saying, thought Tom. It must be in

Chapter One of "*How Not to Get Sued in the Medical Profession.*"

The doctor continued, sensing that his answer had not sated Tom.

"But studies have shown that the most effective course of treatment involves a combination of drugs including anti-depressants and benzodiazepines. In severe cases of delusional disorders, electro-convulsive therapy has proven to be very effective."

Son and mother sat straight in their chairs like they had been shocked themselves.

"Shock therapy? Surely that's not still around." Georgia's face was white—it seemed unimaginable that it had been lit by laughter moments ago.

"It's nothing like you would think. Shock therapy gets a bad reputation, but it's very safe these days. In extreme circumstances, we can even perform lobotomies safely."

The doctor smiled encouragingly, and Tom stared, wondering if the doctor himself had been given a lobotomy and they'd taken out the bit that understood how to interact with other people.

Tom knew that he and Georgia didn't have much in common, but he knew that neither of them felt particularly warmly about taking out a chunk of Danny's brain.

The doctor signalled to the paperwork in front of him, but Tom was captured by the image of Danny, under a medical saw and blue tarps, his skull hanging off like the lid to a cookie jar. The boy he'd caught years ago googling lobotomies, finally getting his wish. Surely the world couldn't be that cruel or that poetic.

"Ok so, I have the exit forms here, I'll let you look over and sign them. They also include some of the vital information that I've gone over today—like signs to watch out for."

The doctor began to repeat himself. That must be the second rule of "*How Not to Get Sued in the Medical Profession*": repeat yourself until a cockatoo could recite your words back to you.

"Someone will need to be home for at least the first three days. Daniel cannot drive or work. He can engage in light physical activity like walking, depending on how he is feeling. You must contact the hospital if you notice anything out of the ordinary."

Like thinking he had lost his soul doctor?

The doctor looked at them both, waiting for their consent.

Georgia glanced at Tom and he felt like he could see her thoughts. She would murder him, chop him up into little pieces and bury his body in the woods if he said anything. He knew she wanted Danny home, more than she wanted answers. Tom could almost see her desperation, like wavy little stink lines pouring out of her body.

She didn't have to worry. Tom couldn't speak. His brain felt impenetrable behind a thick wall of information. It was like being back in school. He couldn't process it all. He needed more time. He felt like he was juggling, working tirelessly to keep his brother and his mother afloat. The weight of his family was on his shoulders. It was stupid, but he really was starting to feel like the man of the house without their father around.

Tom nodded, and Georgia copied him, relief evident in her eyes.

"We will." she said, her words both a promise to the doctor, and a threat to Tom as she cast him one final glare before taking a pen in her hand and signing the out-patient forms.

Danny was coming home.

CHAPTER FIFTEEN
Old Fruit

A single vine of white jasmine brushed against a window of the old weatherboard house, rapping a soft, staccato rhythm against the thick glass. The house was small but trim and it sat neatly against the sidewalk of a wide, oak-lined street. The iron lattice curlings that decorated the front veranda were endearing, and the house had recently been painted a fashionable gunmetal grey. It looked like every other house in inner-city Melbourne, and just like any other, it was worth a fortune.

"The walls are dripping."

"What?"

"I'm in Hell. There's no other explanation for it."

It had taken a moment for Tom to understand what Danny was trying to say. By that point, Dan had snipped the door to his bedroom closed, leaving Tom to wonder slowly to his own room. Once he got it, he realised it wasn't too far from the truth—it was January and the height of summer. The white paint in their hallways seemed to dribble towards the floor like whipped cream sliding off a plump cake. If Tom lay very still on the bed like he was now, he was sure he would be able to hear the floor's laboured breathing, see the warped wood rise and fall gently. The floor was wet, as if it were sweating from its open pores. The city's occupants had been riding a week-long heat wave. It was the third day in a row above 40 degrees and the elderly were starting to shrivel like old fruit. Things that weren't supposed to melt started melting. Like roads. Like train tracks. Most had given up, knowing that fighting the heat was not a battle worth fighting. They sat at pubs, at cafes, sipping sweaty beers, the ambition dripping from them like the sweat rolling down their ironed shirts. Nothing takes the drive from you like heat. There's no room in your brain but to think about how damn hot it is.

As he lay on his bed, thinking about nothing but how damn hot it was, Tom listened as Georgia crept down the halls, and Tom knew she was terrified of waking her fitfully sleeping son. It must be like having a newborn all over again. The old boards creaked and groaned under her, betraying her. Tom could almost hear her grimace.

When they had gotten home from the hospital late the day before and shown Danny to his bedroom, they had hardly seen him since. And now they existed in this strange limbo land, where they waited, and waited. Tom didn't know if it was just the heat, but he was finding it harder to breathe. Like he'd sucked all his breath in, steeling himself before he plunged into icy water.

"Still asleep?" Tom whispered.

Georgia poked her head into Tom's room, her eyes doing a quick scan, taking in the pile of clothes on the floor, the dishes stacked on his desk. Tom felt like standing up and snapping the door shut in her face, just like Danny had done to him moments before. He pushed the urge down. Let her look. If her eyes found something she didn't like... well that was her problem.

She nodded before she began to speak, her voice a soft hiss. "Ok so, I'm home for the next few days, I'll just watch him closely and make sure things aren't getting—he doesn't show any warning signs like the doctor said."

Tom crossed his arms. "I'm at home too."

"You're not working?"

He shook his head. "Took time off."

It was almost true. Cliff had suggested it, and then when Tom had rejected the idea, he'd said in a way that made it clear to Tom that he thought it was a good idea.

"Why?" he had asked the old man, slamming the fryer into its holder. He wondered how Cliff had even known about what had happened.

"Just use the time to be there for your family. Your mum needs you."

"Oh, got my mum's best interest in mind, do you?"

"I'm too old for that—stuff" said Cliff, but as he walked away Tom could have sworn the old turkey's neck had grown red.

Georgia blinked. "Oh." she said, as if the concept of Tom wanting to spend time at home wasn't a completely logical and reasonable desire.

He rolled his eyes. "It's not like I'm a doctor saving lives. It's a chicken shop."

"Okay."

"You don't want me here." he said, sensing the answer.

She paused before replying. "I do, I do. Just—we don't want to overreact to anything. We need to be prepared for whatever happens."

"What do you think I'm going to do? Have him locked up?"

"No." she frowned. "But I just want you to be ready."

"Are you?" he fired back.

"No." she admitted, coming to sit on a corner of his bed.

He itched to push her off.

"But I don't really have a choice," she sighed.

"And I do?"

She looked up at him.

"He's not just your son. He's my brother." Tom said.

Tom took the silence that followed as a personal victory.

"He's been pretty normal since we've gotten home." she said quietly.

Tom didn't have the heart to point out the obvious: that he'd seemed normal because they'd hardly seen him at all.

Morning stretched into afternoon and the bedroom door did not open.

From his room, Tom could hear Georgia's nails lightly tap against the thick wood of Danny's door, almost as if she were afraid to knock any harder and actually get a response. Straining his ears, he heard nothing, and then a string of gentle murmurings, almost like a whispering wind.

Tom poked his head out from his own door. She was standing, almost hugging the door, every muscle in her body tight like freshly tuned guitar strings. Her ear was pressed firmly to the door, a plate of food in her hands. Sensing the presence of her other son, she sighed and smiled weakly at Tom, carefully placing the plate on the floor, as if it were an offering for a hungry stray. It made a soft chink against the floorboards as she set it down.

"He just needs… some time," she said, turning on her heel and walking into the lounge.

The lounge room door snapped quietly behind her.

Tom stared at the plate of food. The chicken was swimming in a pool of creamy mushroom sauce, little green peas bobbing in the liquid like drowning men. He stared and stared at that plate until he saw green spots every time he blinked. His stomach growled. His stomach recoiled. Never in his life had he felt both sick and hungry.

Never in his life had he known Danny to refuse food. Even when he'd gotten his wisdom teeth out, that gluttonous little glob had made them go through McDonalds and get him a cheeseburger. He sucked on the meat patty until he threw up 20 minutes later, smiling stupidly just before he heaved into the brown paper bag.

But now… nothing.

Tom found excuses to walk from the front of the house to the back, just to walk past his room and check to see if, like a little mouse, he'd nibbled at something.

Nothing.

Toast. Soup. Beef casserole—Tom watched as Georgia pushed it all into the ravenous mouth of the bin. He wanted to call out, tell her it was a waste of perfectly good food and he would have it instead, but he couldn't bring himself to eat it. Besides, each meal had sat out for hours before Georgia had picked it up. She kept her eyes glued to the floor, even though Tom knew that she could see him watching her. He felt like a security camera these days, just watching and recording.

The next day, he brought the food to Danny himself. He was the Danny whisperer, he knew it. He would be able to get through to him, surely. No one was closer to Danny than he was. Their bond was unbreakable. The boy had never refused him, could never do anything less than worship Tom. He planned on taking full advantage.

Armed with a plate of the best chicken drumsticks money could buy (courtesy of old Cliff of course) he strode up to Danny's door, preparing to break it down and stuff the legs into his mouth if he had to.

Before he had time to fight it, the furry silence that seeped from under Danny's door threatened to swallow him whole. He could hardly suck in a breath. His arm hung in the air, about to knock, poised like one of those gold Chinese cat statues. Every part of him screamed at him to walk away, to get as far as possible from that room. But it was his brother. He couldn't whimp out now. If your family doesn't come for you, who will? Just like Georgia, he rapped his fingers lightly against the door. He got it now. She felt the darkness too. Silence. It stretched on and on like a monotonous siren, echoing in the hallway, the house, inside Tom's head until he could take no more and knocked again, if only to escape the noise.

Suddenly, he heard a rustling, and the door snipped open. Just a crack. He knew it, knew he had special powers that none other possessed. He would get Danny out of this. He would be the one to suck the skinny little thing through this gap in the door and back into the land of the living.

Living dead. That's what he looked like. It was insane, the amount of weight a person could lose in a short amount of time. Tom cast his mind back to the hospital, when the boy wouldn't lift a spoon to his mouth. Tom's stomach twitched. It had been a long time, he realised, since the accident.

Don't look Tom, don't look there.

"Hey." Tom said, lifting the chicken legs into sight.

Danny looked at the chicken like it was alien poop. "Oh— I'm not hungry." he rasped.

"You haven't eaten anything for days."

The gap of light in the door began to disappear. Danny mumbled something, but it was swallowed up by the darkness as the door closed once more. The door wasn't locked. Tom could have gone in there, could've barged in and shook him until he came back to life. But there might as well have been a giant forcefield around the door. Tom would have slid down and sobbed in the hallway right there and then, but his desire to put as much space between himself and that room had not changed.

He hung his head, hoping big fat tears might come to him, but he just felt cold. Shivering like a wounded dog, he retreated to his own room, the door snapping shut. He swore to God, when he bought a house, there would be no doors. Maybe one for the bathroom, but otherwise, no doors.

Things weren't right. That was pretty obvious, but shit was *really* not right. He knew it in his bones. The doctor warned them that Danny could be different after the accident. But now he knew that every movement Danny made, every expression—even the few words he spoke—screamed that it was not his brother that inhabited Danny's skin, but some ghoulish jellyfish. That was the best way he could describe him. Danny was see through. Tom felt like he would just wobble a bit if he poked him with a stick. Maybe his brain had been sucked out through his ear holes during the crash. Maybe with all the pressure from the injury it had overcooked, and now it was nothing more than a soupy stew.

Stop it.

Like so many times in his life, he tried to beat his thoughts away. He stuck his head in his pillow and blasted the most obtrusive music he could find, trying to suffocate the voice in his head, but it came at him relentlessly, like a driving, wild rain. *Things will never be the same. They can never be undone. Danny won't go back to normal. Remember? Remember the sound? Remember who was driving?*

Don't look Tom. Don't effing look.

He wished he could pass out. He wished his mother would come and find him and cradle his head. But he was alone. There was no one there to save him.

"You've lost your mind."

Tom folded his arms across his chest as he leaned back in his chair. It was all he could say. There would be no fight, no real argument. She always got her way.

Sure enough, his mother bristled. "Why? Right now, he needs some normality in his life. What's more normal than going to school?"

"Yeah, but he's not ready. It's only been a few days. What if it makes him worse?"

She laughed mirthlessly. "Believe, me. He can't possibly get any *worse*. He just sits in his room all day not eating, doing God knows what. I can't really imagine how it could get any worse."

Tom wanted to tell her then to shush, that bad luck was like Bloody Mary. Challenge her, challenge it, and it'll appear.

"Well. That's what I thought about my life a month ago. Now look where we are." he said softly.

She sniffed. "If you see Danny's schoolbag anywhere, can you let me know?"

She left the room. When he had his own kids, he swore he'd never do that. He'd always finish a conversation. He'd rather scream and rage than leave them in silence.

Danny stepped into the room and looked around, almost self-consciously. Tom noticed Danny's white socks kept slipping down his calves, bunching around his ankles. Every few seconds, he'd lean over, like a great sagging tower, to hitch them back up, his school bag slipping from its place between his shoulder blades, smacking him in the head.

"Just leave them mate." Tom said, half amused, half exasperated.

"Ok, good idea." Danny wrestled his feet from his shoes, quickly whipping the socks from his feet and throwing them through his open bedroom door.

"That's not quite what I meant."

Danny shrugged. "Feels better."

"Yeah, but now you look like a hobo."

Usually, Danny's white shirt fit him smartly, outlining his chest and shoulders, but now it was comically large, the sleeves like bat wings. Tom watched as he shuffled into the blazer Georgia had also laid out for him. He'd always claimed he'd rather get detentions that be caught 'looking like a dork', but now he slipped his arms into it without complaint. An image of Danny's first day of school swam before Tom's eyes. Tom couldn't help but compare how Danny looked now to then. Although he looked infinitely less cute now.

"Ready?" Georgia smiled tightly, the smile dropping all together when she saw he was sockless.

"What happened to your socks, sweetheart?" she looked about the lounge room, as if she was half expecting them to be hanging from the mantle like Christmas stockings.

"I took them off."

"They kept slipping down his feet." Tom explained.

"So your solution was to have him not wear any socks?" scowling, she strode into Danny's bedroom, muttering and tutting to herself as if

118

she hadn't heard Danny's admission that he'd taken them off himself. Somehow, it was Tom's fault.

Tom crouched down like a shoe salesman to resock Danny's feet. Obediently, Danny hung one foot in the air, allowing Tom to roll them one at a time onto his hairy feet. Danny teetered, grabbing the top of Tom's head none too softly.

"Why does it matter anyway? They're just *socks*." he said, loud enough that his voice would carry into Danny's room.

She reappeared, her eyes blazing. "They might be just *socks* to you, but in the eyes of his teachers, it's neglect."

Tom rolled his eyes so dramatically they were in danger of being swallowed up by his brain.

"No one is going to call social services because your son's not wearing socks. He's a teenage boy: they're disgusting. We're lucky if they're showering twice a week."

"*We*? So, you don't count yourself in that category?"

"I am not a teenager anymore! How many times do I have to tell you that? And I shower at least once every second day thank you very much."

"You should shower every day, Tom. Put your leg down, sweetie." Danny's leg had been hanging in the air, shaking, long after Tom had finished putting the socks on. Listen to her, fussing over him. Never in their lives had she used those terms of endearment, then all of a sudden, they were flowing out of her like lava. She was fussing about, mussing his hair, fixing his collar. Yep, first day all over again. Tom supposed it kind of was. Danny hadn't been there for a whole month.

The car ride to the school was particularly painful. Ordinarily, Danny would take the tram, but Georgia said she 'didn't feel comfortable' with that.

"If you don't feel comfortable letting him take the tram, how do you feel comfortable letting him go to school all day by himself?"

Her grip on the steering wheel tightened. "He won't be by himself. He'll have his friends and teachers looking after him."

Friends. Tom hadn't the heart to tell her that he hadn't heard from any of Danny's mates. Tom got the feeling either they'd had no idea what to say or that maybe they simply didn't exist. He thought about it then, how odd that was. He'd always thought of Danny as a popular guy, a likeable guy. But Tom had never really met any of his friends. He had just assumed they existed.

"I have an interview with the Head of House this morning, anyway. That should sort everything out." she said.

Tom wondered how long he could stay silent for, before she'd stop talking.

Danny was looking at the white-washed walls intently. There was a fly on the wall and it was creeping towards the ceiling. The fly's wings twitched and ticked. Its black little body hummed relentlessly: brisk and bold against the white of the wall.

"That fly really has your attention hey bro?" said Tom.

They were sitting in the brightly lit school reception, on a squishy bench seat, waiting for Georgia to finish her meeting so that Danny could go to his classes. There were a few other families clustered about the large foyer; a middle-aged man and what Tom assumed to be his daughter were sitting on some rickety desk chairs to their left.

Two young boys were talking to each other, their school bags strapped to their backs, looking at a poster directly in front of Danny and Tom. All around them were colourful signs urging students to sign up for this and that, and motivational posters spouting acronyms for learning and respect. PR companies could learn a thing or two from schools, that's for sure, although for the whole of his schooling life, Tom could not remember having ever signed up to anything. He was sure that if Danny didn't have the migraines, Danny would have joined up to everything. There was no doubt in Tom's mind the kid would have been school captain.

"It's here because of my skin." Danny said, his voice flat like an old tire.

"What? Your skin?" Tom hissed, looking about the room. The schoolgirl locked eyes with him. She'd heard their exchange.

Danny stared at his arm and Tom followed his gaze. Even though his veins seemed close to breaking through the thin sheet of skin stretched over his pale arm, it still looked freckled; the hairs bleached a healthy blonde from the sun. A watch was strapped to his wrist.

"Looks like an arm to me, bro."

Tom cringed at himself. He tended to say little phrases like 'bro' and 'mate' a lot when he was trying to act casual. When he was really trying to hold back, they came spilling out of him. The more he tried to hold them back, the more he tacked them onto the ends of his sentences. He threw another glance at the girl. She was watching them curiously. A sickening thought entered Tom's brain: what if she knew Danny? There was no recognition on Danny's face. Tom wondered how much Danny actually saw of his surroundings. Just for a moment, he wished that he could lop the top off Danny's skull and peer inside. *What* was going on in there.

"What can you smell right now?" Danny asked him suddenly, turning his head slowly to look at him.

"Why, did you fart?"

"No, I just want to know, can you smell anything like... off smelling?"

Tom laughed, "It's a school. I can't smell anything but disappointment and B.O. It's truly hellish."

Danny nodded; his fears confirmed. He deftly slung his watch off with a quick flick of his wrist. It was so quick, it looked for a moment as if he had slipped off his own skin. The watch face cracked against the wall with a sharp thump, and everyone in the waiting room jumped. The girl tugged on her father's sleeve in alarm.

"What was that?" the man said, looking around for the source of the noise. Silently, she tilted her head in Danny's direction.

"What?" her father said loudly, trying to follow her silent cues. She hissed at him to be quiet, glancing at Tom who was giving her a 'go-on-I-dare-you' look. What was he really going to do though, if she blurted out what she'd seen? Start a punch on with a teenage girl in a school reception? He'd be institutionalised.

Tom looked from Danny to the broken watch, his eyebrows raised. "Did you mean for that to happen?" he asked, keeping his voice barely above a whisper.

Danny had no such qualms, speaking at full volume. "Yeah. Hopefully the smell will go away now."

The father looked offended. With a laugh, Tom realised that he thought Danny was talking about him. Casually, the man sniffed at his armpits.

"Danny Carter?"

With a palpable sigh of relief, Tom looked up at the man before him, flashing him a grateful smile. Even though Tom had gone to this school himself, he didn't recognise the man. The Head of House was short and squat like a tomato. He was the colour of one too: from the top of his forehead to the meaty little hand sticking out from his suit, he was a spotty shade of vermilion. His meeting with Georgia had obviously finished. Tom was trying to read his mother's face to get an indication of how it had gone. It was unreadable. The man was smiling warmly at Danny, a trickle of sweat glinting on his forehead under the sharp, fluorescent lights. Teachers were always sweaty. Was that why? Because they were literally always in the spotlight?

Like a lost child, Danny looked from Georgia to Tom.

"Come on Danny, Mr D'Angelos is going to take you to your classes. He just wants a quick chat first," Georgia said.

Dumbly, Danny nodded and tottered off after Mr D, his shoes scuffing on the floor. Tom shook his head and looked at Georgia.

"Danny's failing." she said abruptly as she sat down.

He stared at her. It was unlike her to just blurt something like that out in public.

"Well, he hasn't been at school in a million years. That's hardly surprising."

Georgia nodded. "The Head of House showed me an email he sent them. That Danny sent them when they notified him. A while ago." she looked at him with tears in her eyes. "It was so heartbreaking Tom. He said things in the email that I never thought —"

Tom looked at her, nonplussed. "He never said anything to me."

He felt a sudden sense of dread creep up his spine. "Are you sure we are doing the right thing? Sending him back?"

"What?" she snapped, "He wants to go back Tom. Didn't you hear? He's *failing*. He'll be fine."

At 10:30, her phone rang.

CHAPTER SIXTEEN

Some Kind of Sea Witch

Danny looked at his textbook. It was slippery and hard to read.

"Acc— Acount—"

"Here. You've got to take the plastic off."

A girl gently came to him, her soft hands prying the book from his. Danny's eyes snapped to her face, and he found her green eyes were already locked onto his, searching them. He didn't like it. There was too much in them. They were too green, too big, too expectant. He snatched his hand away.

"Danny, it's Kyraah." she looked around, dropping her voice as their classmates lingered, their eyes and ears tuned to their conversation. "You know me. We're friends."

Danny looked her up and down. "I don't trust the look of you at all." he eyed her suspiciously, taking in her long dark hair and pointed nose. "You look like some kind of sea witch."

Kyraah's eyes flared, but she said nothing, handing the textbook to Leeroy before she sat on the other side of the room.

Leeroy sniggered. "Still terrible with women I see."

He tore off the thick plastic wrapping, tossing the textbook back at Danny. It hit him square in the groin. Pain. Pain like he'd never felt it before. Hot, sharp, throbbing pain.

"Oh, did I get you in the—" Leeroy trailed off, not needing confirmation.

Cottoning on to what had happened, a few others in the class began snickering, watching Danny crumble onto the floor from his seat. Leeroy gently patted him on the back. Their teacher was nowhere to be seen, late to class as usual.

Slowly, groaning like a cow in labour, Danny rose from the floor, his watery eyes meeting his teacher's.

Danny gasped.

Small capillaries like little red rivers crisscrossed their way across the teacher's face, spreading to his sagging cheeks and the tip of his large, bulbous nose. His skin had a translucent quality to it, as if had been worn too thin, like old carpet. At any moment, Danny felt like the man's insides could spill across the floor.

"Wow. You are *hideous*." Danny breathed.

Mr Doerr ran his fingertips through his thinning hair, still wet from his morning shower. He was an ugly old codger, that's for sure. Years of drinking had caused his nose to blow up like balloon, and it had only gotten larger with each passing year, each bottle of whiskey he'd consumed. It's one of the saddest things that can happen to a person: to wake up one day and realise you're ugly and there isn't a single thing you can do about it.

"Excuse me?" Mr Doerr said, trying to rustle up some outrage. After years of teaching, of navigating the waters of teenage emotions, he was, ironically, slow to feel them himself. A good quality for teaching, a bad quality for your personal life.

"Surely, no living man could look like this." Danny said, loud enough for the whole class to hear. Incredulous, Danny looked at his classmates for support. Most were staring resolutely at their textbooks, reading them with a rigour they'd never before demonstrated in the class. Teenagers were heartless creatures, but they weren't mean.

"That is a very strange thing to say." Doerr said slowly, carefully.

Leeroy pulled on Danny's arm gently, in attempt to get him to sit down. Instead, Danny directed his next words at Leeroy instead.

"But don't you think? Look at him! I've never seen anything like it! He must be dead."

Most had given up pretending to read and were looking between Danny and Mr Doerr with a collective expression of shock and fear.

"Dead! I've been called a lot of things before, but never *dead*."

There was weight on his last word. It was heavy and loud— loud enough for some of the students to shift uncomfortably in their chairs.

Danny was smiling broadly. "It's okay."

He was walking towards Mr Doerr like a trained tiger handler.

"I'm dead too."

"I think— I think you should leave." Doerr stammered, pointing at the door. He might have endured years of confrontation, but it didn't mean he was any good at it.

"No, no no." Danny shook his head in wild confusion. "Not when I've only just found you. We need to talk to each other. Help me understand what's it's like." he looked Doerr dead in the eyes. "I'm dead, just like you."

Doerr backed further and further away, stumbling over a wayward chair.

"Sir, do you want me to get the co-ordinator?" asked Leeroy, already half rising from his chair.

"Oh yes, good idea Larry. Go. Quickly now."

Mr Doerr's voice skipped an octave. Before he hurried out the door, Leeroy looked tersely between Danny and his teacher, as if he wanted to stay and protect them both.

Mr Doerr lowered his voice, hoping to create less of a spectacle. The last thing he wanted, was for this incident to become school lore. He knew that was already likely to happen.

"Look, David, I'm not...dead. And neither are you. I'm just... old."

He smiled warmly, quickly dropping the act when Danny's face filled with fresh horror and resolution.

Danny's brow knitted, like a two-year-old trying to understand basic maths.

"But you look dead... and I know I do... and I know I'm not old... so therefore you must be dead. You must be."

Doerr opened and closed his mouth. Reasoning was not going to help him. An idea formed in his mind. He took a step towards the boy, putting a hand on his shoulder.

"How about, I tell you all about it after you have a chat with Mr D'Angelos? Obviously, I can't give away all the secrets of the underworld here in front of your classmates."

"Oh naturally. Why do I have to talk to Mr D first though?"

"Because... well he hired me, didn't he? And it's not a normal thing to hire someone like me... like *us*. So, he just wants to make sure that you keep the secret." he winked a hooded eye at Danny.

Danny tapped his nose knowingly, and as if summoned by their secret agreement, the co-ordinator walked through the door cautiously, as if he was expecting to walk into the scene of a grisly murder. Collectively, the tension around the room eased. Scanning the room, taking in the expectant faces of the students, Mr D nodded slowly, his brain whirling.

"Come on Danny. Let's go have a... chat."

CHAPTER SEVENTEEN

Have You Ever Seen a Fat Angel?

How could she have been so stupid? She cursed herself, over and over again. They say hindsight is a beautiful thing, but Georgia thought it was horrible. There was no lesson to be learned, only pain. Better to never make the mistake to begin with. She realised now that she'd let fear drive her decision to send Danny to school. She was terrified that something was terribly wrong, so she'd refused to believe it, refused to look it in the face. But oh, she had seen it now, and it was an ugly monstrous thing.

She could feel the smugness rolling off her eldest son as he sat silently next to her in the passenger seat. And why not? He had been right. It almost seemed laughable now, that she'd thought it had been a good idea. She stole a glance into the review mirror.

Danny was fast asleep, his chin tucked into his chest, his head lolling forward just like it used to when he was a baby and she would strap him tightly into his car seat. She smiled to herself. He would fall asleep in under a minute when they went for drives. It was like clockwork. He was such a good baby. Such a good kid. How had she been so lucky? She guessed that maybe she was paying for it now. Things can't be perfect forever.

When they got home, no amount of shaking would wake him. Eventually, they'd simply given up and left Danny in the car.

"Must be exhausted. Not surprising, after the day's excitement."

Tom looked sidelong at her. She didn't know why he did that—

said things he knew would irritate her. Did he actually enjoy it when they fought? She frowned, but said nothing, hovering at the front windows, terrified to take her eyes too far from her sleeping son.

The school hadn't said much. Just that Danny had demonstrated some "odd" behaviours. She could see how uncomfortable Mr D'Angelos was; how he tiptoed around her, his mind wholly fixed on getting Danny out of the school as quickly as possible. Legally, the school couldn't really do anything other than send Danny home and press Georgia to set up some psyche sessions. It was almost embarrassing, the lack of power schools had. If Danny had of punched another kid in the face, he would have gotten nothing more than a few days off at home.

By the evening, Danny was sitting straight backed against the throne of an armchair, his eyes fixed on the TV screen, completely oblivious to the chaos he had caused.

The next day, the house was quiet. Georgia had sent Tom out, saying she needed some alone time with Danny. In reality, it couldn't be further from the truth: she didn't want to be left alone with Danny. She'd felt like the worst mother in the world to admit it. She was supposed to be strong, to know what to do—it was her son. She felt like she was scrambling to find an instruction manual: "How to Reassemble Your Teenager". Her eyes glanced towards his bedroom door. If he just stayed in his room, then everything would be ok. She could help him later; she would be able to figure it out then. But right now, she had nothing to give him. As if her look towards his door had triggered it, it creaked open. She swore to quietly to herself, before fixing a smile to her face.

He was thin. She knew he had thinned out in hospital, but for the first time, she realized how much weight he must have lost. He couldn't really afford to lose much to begin with, so the difference of a few kilos was painfully obvious: his cheekbones were sharp ridges in the plains of his face. She looked into his eyes. They were bottomless valleys.

His expression changed very little when he looked at her. He did not look at her with spite, with hope or even with recognition. He just looked.

"What are you doing?"

To hear his voice was a shock. Like his eyes, it was flat and edgeless. "I was going to go to the shops."

It was a lie, but it came easily. She didn't know why she said it. He nodded and turned back into his room, reappearing at the door a moment later with his shoes in each hand, holding them like serving platters.

"Oh no, sweetie, I don't think that's a good idea."

"Why not?"

He stopped halfway into wiggling his feet into his shoes. She almost wanted to bark at him to undo the laces and put them on properly.

"You're tired, you've had a hard time, surely you don't want to follow me around the supermarket for an hour?"

He stood up and looked her dead in the eye. "I don't want to go to the supermarket. I want to go to the cemetery."

She looked at him softly. "Why? Do you want to see Al?" it wasn't really a question. He was the only person they knew who had passed away. Even though she thought he was rotten to the core, it had been obvious to her that Danny had been shaken by his death, even though he had hardly known the man.

She did not want to be here. Every part of her was screaming to leave. It reminded her of all she'd lost in her own life. But how could she deny her son the only thing he'd wanted? She was eager to please him, hoping that his interest was a sign of something returning to him. Maybe it was good for him to be here. He had to make his peace with what had passed. She knew that wasn't really possible. You always carried loss with you. The best a person could hope for was that it wouldn't drown you. That it was a weight you could manage to shoulder for the rest of your days.

The beauty of the place frustrated her. The grass was a rich green, and it folded gently over the rolling hills in the wind. Pink, purple and blue pansies sprouted from the garden beds. Headstones in varying degrees of decay littered the landscape in an eclectic, almost artistic mix of shapes and sizes. This place had no right to look this way. The sun had no right to be shining. But if this is what Danny needed, she could face it. The dirt on Al's grave would still be fresh.

"It's this way Dan." she said, gesturing towards a line of

headstones. "Allan Wilks." she whispered softly, reading the name written on its shiny new plaque.

"Benjamin Meyers," Dan said loudly.

She turned around to find him about 20 meters away, on his knees in front of a large, ancient cherub.

"Died 1912. Forever loved by his wife Susan and young son Michael."

"What are you doing?"

He ran further down the line of headstones and stroked a large, chipped stone.

"Bethany Holt. 1947. Our loss is heaven's gain."

She stared at him open-mouthed. His movements were erratic, frenzied, as he darted from grave to grave, reading the headstones and stroking them with awe. A cold realization dawned upon her: he had not come here to see Al. For a while, she couldn't quite place the emotion that slid through her as she watched him. Anger never crawled down her body like this. Sadness always hit her right in the chest. She knew those emotions well by now, and this one came from a different place.

She was afraid. She was afraid of her own son.

Yes, scared for him, but also afraid *of* him. Her fear doubled when she recognised it. Ironically, when you realise you're scared, it makes you more afraid and maybe that's actually what fear is. You can't really be scared unless you know you're scared.

She had no idea who or even what he had become.

She was thankful though, that no one else had dared to brave the heat to visit their loved ones today, even if she did wish there was someone around to help her. She felt like a wild animal had been let loose. How was she supposed to catch him and take him home?

When they were younger, the boys would go to children's parties and run around all day until they finally collapsed, their little faces mucky with chocolate and tomato sauce and she would just sit and watch, waiting for them to run out of energy. She turned back to her car, thinking that she might as well sit in some air-con and wait for him to tire himself out like she did all those years ago.

The sun was starting to drift towards the horizon when she finally found him lying on his back, not too far from Al's grave. Danny's eyes fluttered open and turned to her.

She awkwardly knelt down in the dirt, her skirt stretched taut across her backside. She placed her hand tentatively on his. He didn't pull away, but he didn't reach for her.

"My flesh is melting," he said, laying a hand across his forehead.

"No, you're just extremely sunburnt." for someone who'd sat in a car for the past two hours, she was exhausted. "Can we go home now Danny?" she asked softly.

"This is my home. This is where I belong."

She only had one more tool in her parenting belt left to use.

"What do you want? If you come home with me now, I'll give you anything you want." she was not above blatant bribery.

He smiled at her, his eyes filling with warmth. "There is one thing I want."

She smiled with relief. "Anything. Anything that's going to make you better."

"I would really like to have a funeral please."

Jesus. The last time she'd had a cigarette, had it been the night she'd met Simon? She drew a breath, her head hanging out the kitchen window and the embers of its end flared. She remembered walking onto the porch and seeing him, seeing the tilt of his jaw, the way his eyes had raked over her as he sucked on the end of his own, smoke billowing around him and his friends. He'd seemed like such a man then, and she'd felt safe. Smoke and mirrors. Jam a cigarette into a guy's mouth and he suddenly becomes James Dean.

"Gross."

She turned to see Tom watching her, shaking his head.

"There was a time when this was cool." she said defensively.

"That time has long since come and gone."

He took the cigarette from her fingers and took a long drag. "I'm so glad this is so bad for me. Otherwise you wouldn't be able to pry one from my lips." he flicked it out the window. "I've never seen you smoke before."

"I haven't. Not in about 20 years."

"So, why today?" he sounded like he didn't really want to hear the answer. "I take it your mummy son day was…relaxing."

Before she could even think about what she was saying, it was spilling out of her. Vaguely, she thought she should stop herself, keep the knowledge to herself. She was the mother. She wasn't supposed to do this to her son. It was her burden to bear.

"Jesus."

He was looking at his shoes, those mangy old tennis shoes he always wore, but she could see the colour had drained from his face. She shouldn't have told him. But it's not like he wouldn't have found out. Danny thought he was dead. *Dead.* There was no hiding it from him.

"Tell me you've got another cigarette."

It was the dead of the night. She'd always considered herself to be an early bird, but more and more she found herself craving the calm the darkness brought. It was the only time she really felt like she could breathe. In the quiet, she imagined she could hear the house breathing with her. A part of her wished that Simon was still there, to fill some of the night silence. He would wrap his arms about her shoulders and plant a kiss on her temple and then she would know she was not alone. But if she was honest with herself, she couldn't remember a time his company had ever made her feel any less alone. It was no fault of his. Even though he had his flaws, she imagined it would be the same with any man. There was a part of her that no one else could touch.

Her nails clacked against the keyboard as she began to search for answers: *Brain trauma. Behaviour. Changes. Treatment.* She felt like she had in university when she would put off studying for a final exam. The same sense of impending doom loomed over her. It had been too much to think about seeing the words before her. Her fingers itched to slam the laptop closed. What would she find out about Danny? And more importantly, what would she actually be able to do about it? It felt too huge. She felt too weak. But at least, in her room, it was her knowledge to keep. If no one else knew about it, then they couldn't blame her for failing to do something about it. They could deny it to themselves all they wanted, but the responsibility was squarely on her shoulders. Mothers were supposed to keep their sons safe.

She skim read paragraphs from the search. Her skin felt dirty, like she'd been looking at porn for hours on end.

'Studies suggest that 42% of people who have suffered from a traumatic brain

injury will also suffer from a mental illness. Such illnesses can include depression, anxiety and personality disorders. The patient can often become frustrated and quick to anger. These conditions can be treated, but often they are a permanent result of the injury.'

Her blood went icy.

Permanent.

Scrolling further down, she paused over the section on 'treatment'.

'Treatment can include small changes such as regular physical activity; healthy eating and adequate sleep; family and peer support; and psychological therapy for mild-moderate anxiety and depression. Severe depression and mental illness requires intensive support from mental health professionals. Hospitalisation and medication are often recommended as a course of treatment.'

She almost laughed out loud. Yeah, a plateful of broccoli and a quick run around the block; that'd solve everything. But as sceptical as she was, it was something she could start with, even if the doctor had said no vigorous exercise. She felt like she had to do something *now*. She'd try the whole healthy eating thing, but how was she supposed to get him to eat broccoli when he'd hardly touch fried chicken?

She felt like a child again. The computer was a mirror and she found herself staring into the vast plains of her own ignorance. All she knew was that medicating Danny was not an option. Not after the migraines. She was done, Danny was done, with doctors and pills.

Her fingers hovered over the keys. She dared herself to type, the question burning in her brain: how many of those that were mentally ill became... fascinated with death like he was? Was that normal for people brain injuries?

She added 'delusions' to the list in her search. The first hit seemed promising. She began to read with trepidation:

'Studies have shown that patients with traumatic brain injuries can experience personal delusions. Persons with traumatic brain injuries and schizophrenic disorders often have difficulty separating fact from fiction, as lesions on the right side of the brain often overstimulate the left hemisphere, responsible for creative narration.'

She snapped her laptop closed. So, in his distorted reality, it was completely believable that he thought he was dead. It occurred to her that he probably thought he'd died in the accident. It kind of made sense. Blacking out seemed close to dying. She recalled the few times she'd taken anaesthetic in her life. It felt like sinking to the bottom of the deepest ocean. Each time she'd been a little disappointed when the nurse shook her awake. There was peace there. Maybe that's what Danny's brain was looking for. Maybe he had chosen to sink to the bottom of the ocean rather than surface and face everything that had happened.

After hours hunched at the computer, her back felt like a slab of cement. She rubbed her aching shoulders, again thinking about all the time she'd spend in the past cramming at her computer. She would either pass or she would fail to help her son. There was no in between. Understanding what was happening to Danny brought her no comfort. Like she'd feared, it made it all real. And it was her problem to solve.

She really didn't know if she'd done the right thing. When they were little boys, she'd skirted around buying them a dog. Like any child, they'd begged and cried and made promises themselves, assuring her they'd train it, wash it, play with it every day. So she'd mhmmed and given them "*I'll think about its*" and "*Ask your fathers*" until one day, they stopped asking.

But this time, she hadn't done that. She'd outright *promised* Danny that he could have a funeral. A promise to a child was different. It was contractual. Not that she really thought it would make a difference anyway. This new Danny was more determined than he'd ever been. She had a feeling he'd get what he wanted, one way or another. Better to agree to it on her own terms and get something out of it. She'd told him that if she was going to give him a funeral, then he had to eat whatever she gave him. He grumbled, and she caught the words "counter-productive" and "pointless" in his mumbling, but he nodded all the same. With even less enthusiasm, he'd promised to accompany her to the gym.

"Why on earth do I need to exercise?" he'd said, crossing his arms, looking like a grumpy toddler, squirming in the armchair before the TV. When he wasn't in his room, which wasn't often, he was sitting in that chair. He hardly ever used to sit there.

"Because. It's one of my conditions." she stood in front of him, blocking the TV.

"I don't know about you, but I can't think of any reason why a dead person would need to exercise."

"Well, in all the stories and all the pictures, have you ever seen a fat angel?"

His eyes narrowed, and she knew she'd scored a point. "I'm not an angel."

"And if you've died, why can't you be an angel?"

His eyes bored into her. "Because I'm not in heaven."

A chill swept over her, and she wanted nothing more to turn and run from the room, but she stood her ground, pretending to see the error in her questioning.

"Right, I see. Well in that case, to run away from the devil? I've heard that in hell, Lucifer personally tortures anyone he can catch."

Danny's eyed widened, and she instantly regretted her embellishment. She came over to him quickly then, wrapping her arms about his shoulders. He stiffened under her touch.

"No, no sweetie," she said, smoothing his hair, "I was just kidding."

Danny still looked unconvinced.

She pressed her advantage. "At any rate, if you're really worried about—*that*—then you really should work out with me." she flashed him an encouraging smile, and lightly shook his shoulders.

He nodded dumbly, and she gave him one last comforting shoulder rub before she stood up to leave. He caught her in the doorway.

"I still want my funeral." he said sternly, like he knew her renegade thoughts.

She hoped she'd distracted him enough that he'd forgotten, but she gave away none of her disappointment.

She smiled brightly at him. "Of course."

But she had not promised *when* he'd get his funeral or *who* would attend. Those were details that could be handled, hopefully long after she had gone, once Danny had lived to a ripe old age. So it wasn't a lie. Not really. One day someone would plan a funeral for him. But it wouldn't be her.

He was dressed in baggy grey shorts and a white singlet. She had tried to persuade him to wear a t-shirt, but he said he felt hot all the time and didn't think he'd ever need to wear pants or long sleeves ever again.

She was dressed in gym pants, the lycra moulding to her hips. She wasn't thin, she was curvy and always painfully aware of how her bottom jiggled when she walked. The orange of her t-shirt offset the darker hue of her skin. There was something in her heritage, something exotic, that shimmered on her. The boys had missed it; they had always been as white as delicate little snowflakes.

Danny stood on the treadmill and looked at her, then cast his eyes over the moving figures about him. "Nothing is happening."

Georgia leaned over the bars of his treadmill and pressed the quick start button for him. It clunked into motion, crawling along at its safe start up pace. Still, he nearly tipped over the edge, until she barked at him to lift his legs up and walk like a normal human being. He lumbered forward and she pressed the buttons *up, up, up* until he was forced into a jog. With caution, she began her own workout, one eye fixed on her son and a small smile playing on her lips as she listened to him rasp for breath.

"I'm starting, to get really tired." said Danny through great racking breaths.

"Push through. You'll be right. It's just mind over matter."

He almost tripped over his feet. "I think I'm going to stop."

She reached over and put a comforting hand on his shoulder. "Keep going, keep going! You'll feel great after, trust me."

"Nah, I want to stop. Can I stop?"

She sighed her assent and as soon as she nodded, he locked his legs into place and swayed forward a fraction before he was flung like a pebble from the machine.

Had the moron never been on a treadmill before?

His back hit a spin bike, the first in a neat line, ready and waiting for the next class. The bike rocked violently and tipped onto its side, careening into the next one. Down and down they went, each with a thunderous crash. When the last bike hit the floor, all eyes turned towards them. Danny's lanky arms were draped over the first bike and his face set in shock and surprise. Georgia swallowed the laughter that bubbled up from within her, knowing she absolutely could not let it escape her. What was wrong with her? Laughing at her son, her sick son, who could be hurt? A small part of her wanted someone to see, to look at her with disgust, to call child services on her. It would be over then. If her children were taken away from her, she would be guiltily absolved.

Her heart would ache for them.

Wouldn't it?

Of course it would. It was just that… they took pieces from her.

CHAPTER EIGHTEEN

Mad Hatter Nonsense

Tom was starting to think the couch cushions were glued to his brother's bottom. The kid had watched more TV in the last week than he'd watched in his whole life. And that was saying something. Better than being in his room though. Although, if he were being honest, a small part of him preferred it when Danny was in his bedroom. He couldn't really want that though.

"Hey, mum told me about what you said the other day."

It had taken Tom all day to work up to this conversation. He paused, hoping Danny might offer him an explanation, but he just blinked up at him from the couch.

"What did you mean when you said you wanted...a funeral?" Tom tried to keep his voice casual, but it broke on that last word. He already knew what Danny had meant. He just hoped to God they'd gotten it wrong.

Danny turned to him, and his face serene. "Well, I would have thought it was obvious." he said mildly.

Tom raised an eyebrow, waiting for him to continue.

"Well, why would anyone want a funeral? Because they'd died of course."

Georgia sucked in a sharp breath but remained silent as Tom's mouth became a hard line. She floated in Tom's peripheral vision, standing in the furthest corner of the lounge room.

"So, you think—" he couldn't believe he was saying it, "You think you need a funeral because you have *died*?"

Clapping filled the room. "Well done for figuring it out so quickly!"

Little bastard. God give him patience.

"And can you tell me how that is possible?" Tom spread his hands out and spoke slowly, as if he was talking to someone very young.

"Well, I was alive and now I am dead." Danny replied, as if he were speaking to someone equally stupid.

A sigh escaped from Tom's lips. *Walked straight into that one.* Time to try a different tact. "But you're breathing and walking and talking."

"Yes. Well spotted."

Apparently, the dead are giant smartasses.

"Dead people don't do those things."

Danny shrugged. "What can I tell you? Just because it doesn't make sense it doesn't mean it's not true. Like the Earth being round. That just does not make sense to me, but apparently, that's how it is. Some things just are and we have to accept that. We don't always need an explanation."

It was Alice in Wonderland logic. Mad Hatter nonsense.

"That was equal parts beautiful and insane." Tom said and Danny tipped his head in acknowledgment.

"As beautiful as it may be, I think you can understand how mum and I can't just *accept* that you are dead."

"It would be much easier for us all if you did."

It dawned on Tom that Danny was not going to make this easy. All his life, Tom had been the smartass, the one able to argue his way out of anything, but Danny's belief in this was so real, Tom would sooner be able to convince Danny to detach his own arm and give it to him.

"Is there no way we can convince you otherwise?" Tom asked. He might as well have his suspicions confirmed.

Danny laughed. "Have you ever heard of anyone trying to convince a dead person that they're not dead? I think that's pretty pointless, don't you?"

No. Yes. Why was what he was saying making sense? Tom looked at his mother helplessly. She looked like a corpse herself.

"I don't know how to help you, Danny." Tom said quietly.

Danny looked earnestly into his eyes. "You can help me, Tom. Give me a funeral."

A knock echoed through the house, and they froze. Just as well, thought Tom, because he had absolutely no reply. Slowly, Tom inched towards the hallway, carefully poking his head around the door. He could see Mickey standing on the ramshackle porch, as if she were about to light a bag of dog poo on fire and leave it on their faded welcome mat. Tom could see she was trying her best not to look through their stained-glass window, but they made eye contact, and Tom wondered if he would have answered her knock if they hadn't.

He took his time coming to the door and she stepped back, pretending to inspect the cobwebs in the eaves of the porch. The door cracked open and a sliver of Tom's face appeared out of the dark hallway.

"Hello." she said.

He could see her taking him in, her eyes stopping at his nose. She said nothing, and Tom wondered if she knew what had happened to his nose. He had no intention of telling her.

"Hi." he said, his voice impassive.

Mickey looked down at her feet. "I brought you guys a pie."

Did she make a pie because that's what they did in movies? Why pie? Was it a particularly sympathetic food?

It was a few seconds before he remembered his manners.

"Thanks."

He made no move to take the pie from her hands, so she pushed it up towards his chest like she was offering a sacrifice to an ancient god.

"I just wanted to see— to make sure that you were okay, I mean, your family was okay with everything that happened."

"We're fine." he looked down at his hands. "Well, thanks for the pie."

He raised the pie in acknowledgment and Mickey gave no protest as the door slowly closed in her face, almost nipping her nose.

"Well, that was rude."

Tom heard his mother's voice and turned to see her leaning on the wall behind him, her arms crossed about her torso.

"I know, but I think she was only trying to be nice."

"I meant *you*."

"Oh." he paused. "Well, I just didn't really think it was any of her business. Surely you of all people don't want people sticking their noses in it?"

She looked affronted. "What do you mean by that?"

He rolled his eyes, starting to walk down the hall.

"C'mon. You're not honestly going to explain it to people, are you? Even I don't know what is going on or what I'm supposed to say. The kid thinks he's died. He's having some sort of episode, and we have no idea how long it's going to last for— until his head heals. Whenever that's going to be."

She sniffed. "Why do we have to say anything? We'll just say he's not feeling right since the accident."

He levelled her a look. "You really think you're going to be able to hide it?" Tom shook his head. "I don't know how you can stomach it: all the lying. Makes me feel sick."

"You just shut the door in that girl's face!"

"Yeah, but I didn't *lie* to her. Lying's different. Lying splinters your soul."

For dramatic effect, he made sure he ran down the hall before she could reply. He was right, he knew it. He hadn't lied to Mickey. He just didn't want to have explain what was happening to Danny. It was private; he didn't even know how she'd found out in the first place. They just needed time. Time to make sense of it all. Time to pull themselves out of the rabbit hole. That's exactly how he felt. Like he was plunging headfirst down a well. It felt like there was nothing he could do to slow down, to stop his stomach flipping over and over.

He wondered when he would hit the bottom.

CHAPTER NINETEEN

Possums in the Roof

Tea slopped down the front of Georgia's white shirt as the rapping on the front door sliced through the house. Sitting next to her on the couch napping, Tom let out a small yelp and sat upright. Georgia swore and froze in her armchair, waiting.

The knock came again. Loud. Assured.

They were being circled by sharks. Why couldn't people just leave them alone?

Georgia looked at Tom before she crept forward, keeping a wide berth from the large, netted curtains that faced the street. She'd always hated the curtains she'd inherited with the house; the scraps of pointless, frilly lace that draped across every window, marring her view of the spectacular oak-lined street. In this moment though, she was glad she'd never ripped them down with her bare hands like she'd intended. She peered into her hallway, to try and gain a profile of the intruder.

Georgia squared her shoulders: there was no mistaking the thin, stooped body. The woman looked ready to knock again. Georgia cursed softly. Her mother came from a generation that wouldn't, *couldn't* understand what was happening inside her house. Her house was a delicate cocoon. She was working hard to weave even a fragile functionality about her life. She loved her mother, but in this house, in her world right now, she was not welcome.

"Don't answer it!" Tom hissed behind her.

"She'll just keep knocking if I don't."

"No, let's just hide."

"What are we, five year olds? It's going to happen Tom. If not today, then tomorrow. People want to come and see Danny. We can't be prisoners in our own home."

"I know, but I don't think I can pretend that everything is fine." he tugged on her hand, trying to lead her away from the door.

"Let go of me!" her voice raised on the last syllable.

A pause and then— "Georgia?"

Tom turned and ran on his tiptoes to his bedroom. Georgia waited until his door snipped shut before she slapped a smile on her face and poked her head through the front door.

Her mother looked at her curiously, craning her thin neck to peer into the hallway.

"Hello, I almost thought you weren't home for a moment?"

It was incredible really, Georgia thought, how her mother always managed to sneak a question into everything. Georgia held her silence and, uninvited, her mother shuffled to the door. Despite the heat, she was bundled in a thick-checkered coat, her hair pulled back into a tight bun that emphasized the high border of her forehead. Even now, when the beauty slid off with each passing year, her face was perfectly made up. Georgia cringed at the noise of her mother's shoes —Danny was asleep. Silently, she pattered after her.

"So," her mother said as she settled herself into one of her rustic kitchen chairs. "Where's my grandson? He's been back home for a week now and I've hardly seen him."

Georgia picked at the foil covering the lasagne that had been thrust into her hands.

"He's out. He's a young boy. They're supposed to be busy. He's out all the time. He is *very* popular."

"Are we talking about the same kid? Because I remember he sat on that couch—"

She pointed emphatically to the lounge. She was always doing that, gesturing, throwing her arms about. It was a family trait.

"—for three days and spoke to no one when one of those Harry Potter books came out."

Georgia gave a small relenting smile as she remembered him curled up, his long legs tucked neatly underneath him, his eyes straining and wincing as he became oblivious to the night falling around him.

A creaking groan sounded from deep within the house, pulling her from her thoughts. She looked quickly at her mother.

"What was that?" her mother had half gotten out of her chair.

"Possums." Georgia said quickly. "We get a heap of them here. All in the bloody roof."

She cursed herself. Possums? She could have just said Tom was home. She followed her mother as she ignored Georgia and poked her head down the hall. Georgia followed suit and saw, to her relief, nothing but her gloomy walls. *He's gone back into his room. If there is a God, he'll be back in his room.* Her mother backed slowly into the kitchen.

"That was stra—"

There was another loud groan from the hallway. It could not be mistaken for anything but the weight of a human body on an old, wooden floor.

"There is someone is this house." her mother's eyes were wide with certainty and fear.

"Tom's home. Tom!" she yelled. There was no response. She patted her mother's shoulder. She wasn't ready to give it up. Wasn't ready to show her everything. She leaned in closer to her mother.

"I'll have a quick look. You stay here."

"Georgina, no!" her mother hissed as Georgia jumped up and crept down the hall.

Georgia almost would have found it funny. Almost. She peered into the closest room, the bathroom. It was as it had always been—large, underwhelming, and unoccupied. Danny's door was shut. She crept to it and hovered her ear over it, but no sound passed through. She took a tentative step back. If he was in there, she did not want to disturb him. She didn't bother going any further; she really just wanted to make sure Danny was tucked away.

She returned to her kitchen to find her mother wide-eyed and frantic.

"No one there. Maybe Tom was walking around with his headphones in and didn't know we were in here."

Her mother sighed and leaned back. "This house is creepy. It's lovely from the outside, but dark and creepy inside."

"Thanks Mum."

"You know what I mean. It's not your fault. I mean, you could have done something with the interior design, gave the walls a lick of paint, but it's just one of those houses. No matter how it looks from the outside, it'll always have this... air about it."

"That's much better. Thanks."

"Don't be snarky." her mother frowned at her and stood up. "I'm just popping to the loo. Flick the kettle on, won't you?"

"I hope you fall in." Georgia muttered after her.

Parents. Surely, they must know how infuriating they are. Her thoughts stilled as a strangled scream floated into the kitchen. Georgia had nearly made it through the visit without revealing their secret. She careened into the doorframe as she skidded into the hall and then the bathroom. Her mother stood close to the door, her hand slack on the light switch, still in the action of flicking it on.

A man stood by the bathroom window, pressed against the wall as if he'd somehow walked through it from outside. He was hairy and stout, no older than forty. The women did not move, as if he were a wild animal that might spring into action from their slightest movement.

He spoke first. "I was just fixing the window for you. Your husband rang and asked me to help him out. Got to go now though."

He strode towards the women with his head down, pushing past them to enter the hallway. His hurried footsteps died away and a door slammed before the two had said a word. Her mother snapped the bathroom door shut and pushed her hands against it, as if her bones wouldn't shatter the second someone pushed back.

"There was a man inside your house Georgina!" her mother's voice tipped upwards with each syllable, edging towards hysteria.

"I know, I know. It's okay, I don't think there's anyone here now," she paused for a moment, before a barb of fear twisted into her. "Danny!"

"I thought Danny was out?"

"He's not out," she snapped.

"Tom!" no answer. "Should I open the door?"

She half hoped her mother would stop her, but she knew she couldn't leave the boys out there. She took in a breath. It was ridiculous. They'd heard the man leave. There was no one out there. Just her sons. The sons she'd brought into the world and sworn to protect. If she was about to be violently murdered, then so be it. She'd die a thousand terrible painful deaths for them. Except for maybe being burnt alive. Or drowning. Or torture of any kind.

Slowly, she turned the knob. Her mother cringed against her as they pushed the door open and looked into the hall. A man stood before them, naked save for the saggy black underwear that stuck to his skinny legs.

They screamed.

He screamed.

"Jesus Christ Danny!"

Her mother had covered her heart with a bony hand. He'd always been a stealthy little thing. Had always been able to sneak about the house undetected, sneak in after a late night out.

"Put some pants on!" yelled her mother.

Because that was the priority of course— not their safety: decorum.

At last, their voices had raised Tom. He poked his head into the bathroom.

"Oh, just in time." Georgia rolled her eyes at him.

Tom looked between them and his nearly naked brother and grinned. "Well hello grandmother."

"We just had a break in Thomas."

"What?" the amusement slipped from his face and he strode towards them.

"Someone broke into the house." Georgia confirmed.

"What happened? Are you okay? Danny are you okay?"

He shook Danny's shoulders before marching off to inspect the rest of the house. Georgia felt the fear slowly leave her body.

Danny's eyes shuttered. "No. I'm dead."

"What?" her mother turned her attention to Danny.

He looked at her curiously. "Tom asked me if I was okay. I'm not okay. Because I'm dead."

Georgia forced herself to laugh. "Oh, don't worry mum, he's just being dramatic. Did you see anyone Tom?" she asked as her eldest son reappeared.

"No, I was in my room the whole time."

She reluctantly turned to Danny. "Danny? Did you see anything?"

He looked down and examined himself, in a way that reminded her of a small child.

"I was in my room."

Tom strode down the hallway to the back door. The tattered back fly screen was open which was normal, but the back door was slightly ajar. He snapped it shut and slid the deadbolt across. Watching him, she was surprised at how quickly the fear had dissipated. Usually, he was the cause of her stress.

"So, what do we do now?" her mother asked, looking between Georgia and Tom.

"Well, what else are we supposed to do?" asked Tom

"Call the police?" said his grandmother incredulously.

Georgia rolled her eyes. "Oh, but what are they going to do? Send a squad over to see if he's still here? He's gone. We frightened him off. I'm sure he's not coming back."

Her mother's eyes flew wide open. "Oh my god Georgia did he take anything?"

Georgia hadn't even considered that as a possibility.

She looked at her two sons. "As long as we are safe, I don't even care."

"I really think you should have called the police."

Her mother sniffed into her teacup. They were all sitting in the living room, with the exception of Danny who had taken to walking laps of the house. He would reappear every few minutes, and Georgia watched her mother's eyes flick to her youngest son, taking in the erratic movements, the ping-pong eyeballs darting about in his head.

"What is wrong with that child?"

Her mother had broken the momentary silence of the room, gesturing at Danny. He stopped pacing and looked at her, and then looked towards his mother.

"He's... okay. He's just trying to cope with the accident."

"He is acting like a mental patient."

"Like I said, he's still recovering."

"Is that *normal*?" her mother asked slowly.

Georgia threw up her hands. "His brain swelled like a balloon inside his skull. I don't think *normal* will be happening for a while." Georgia noticed Danny's jocks had begun to ride up on his left cheek.

"What are you going to do Georgia?"

You. What are *you* going to do? She hated her for saying that.

Danny poked his head back into the room and began to speak before she could answer. "Don't worry grandma, we have a plan."

"Dan—" Georgia started.

"I am going to have a funeral. Things will be better then. You're welcome to come," he added earnestly, like he was inviting to her to his fifth birthday party.

Her mother looked like someone had slapped her across the face. So, she knew. Georgia felt a savage sense of satisfaction.

Her mother let out a strained laugh. She looked around at them all, waiting for someone to tell her it was a joke. A small part of Georgia had hoped she'd understand and as much as she didn't want to admit it—take charge. But, maybe for the first time in her life, it looked like her mother had no idea how to act. In her world, hurt was a broken bone. Sickness was a flu. She might know everything, but she had no clue about this.

CHAPTER TWENTY

A Dead Spider in the Cookie Tin

They had no idea he was gone, he was sure of that. They thought he was tucked up in bed. To be fair, that is usually where he would be. He knew what they thought. He saw the way they looked at him, danced around him like he was some sort of apparition. Well, maybe they weren't too far from the truth.

It had been difficult to climb out the window. It had been years, perhaps decades, since anyone had replaced the fly screen and over time, its screws had melted into the wood of the window frame. The pliers had ripped into his fingers as he wriggled the screws back and forth. But eventually, he'd been able to slide out into the night.

Sitting on the faux leather seat near the back of the bus, the heat was stifling, even at this hour. With every movement, his butt cheeks peeled away from the seat with a soft squelch. He was on the 37 heading east, away from the city.

A young couple were sitting two seats in front of him. The girl was rambling to the man, her words slurring intermittently. Danny noticed the man stroke her shoulder softly, dotting her forehead with sporadic kisses. It was kind of nauseating, but kind of beautiful. He tried to peer in, imagine what it was like to be her, to be him, but he felt like there was a force field pushing him back. He could not be a part of their bubble. He could never know what it felt like to love her. He could never know what it felt like to love him. No one can really ever have any idea what's inside someone else's head. He'd always struggled with that concept. It amazed him, how a person could live their life, think their complex thoughts, look in the mirror every day and no one else would ever know what it was like to see that reflection.

Would a person be shocked if they could grab a pizza cutter, open up his head and peer inside? Danny imagined them reeling away, staggering back a few steps and then carefully placing the lid back on with a shudder as if they'd found a dead spider in the cookie tin. He'd always felt that way, like his brain worked differently, independently to all the other brains, like they were all connected by intricate strands of webbing, but at some point, his had been snipped away.

But for the first time in a long time, he felt drawn to people. He wanted to speak to them, to feel something when he looked into their faces. So, he was going to them. To his people.

The buzzer gave a muted bleep, announcing Danny's stop. The heat had not dissipated at all. It hit him square in the face as he stepped off the bus and into the black, still street. Danny knew where to go. It loomed in front of him. He skirted the bright lights that heralded the front doors, instead heading for the back carpark. Hospitals were like Christmas trees. The front busy, the back bare. A small, discreet path hugged the outside wall of the hospital. Danny followed it and eventually he came upon a fire door, left slightly ajar. It made sense. It was the easiest way to get into the back carpark, but surely hospital staff closed it at night? Visiting hours were well and truly over. Anyone could just walk in there. Danny shook his head at their lax security and slithered through the opening.

He expected alarms to sound and hospital staff to tackle him to the ground, but not a single soul was there to greet him when he stepped into the corridor. It was quiet, but he could sense the presence of living bodies close by. He wasn't about to go looking for *them*.

Down. It had to be down. Everything he'd learned from pop culture told him that was where he needed to go. After minutes of searching the floor, he spotted an unassuming stairwell, leading downstairs to a dim floor. Unlike the one he'd just come from, there were no corridors leading off to individual rooms. Instead, he found himself standing before double doors, marked with a stop sign that read: "All visitors must be accompanied by hospital staff".

Danny pushed the doors open and found himself standing in a

cramped and sparse foyer. In front of him was a large pine desk that didn't look too different from the kind you'd find in the reception of a second-rate hotel. To his left, there was a trio of plastic chairs. There was nothing else in the foyer, apart from the medical announcements that littered the room: *'please wash your hands'* was stuck to the walls in several places around the room. Maybe hospitals had to put that kind of stuff up—legally they were obligated to ensure the public knew that not washing your hands led to you having dirty hands.

Danny also noticed several posters that provided the number to a grief counselling hotline. An array of flyers littered the counter, advertising the numbers to local funeral homes. All in all, it was a bleak set up. Whoever was in charge knew there was no point pretending this place was something other than what it was. They knew that no amount of flowers or wall art could make people forget why they were here.

Surprisingly, there was no one manning the counter. Danny had half a mind to write to the hospital, informing them of their poor security. But it's not like they needed to do anything to keep the people in here. He chuckled to himself. Oh no, in fact, people were *dying* to get in.

Throwing one last glance around the room, Danny jumped the counter to push open the door behind it. Another serious sign was stuck to it: 'STOP. You MUST be accompanied by a member of hospital staff beyond this point.' He snickered to himself. *Ooo capital letters, that'll stop me.* He wasn't really doing anything he shouldn't be. He only wanted to have a chat.

Beyond the foyer, the morgue had an open house plan. Through large, tempered glass windows, Danny could make out rooms that looked like science labs.

"Oh sh—"

He'd been so busy taking in the labs, he'd almost cannoned into the man before him. It took Danny a moment to realise the man in the chair in front of him was asleep, sitting behind a desk scattered with paper. The man's bleached white hair and the sagging bags under his eyes aged him beyond his years. The lanyard around the man's neck indicated that his name was 'Gordon' and he was a morgue supervisor. One earphone dangled down his scrubs, the other firmly planted in his right ear. Even from his few feet of distance, Danny could hear heavy metal blaring from the headphones. Danny smiled. It was more likely that the corpses in the rooms around him would wake before Gordon did.

The first door he tried was locked, as was the second, third and final door. He would have deleted the draft of the letter he'd been writing in his head to the hospital if he hadn't of been able to simply grab Gordon's keys from the desk as he slept, his head bent at an awkward angle.

It was significantly colder inside the lab. It reminded him of when you go to the supermarket and walk through the meat section. He'd always be in shorts and a t-shirt, unprepared for the cold that hit him, like he was now. Always bring a jacket. It was just good sense. How hadn't he learned that life lesson yet?

There were no slots in the walls; he didn't have to go fishing around like he was looking for a tray of ice cubes. Three white body bags on metal trolleys were in the centre of the room. Carefully, Danny unzipped the left bag.

A middle-aged man lay splayed before him. His face was bloated, almost transparent. A great, puckering slash ran the length of his torso from, Danny could only assume, when the autopsy had taken place. A great grumbling moan sounded from the back of the man's throat and Danny watched as the man squinted at him through one eye, before he mustered enough energy to open the other. His eyes were dilated, and Danny gasped as the man sat up, exposing a great gash to his balding head. The man sighed and looked around.

"Am I where I think I am?" he asked, taking in the white walls, metal trays and finally, the stitches across his body. "Oh damn. I don't know how I slept through that."

He gingerly touched one of the stitches in his abdomen.

"Sorry?" Danny offered hesitantly.

Was that the right thing to say in this situation? He'd never had to offer condolences to a corpse before. The man nodded slowly, sighing and stretching his arms.

"Well, this sucks. Whoa." he sniffed the air before him. "Don't come too close. My breath stinks. Pardon me." he smacked his lips together in distaste. "God, my lips are so dry. There isn't anything to drink around here is there?"

Danny fished a water bottle from his backpack and tossed it to him.

"Don't have anything a little more... *colourful* than water do you?" the corpse asked, winking and shaking the bottle suggestively before taking a few gulps.

Danny rolled his eyes. "Sorry. I didn't think to bring a bottle of Jack to morgue."

The corpse gave a racking laugh that seemed to reverberate through his chest cavity, as if there was nothing inside to soften it, which Danny realised was probably very close to the truth. The corpse reached out to give the bottle back to Danny. Danny shuddered.

"That's ok, you keep it."

The corpse nodded his thanks. "I'm Barry by the way. Baz or Bazza if you like."

Barry extended a hand and Danny shook it. It was cold and the tips of his fingers were dark, almost black. Danny eyed the gash on Barry's head. It looked sticky and wet and red and gooey and he absolutely *had* to stop looking at it. Baz followed his eyes questioningly, and brought a finger to his bald crown, his black eyes widening in horror.

"Don't! Trust me. Don't touch it." warned Danny.

Barry nodded, and obediently snatched his hand away, tucking it into his naked lap. Danny wished his eyes hadn't followed the movement.

"How... how'd it happen?" Danny asked tentatively.

"I..." Barry looked as if he was trying to pull a long-lost memory from a dark corner of his brain. Maybe it had been stored in the section that was now missing. Danny's eyes darted to the gash again. *Stop it.*

"I fell... through a table... a glass table."

"Clumsy." Danny said mildly.

"No. I lost consciousness." Barry sighed. "Because I had been poisoned."

"Oh damn! What did you do?" Danny half laughed, before he remembered where they were and what the outcome had been for Barry. He wiped the smile from his lips.

"I tell you I was poisoned and the first thing you ask is what did *I* do." Barry rolled his eyes. The effect was nauseating.

"Ok then, who killed you?"

"My wife."

"And what did you do to make her want you dead?"

Barry let out a puff of hot air and threw his hands up. Danny reeled back, blinking.

"Oops sorry. I told you my breath was bad. Yours isn't much better." he said accusingly, casting an eye over Danny. "And what, exactly, happened to you?"

"I had a car accident."

"And?"

"And then I died."

Barry frowned. "You don't look very dead."

"Could say the same about you. I mean, if it wasn't for the stitches, and the yellow skin and the black hands and the—" Danny's eyes trailed to the wound again.

No, no, no. Eww gross.

"Well, she was smart about how she did it, that's for sure. Didn't leave much of a trace. Except for the eyes."

He opened them further to show Danny his dilated pupils, as if he hadn't already noticed. Danny feinted polite interest. They were almost as unsettling as the head wound. Almost.

"Do you think they'll catch her?"

"You'd think so," he scoffed, "Even the cops at the scene knew something wasn't right. A healthy man doesn't just keel over, frothing at the mouth."

Personally, Danny thought he looked far from healthy. His belly was paunchy, his face haggard. He had the distinct air of a man who had never denied himself anything.

"But the thing is, I was diabetic. My wife waited until I'd had a few drinks. Then she pumped me full of insulin. Pretty brilliant really. Or opportunistic—however you want to look at it."

"Diabetic. And a drinker." Danny said.

Barry shrugged. "I'm many things. But I'm not perfect."

"So, why'd she do it?" Danny asked again.

"I don't know," Barry said simply. "We'd gotten tired of one another, you know? Is that enough reason to murder your husband? Because you're sick of looking at his ugly face every day? We had money. It wouldn't be that. Maybe she had a lover. She was a wily minx for sure that one. Who knows? You don't get all the answers when you die."

Danny nodded eagerly. "It's like that for me. I really thought everything would be different once I'd died."

"Like how?" Barry crossed his arms and absent-mindedly began to roll his head slowly, loud cracks reverberating about the room. Danny shuddered, but ignored them.

"Like I'd feel at peace and all that. But I don't really feel any different." Danny sighed. "I feel so… dead. Do you know what I mean?"

Barry raised his eyebrow, gesturing to his stitches, but when Danny didn't react, he answered. "I feel like I did before I died. I feel like exactly the same man. Minus a few brain cells."

Danny looked at the wound again. Goddamn, it was like a piece of raspberry pie—once you cut it and the insides spurt out from the pastry and you have to basically scoop it out of the tin.

"So you're okay with being dead?" asked Danny.

Baz opened his mouth, and then closed it looking thoughtful. "My first instinct was to say no, considering the whole murder thing, but now that I think about it, I guess… it is what it is. I feel like I did before." Barry shrugged. Danny was silent. "What about you?"

"I don't know." Danny said flatly.

"Are you unhappy?"

"I don't know."

"Well, that's good. I've heard the unhappy dead make for mean ghosts." he winked and then looked over Danny with interest again. "So, I wonder what you are then? Dead? Alive? Somewhere in between?" he raised an eyebrow. "A zombie perhaps?"

Danny narrowed his eyes. "I told you, I'm dead. And I'm not a zombie. I'm just—"

The door to the lab gave a quiet squeal and Danny wheeled around.

"Stay there. Don't move. Or I'll lock you in and call the cops."

Gordon stood by the door, eyes wide open, a shaking arm outstretched towards Danny. Danny jangled Gordon's keys at him and Gordon's mouth formed a silent, comical 'Oh.'

Danny faced him, his palms open. "I'm not up to anything weird. I was just here to have a casual, friendly conversation. That's all."

Gordon looked between Danny and Barry.

"That's… really not very reassuring." Gordon massaged his

eyeballs. "Come on man, please tell me you weren't up to anything weird. I'm gonna get in so much trouble."

Danny stood up in what he hoped was a conciliatory move. "Look it's ok. Barry is really my uncle. My dear Uncle Barry. Him and I have always been close, but my dad and him had a falling out—because of the drinking. So I never get to see him. And when I heard what happened… I had to see him. I'm sorry."

The lie came to him so quickly, he surprised himself. It made him think of Al. He was in the ground now, but had he come here too? He hoped not. It didn't really seem like a peaceful place. Maybe that was his fault though. It was probably bad manners to wake the dead. He hoped Al felt peace.

Gordon looked like he was fighting an internal battle.

"I get it, but why'd you have to break into the morgue? And at night-time too." his voice was almost pleading.

"Well, I didn't exactly have to break in did I? And now was the only time I could come. As I said, dad *really* wouldn't have approved."

"You're just a kid. Kids do stupid stuff. But you better get out of here."

"Absolutely. Can I just have one more minute with good old Uncle Baz?"

Gordon hesitated and Danny jangled his keys. "How are you going to explain this, Gordon? Let me have a minute more, and no one has to know how I got in here."

"Ok. But I'm watching from the window."

Gordon narrowed his eyes and backed out. As promised, he stood at the window with his arms crossed. Danny turned back to Barry.

"Barry?"

"Yes Danny?" he asked, as if no interruption had taken place.

"Why am I stuck here? Why can't I go where you are?"

"If you can't pass over, doesn't that usually mean that you aren't at peace? That something is missing?"

"Yeah."

"What is it then?"

"I lost my soul."

Tap. Tap.

'Times up.' Gordon mimed, pointing to his wrist. He wasn't

wearing a watch, but Danny got the message.

"Thanks for the chat, Barry. I'll leave you alone so you can rest in peace. I mean—I didn't mean—"

Barry waved a hand at him dismissively, folding his legs into his bag. He laid down.

"It's fine. I can't remember the last time I had a good night's sleep."

He looked wistful as he reached down and zipped the bag up over his face.

It's just me. Just me in this big wide world.

Danny knew it, of course he knew it, but he'd never looked it dead in the eye before. He'd kept his back to it all his life. Like when you're a kid and you think there's a monster under your bed, so you just screw your eyes shut and hope to God that when it eats you, it swallows you whole, quick, instead of munching on your flesh and slurping on your bones.

There were some people though, that never knew it. Never had the fear of monsters under the bed. Never realized they were alone to face them. Baffling. How could you not know? Or did they know it and wanted it so badly not to be true they'd tried to fill their space with children and friends and cars and clothes. When he looked at them though, they didn't seem empty. He watched for the cracks, the look that he knew well. He never saw it in those people. He saw it in some people, the other ones, but never as much as he saw it in himself. It made him feel like a black speck in the ocean. Like he was somewhere in between two shores.

CHAPTER TWENTY-ONE

Chopping Logs

Sporadically, the door would rattle and the golden knob would slowly turn. The door would open a crack, only to be snapped shut moments later. Odd thumping noises sounded from the room, and the light would often shine brightly in the middle of the night, seeping under the door and into the dark hallway.

When Danny did open the door, a wraith-like creature would flit from room to room, hovering in doorways, muttering to himself. He was a very active ghost. He must have some sort of agenda, to be so animated in his haunting. It was unnerving, never knowing when he would appear. You could be on your way out of the kitchen, carrying a hot cup of tea and then bam! There's Danny. And there's your tea. All over the floor.

Or you could be in bathroom, like Tom was now, minding his own business while he *did* his business, and then suddenly the door would start creaking its way open. You've never felt more powerless in your life, than when you're sitting on the toilet, and the door starts to open. The toilet was too far away, so there was nothing Tom could do about it, except sit calmly and stare into Danny's eyes as he pushed the door open. Had they never even stopped to think about putting a lock on the bathroom door?

"Hi." Tom said conversationally, as he waited for Danny to say something.

But Danny just stared, his eyes going to Tom's pants bunched around his ankles and the phone lit up in Tom's right hand.

Tom followed his gaze. "As you can see, I'm kind of in the middle of something here."

Danny shifted his gaze, carefully inspecting the walls. There wasn't much to look at. It was a bathroom. Shower. Bath. Toilet. Basin. That was pretty much it.

"What do you want?" Tom said, laughing.

How he could possibly find this funny, he didn't know. But as he stared into his brother's face, he recognised something there. He was averting his gaze. His cheeks were flushed.

"You need to go!"

Danny gave a small nod, squirming with discomfort. Tom burst into laughter, but quickly stopped himself, not liking what it was doing to his body in his present state.

"You realise don't you, that dead people don't need to do *that*."

"There's an exception to every rule." Danny said haughtily, moving further into the room.

Tom put his hand up, nearly dropping his phone into the toilet bowl.

"Whoa. Hold up there. What are you doing?"

Danny's brow furrowed. "I told you. I need to..." he gestured to the toilet and hooked his thumbs into the waistband of his shorts.

Tom yelped. "Yeah, I get that! But I'm on here! El occupado!"

Danny's hands remained on his shorts, looking at Tom with a blank expression.

"If you pull those pants down, I swear to God..."

Like a robot programmed to obey only its primal directives, Danny slowly pulled his pants down.

"Ok. I'll remember that. And you've forced me to do this," Tom took a deep breath in. "Muuuuuuum!"

Instantly, Tom heard the sound of heavy footsteps coming towards them. Georgia burst into the bathroom, blinking rapidly as she took in the sight of her youngest son's bare bottom. She thought she had it bad. Tom had a first-class seat of the front view.

She clamped a hand over her eyes. "Why is he naked Tom? Why are you on the toilet?"

She asked the questions, but it was clear from her tone that she was really didn't want to hear the answers.

"I'm filing my taxes."

She ignored him. "Danny, sweetie, why are you naked?" she almost begged her last few words as she groped to find the profile of her son.

"Mum you should not do that with your eyes closed. You're asking for trouble."

"Shut up," she growled as she found Danny's shoulders, "What is going on here Tom?"

Tom sighed, looking at his phone. "The fruitloop needs to use the toilet."

"Don't call him that." she snapped.

Danny let out a small groan, bringing a hand to clutch at his intestines. Tom raised his eyes in alarm and Georgia swung into action.

"Come on, you can use my bathroom."

She grabbed his shoulders and steered him away, not bothering to pull his pants up. She fixed her gaze straight on, not even looking down as Danny stumbled, his ankles getting caught in his pants. Eventually, he shed them entirely, and they remained on the bathroom floor as if to remind Tom that what he had just experienced was real—he hadn't just passed out the toilet and hallucinated. None of it felt real. How was it that his old life had been swept away so easily? He didn't even get to say goodbye to it. It just morphed into this.

Whatever *this* was.

Georgia stormed back into the bathroom. Presumably, Danny had made it to the toilet.

"God? Can't I get a moment of privacy around here? A man needs peace and quiet when he's chopping a log."

"What is wrong with you?"

"Constipated most likely."

"This is what I'm talking about. Why do you have to make a joke about everything?"

For the first time in his adult life, she loomed over him, her hands on her hips, her mouth a hard thin line.

"Oh mum stop—"

"No, I'm sick of it. Your brother is *sick* and all you can do is make jokes."

"Sick? Got a bit of a runny nose, does he?"

"Stop it Tom!"

"That wasn't a joke!" he almost stood up then, which would have been a big mistake.

"You think I don't know that Danny's *sick*. I have no idea what I'm supposed to do. I feel like a smacked ass. I'm a pen with no ink. A priest with a giant—" he stopped, remembering it was his mother he was talking to.

"Sometimes I just have to laugh about it. And I know that's wrong and it's messed up, but I can't help it. If I don't laugh…"

There was quiet for a moment as she huffed in a few breaths.

"You're right."

"Excuse me?"

She rolled her eyes. "It is better, being able to laugh sometimes."

He nodded. "Sometimes, it's all you can do."

"Like now?" she said slowly, reaching out to the toilet holder and snatching the roll off.

"Nah, that's not funny."

She grinned at him, picking up the basket of spare rolls as well.

"No mum, seriously don't—"

"Enjoy!" she cackled as she backed through the door, snicking it closed with a bump of her hip.

He smiled to himself. The joke was on her. After all the commotion, he no longer needed to go. It had shot back inside like a scared little turtle.

CHAPTER TWENTY-TWO

A Chase Between the Gravestones

Danny could not stay still. Something in him demanded he move, that he get out of the house. He couldn't think with the walls pressing in on him. It seemed smaller, a different place than he remembered. It didn't feel like home, not like the graveyard where the moon hung high in the sky and he could prowl the grounds as much as he liked. They had no idea about his night-time adventures. They thought he was safe in his room and they were safe on the other side of his door. He knew what they were thinking. They thought he was out of his mind. But he was finally thinking clearly. Barry's acceptance of his own death made him realise that he needed to embrace his own. He'd scoffed at Barry at the time, but maybe he was right. Maybe he was an angry ghost, haunting the halls of their house, scaring its occupants, his family. Maybe that's why the house felt different. Because of him.

He sighed into the grass and looked over at the rows of headstones surrounding him. Those below the ground were his true kin. Maybe he didn't have to go back. Was there any reason he couldn't live in the graveyard forever?

There was one reason. He didn't belong. He was like an underage kid trying to get into a club with a fake ID. How could he stay here, be accepted into the ranks of his comrades, if they saw him as an impostor?

There was no other way. He had to have a funeral.

Then the rest of my life can begin, he said to himself.

He heard a soft voice coming from his left. "How inspirational."

Danny let out a little yelp. He had no idea he had company. He madly craned his neck, searching for the source. Big black boots stepped into his line of vision and his eyes travelled upwards, taking in a pair of bare thighs, creamy in the moonlight. His eyes travelled higher still, almost disappearing into the back of his skull as he noted the rest of the girl's profile. Despite the boots, she was short, just like her skirt and bright red hair. It really didn't seem like appropriate attire for the location.

"You're dressed funny."

She raised an eyebrow at him. "Well, I am in a graveyard at night. You didn't really expect me to be normal, did you?" she plonked herself down next to him. "So, what brings you here this fine evening?" she was talking to him like she'd known him for years. Maybe she did.

"We don't... know each other, do we?"

She looked at him, grinning. "No, but I kind of feel like I know you already."

"You're weird."

She gave a loud, obnoxious laugh that sliced through the quiet night. "Two for two."

"I'm dead." Danny said.

She didn't miss a beat. "Hi Dead. I'm Peet. Well it's Peeta, but I prefer Peet."

She saw the less than impressed look on his face.

"Not a fan of dad jokes, got it. Well Dead, we do have something in common," she inhaled deeply. "I'm dead inside too."

Danny sprung upright, and Peet jumped several feet into the air.

"If I wasn't before, then I am now." she clutched a hand to her chest, checking her vital organs weren't still floating in the air.

"Really?" Danny breathed, oblivious to the fright he'd given her, scanning her body for clues.

Mischief danced in her eyes, filling them with life. Even in the moonlight, he could see her cheeks were rosy. There was nothing wrong with her circulatory system, that was for sure.

"Are you sure about that?"

She nodded solemnly. "I saw an old lady fall down some stairs the other day and—*I laughed.*"

Danny sighed. "You're lucky. I can't even remember the last time I laughed."

"I can't remember the last time I was serious about something. I had a pap smear the other day and I could *not* stop telling dirty jokes."

Danny shuddered.

"Oh sorry was that a bit too much? I have a habit of doing that. No filter. Just don't really care anymore." she gave another one of her barking loud laughs.

"Because… you're dead." Danny said slowly.

"I guess. I wasn't always like this. But one day I just… stopped caring. Nothing really seemed to matter very much." she bought a hand to her face, sweeping her hair back. "Look at me, yapping on and on to some stranger, sitting in a graveyard at night-time. I've *really* lost it."

"Lost what?" Danny said, his eyes alight.

"You're an intense person Dead."

He sighed and sat down again. "It's just that—I've lost something too."

"Your house key? Explains why your here." she smiled, by Danny looked at her solemnly.

"No. My soul."

Peet smile dropped from her face and she looked at Danny for a few moments. "That is an irreplaceable thing to lose. You would have been better off dropping your phone down the toilet."

Danny nodded. He didn't need to reply. It was just nice to have someone believe him, to understand how he felt. He was empty. There was a hole in his heart.

"What are you doing here anyway?" he asked.

"I've found graveyards to be a *great* place to pick up guys."

"Oh, is that why you're dressed like that?"

"Like what?"

"A prostitute."

"I'm dressed like a whore because I am a whore."

"Are you really?"

"I could be." she eyed him slyly. "None of your business really, is it? What I wear is no one's business. Where I go is no one's business.

Would you like to know what I had for breakfast? Well guess what—"

A light flashed across their faces.

"Oi!"

Danny heard the jiggling of metal and heavy footsteps pounding on asphalt coming towards him.

"Great to meet you Dead." Peet said, winking. "But it's time for me to dash."

With a flick of her skirt, she was off, giggling and whooping into the darkness.

Shit, Danny murmured to himself. Why was it always him getting caught in strange places? Surely there were proper criminals out there, hurting and killing people. It's not like there was anyone here he could murder. He dragged his body upright, preparing for a chase between the gravestones.

He heard ragged breathing behind him. "Stop! This... out of... bounds!"

Danny felt like a prized stallion, leaping and prancing between graves. He sprung right over a large, newly polished stone, grabbing the arm of a smiling stone angel, the darkness making her look strangely menacing as he ran around her, losing his quarry within the rows. He stopped behind a large oak tree, sucking in breaths as he crouched against the trunk. It was only once he stopped that he realised just how out of breath he was. His mother was right: even for the undead, fitness was important. Gasping, he desperately tried to fill his lungs with air. He tried to silence himself, pressing his hands to his chest, but it rose and fell as quickly as before, his rattling breaths betraying his position.

Laughter sounded close by. "A bit puffed, are you? No need to run anymore. Got you now."

Danny realised he was trapped. Behind him was a large fence, too high to vault over. He peeked around the trunk and spied his quarry. He was a portly man, a ring of fat about his middle, but Danny was wary of him now, since apparently, he couldn't run more than a few 100 metres without fighting for air. What had happened to his body? If he could just make one last run for it, he could dart around the guard and make a break for it.

Without another thought, he sprung from his hiding spot, but the guard had moved closer to his position. Danny lunged forward, but the man caught him and brought Danny crashing to ground. He landed painfully on his back amongst the dirt and leaf litter. The guard cackled to himself, a hard boot pressing into Danny's intestines.

"Boy, you move slower than a stoned turtle." he gave an extra hard poke with his toes into Danny's ribs. "You just sit tight. The cops will be along any minute. Then you can explain to them what you're doing creeping about the graveyard at night-time." he sniffed, and Danny sighed, staring into the sky.

It really was a beautiful night.

CHAPTER TWENTY-THREE

You Can't Trust Strangers

"Hang on, he what?"

Georgia was standing at her front door in her dressing gown, staring nonplussed at the two police officers gripping the elbows of her youngest son. She was wide awake, despite having only woken up minutes ago. As it turns out, insistent knocking at 3am in the morning is a *very* effective wake up call. She was hardly relieved to see the police standing at her front door, holding her son, but she was glad it wasn't another burglar. Although, a thief would hardly knock on the front door.

Danny was staring at a spot over her shoulder, his eyes unfocused.

"He was in a graveyard ma'am." the older of the two officers said. He had a bristly moustache and a belly that was beginning to round.

"He's been in his room." she said weakly.

The cop cleared his throat, not wanting to contradict her. "The night manager called us. Said he was hanging around by the graves. Maybe with a girlfriend."

"A girlfriend! That's impossible."

The cop shrugged. He didn't get into the job to sort out family dramas.

"He'll be right with you?" he glanced between her and Tom.

She could tell he'd put together that she was probably a single parent, struggling to deal with rebellious teenage boys. If only her problems were that pedestrian.

"Yes, yes of course."

He looked her over, scanning her face with sharp eyes. "Are you sure?" he asked slowly.

She forced herself to look at him. "Yes. Thank you, officers."

They both nodded politely and then turned back to their car, leaving the three of them on the threshold. Once they pulled away, Georgia fixed her eyes on Danny. Should she shout? Cry? She wanted to do both. But she just stood there, her feet locked in place.

Finally, Tom broke the silence. "Should I… make us all a cup of tea?"

She nodded dumbly, and he gently pulled her back into the bowels of the house. She grabbed Danny's arm, and the three of them trailed into the kitchen like a paper chain. As she wrapped her shaking hands around a cup of weak earl grey, she told herself she was in control.

"So, are you sure we can't put a lock on his door?" Tom asked.

"A locked door won't keep me in."

Tom and Georgia looked at each other, surprised to hear Danny speak.

"We aren't going to lock you in Dan." she pushed the cup of tea into his palms. "But it's not safe out at night by yourself."

"I wasn't alone."

Georgia and Tom looked at each other again. "You can't trust strangers Danny."

"She's my friend. And unlike you two, she understands me. She wants to help me."

Tom choked on his tea, nearly swallowing the tea bag whole. "You can't possibly think we don't want to help you."

Danny narrowed his eyes at him. "If you really wanted to help me, you'd let me have a funeral."

Georgia couldn't help but feel like Tom had walked them right into a bear trap. Danny turned his glare to Georgia.

"I've done everything you wanted. I exercised—"

"You went to the gym *once.*"

He continued like he hadn't heard her. "I've been eating your disgusting food. I've upheld my part of the deal."

"Danny it's not like we'd be throwing a party. We would be pretending that you'd d—" she stopped, realising that he wouldn't take kindly to her words. "What will people say?" she asked weakly.

He reached out to pat her shoulder. "Probably 'my condolences' or 'sorry for your loss'."

Georgia put her head in her hands and Tom took over.

"It can't happen Danny. Not that we don't want to do it for you, but people won't understand. They'll be offended."

"I don't care what people think. This is what I want. If it doesn't happen, I'll keep going out. I'll find others that will help." he gave them a look, daring them to challenge him. "You can't stop me."

Georgia didn't like the look in his eye one little bit.

"Are you ok?"

She considered all the different ways she could answer the question.

Yes.

eye roll. Teenage boys. Giving me a hard time.

Danny's just… not doing well.

My son thinks he's dead and I have no idea how to help him and every day I wake up worried that something is going to happen to him but I can't tell anyone.

As ridiculous as each reply seemed, none seemed as impossible as answering with a simple *no*. When people asked that question, were they really prepared for that to be the answer? Looking into Mel's sweet, earnest face, she didn't think so. She might think she wanted to know the answer, to help even, but Mel didn't have kids. She was a part-time yoga instructor. What could she do about a teenage boy that snuck out to graveyards in the dead of the night?

"I'm fine." Georgia replied, dragging a smile to her lips.

The food in her mouth felt like chunks of dry wall. She didn't really know what that was, but it sounded like it would be an unpleasant thing to eat. She looked around her then, acutely aware of the strangers surrounding them, laughing and chattering over their coffees.

Mel picked up her knife and fork delicately. "How's Danny?"

"He's… okay." Georgia almost felt bad for Mel. She couldn't help but be reminded of the conversations she had with the boys sometimes. When she'd asked them how their day was and all she'd get back were monosyllabic words and grunts. Maybe they'd felt like she did now: like there was no point trying to explain what her life was like to someone who'd never lived in it. It's not that she didn't appreciate her friends concern, it was just… pointless.

Mel nodded slowly, keeping her eyes on her breakfast. Georgia could see that she wasn't fooled.

"The funniest thing happened in the class I took last night." Mel paused, and Georgia knew it was to give her the option of continuing.

"Oh yeah?" Georgia felt a weak rush of gratitude towards her friend. Mel wasn't stupid. She knew things weren't okay. Georgia didn't even know it until Mel gave it to her, but what she really wanted was a distraction. How were some people so attuned to the needs of others? She'd underestimated her friend. She would have felt shame, but her body was numb to it. Maybe if you feel too much of something, you just stop feeling it anymore.

CHAPTER TWENTY-FOUR

Zombie Babies

Tom was in his bedroom, reading, when he glanced up to see Danny standing in the doorway. Tom had the impression that he'd been there for a while. What felt like a cold finger trailed down his spine and he shuddered.

He arched an eyebrow. "Yes?"

He was really not in the mood for Dannyisms today. Since their last conversation he had just felt... sick. Powerless. Tom knew Georgia felt the same, even though they'd barely spoken since. Silence was becoming their constant passenger.

Dan looked down at his hands and shuffled his feet.

"Are you... nervous?" Tom sat up, begrudgingly interested in why Danny had appeared in his doorway.

Dan blushed, but ignored him. "I just wanted to ask you something."

He was looking at the ceiling as if Tom was hanging from it like a big bat. Tom raised his eyebrows and motioned for Danny to spit it out. Just because he was interested, it didn't mean that he had to make it any easier for Danny.

"I—there's this girl."

"Ah," said Tom, leaning back against his bedhead, his arms spread behind his head. "There always is." his eyes narrowed. "The graveyard girl?"

Tom had no idea what had happened to the girl from the party, the night of the acc—he forced himself to shake the memory away.

"She's an angel. She's the most beautiful creature I've ever seen."

"Ok, hold up there buddy. Just slow down a bit."

Danny's eyes and mouth looked like they were melting off his face.

"She's just a girl Dan."

Danny's eyes snapped to Tom. "She is *not*. She is a siren. Sent by God. To me."

"No, Danny, no." Tom swung his legs off his bed, ready to jump to his feet and throttle the boy.

Danny just smiled. "I'm going to ask her to marry me."

"You cannot—" Tom took in a deep breath. He smiled serenely. "You know what Danny? You do what you want. You want to get married? Sure. Go for it. I wish you both every happiness."

He pretended to go back to reading his book. *Their mother was going to kill him.*

Danny grinned. "Great. Now I wanted to ask you about *sex*."

He said the word like it was a candy he'd sneaked from the chocolate box.

Flecks of spit landed all over the pages of Tom's book as he spluttered and coughed. "You are not."

Danny blinked. "Tom. We are in love. It's a beautiful, natural act when two people love each other."

"And you know this? She's told you she wants to get…" Tom raised an eyebrow suggestively. "Freaky."

Danny just stared at him blankly.

Tom sighed, putting his book down onto his coverlet. "You've had no interest in anything and now all of a sudden you want to have sex." he puffed in a few quick breaths.

Dan shrugged. "The heart wants what the heart wants. So… do you have any tips?"

He really didn't. The last few times, he'd barely fumbled his way through it. He wasn't about to tell his brother that though.

"When you're better, I am never going to let you forget that you came in here asking me for sex tips. The old Dan would be mortified."

"I'm still the same person Tom."

Tom gave a hollow laugh. "Yeah, and I'm Batman."

He would not get involved. He wouldn't. He wouldn't.

"If you lay a finger on that girl, so help me god, I will cut off your gonads."

"And deprive yourself of future nieces and nephews? I don't think so."

"How can you procreate if you are DEAD!"

"I'm not going to get her pregnant, don't worry."

"Oh right, so you know how it all works then?" said Tom, inadvertently eyeing Danny's crotch.

He thought about Tom's answer seriously. "I think so. I did a bit of googling. I think I have the basics—"

"Ahh okay stop." Tom clasped his hands over his ears. "I can't hear you."

Danny blinked in confusion. "Well, that's because your hands are over your ears."

"Can't hear you. You should probably just—" Tom mimed turning around and walking out the door with his fingers.

"THAT'S PROBABLY BECAUSE—"

"Ah Jesus, stop yelling. I know why. God, you really have lost all sense of humour."

"I already know that." Dan said.

Tom considered him through narrowed eyes. "I actually can't tell if you are being serious or not. Talking to you is like swimming in a pool with a blindfold on: I have no idea what direction our conversation is going in or when I'm about to hit the bottom of the pool."

"Speaking of swimmers, do you have anything I can use to protect my boys?"

Tom breathed in deeply, gulping down the air. Control. He had to maintain control. Smiling, his lips firmly glued to one another, he silently fished an arm into his bedside drawer, sifting through the junk he'd collected over the years, searching for the unmistakable square packets. His hand locked onto them and in one deft motion, he flicked them up into his palm and lobbed them at Danny. They showered him like gold confetti, raining down onto the floor, a few slipping under Tom's bed.

"Whoa, that's a lot. I don't think I'll be able to use that many, but I can try."

Danny's face was so earnest, like a kid promising their parent that they would do their best on their maths test. Tom could almost laugh. Almost.

"Go nuts."

He was dead.

Or as good as dead. Georgia would peel off his skin and broil him whole once she'd found out that he'd aided and abetted Danny's sexual escapades. Tom was sitting on his bed, his door closed, his thoughts churning about his conversation with Dan. She might never find out. But like most things concerning Danny these days, he had a bad feeling about it. He ran through the possible outcomes in his mind: zombie children were obviously high up there.

A jangling of keys from the hallway sent a final, painful crunch through his chest. Tom's head snapped up, and he leapt into the hall. Danny looked up, halfway through tugging a jacket on. Absentmindedly, Danny patted his pockets, checking that his possessions were where they needed to be: Keys? *Check.* Phone? *Check.* Wallet? *Check.* Condoms? *Check.*

"So… you're going out now?" Tom asked tentatively.

"Well, I don't need my house keys to get into the house if I'm already in the house, do I?"

Touché.

"That's not really what I meant. I meant… are you going to see that girl *now*?"

Dan shrugged, taking one last look about the hall stand to make sure he hadn't forgotten anything.

"As good a time as any, really."

"But it's the middle of the day!"

"Do penises stop working between the hours of 2- 5pm on Saturdays?" Dan asked mildly.

Why could he never tell if the prick was serious or not.

Tom ignored him, pressing on. "And how are you getting there?"

God, with each passing day he was starting to sound more and more like his mother. Danny was saved the task of replying as a car horn gave a polite toot. They both stuck their heads out the door. A red Barina flashed its lights and then reversed to park on the other side of the street.

Hope they're not planning on doing it the car. There's barely enough arm room in there to make a three-point turn.

Danny inclined his head as way of a goodbye, and the front door snapped shut behind him. Engulfed in silence, Tom danced on his toes. This was not his responsibility. He didn't sign up for this. He had his own life and his own problems. Swearing to himself, he scooped his car keys out of the bowl on the hall stand and ran out.

This was not going to work. Surely, they'd notice immediately that Tom's piece of crap car was following them, and they'd pull over and ask him what on earth he was doing following them. Did he have nothing better to do on a Saturday afternoon than follow his brother around? No. But that was besides the point.

The little Holden was still parked across the street. He looked over at them. They were completely oblivious to the outside world: he could see the back of a girl's head. She fiddling with something on the dash, and Danny was looking at his phone. Ah, so he did still use it. It was strange to see him using a phone. It seemed too normal.

He could do this. With a final glance around him, Tom lifted his hood from his shoulders. How convenient, that he happened to be wearing a jacket with a hood on it. It must be a sign. *Stalk*, said God, *stalk*.

Once he was behind the wheel, he slunk down in his seat and quickly popped open the glove box. Bingo. Sunnies. Stalker profile 99% complete. All he really needed was an overgrown moustache, but he'd never really had much success in cultivating facial hair. He glanced into his review mirror and watched as the reverse lights on the Barina sprung to life. Willing his car to behave and turn on quietly, he turned his key. The little motor purred to life softly.

"That a girl." he said, stroking the wheel softly.

Quickly, he chucked her in reverse, and spun out of their narrow driveway, the wheels crunching on the stone. The Barina was at the end of the street, indicating a left turn. Perfect. He sped up, waiting until the red car turned the corner before he followed.

Danny's girlfriend drove like a balding 40-year-old man in the midst of a mid-life crisis. Sweat collected at the back of Tom's neck as he tried to keep up as she swept through the streets. He swore at one point that two of her wheels lifted off the ground. God, the two of them were in a hurry, weren't they? He supposed they were teenagers

—slaves to their raging hormones.

Ten minutes and one mild heart attack later, Tom, still a good 50 metres behind the Barina, saw it slow to a halt outside a park. *Here? Really?* Tom looked around as he pulled over and killed the engine. He supposed it was a quiet spot. The park stretched as far as the road ahead of him, and there were no houses lining the perimeter. Or shops. Just a footpath. It made for a nice walking track. Racking his brain, he tried to place where he was. He'd never really been in this part of town before. All he knew that was done this way was...

The cemetery.

This wasn't a park. This was the *cemetery*.

His face twisted in disgust.

"That sick b—" Tom mumbled to himself, shaking his head as he unbuckled his seatbelt.

Tom opened his car door and watched the pair from the corner of his eye. From this distance, he noticed that the girl was short, and her skirt barely covered her butt cheeks. Big, black boots came up to her knees. If he didn't know any better, he'd say that Danny was out with a hooker. He shook his head, hoping it was far from the truth, and watched as the pair crossed the road and walked slowly up the leafy, tree-lined path leading into the heart of the graveyard.

It always amazed Tom how beautiful cemeteries were. The gravel crunched under his feet and he cringed, hanging further behind them, waiting until they disappeared over the crest of a small hill. Small groups of people looked at him and gave him small sympathetic smiles, noticing the sunglasses, the hunched posture. *Poor little lamb,* he heard a woman murmur as she passed by.

Lady, you have no idea, thought Tom. He strode up the hill, only to find that he had lost sight of them. Crap. He spun around in circles, seeing nothing but an endless number of paths leading through rows of headstones. Panic swelled within him. He couldn't come this far and lose them. Why had Tom let him out at all? This was all going to come back on him. He should have fought him, tooth and nail. Should have tackled him to the ground, pummelled him into unconsciousness and dragged him back into the house, back into his room. Whatever it took, he should have done it. Because it was his brother. And if he had to hurt him to keep him safe, then he would.

A thought flitted into his mind. *Wasn't this the cemetery Al was buried in?* Tom didn't know what to make of that. Had Danny been visiting his grave in secret? If he was, then maybe he was more rational than they thought. Despite everything, a small bulb of hope planted itself in Tom's chest.

Craning his neck from behind a statue of an angelic cherub, he spotted them walking up to Al's site. He looked down the aisle, frowning. There was no way he could follow them without being spotted, but in the next row, a large oak tree offered some shelter.

Ducking and darting from one spot to the other, holding his hood around his face like a maniac, Tom made it to the tree, peering around the trunk so he could keep an eye on them as he eavesdropped. Really, if there were awards for stalking, he'd have to be up for at least an honourable mention.

Danny and the girl stood, hand in hand, before the grave. They turned to face one another, and Tom saw the girl's face. It took him a moment before he placed it, sucking in a breath.

Peeta.

He wanted to heave up his lunch. Danny's secret girlfriend was Peeta. How had this happened? He supposed that they had never really met. The last time Danny saw Peeta, he would have been a little kid. Danny hadn't gone to Al's funeral.

Suddenly, a smile spring to his lips. He stepped out from behind the tree.

"Well, well, hello Peet." Tom said smiling.

Peet's head snapped up and dropped Danny's hands. "Who the hell are you?"

Whipping the sunglasses and hood off, Tom strode towards her, his smile deepening as he saw recognition flash across her face.

"Tom?"

"That's right. Long time no see."

Danny waved at him and Peet looked at Danny in confusion.

"Do you know him?" she asked Dan.

"Yeah, he's my brother." Danny said, as if it were a simple fact. Which it was.

"He's your..."

The look on her face was everything Tom wanted it to be.

Tom let himself laugh. "That's right, he's my brother."

A faint flush worked its way up her neck. "I've just been trying to help him."

Tom scoffed. "Yeah, help him with your—"

She advanced on him, and he took a few steps back. She was almost as tall as him, and he hated to admit it, but she carried twice as much muscle.

"You have no idea what you're talking about. You know nothing about me. Or about Danny. Danny has opened up to me. We talk about what happened."

Tom scoffed again. He wondered when exhaling had become his only form of comeback.

"It's true. We talk about how he *feels*."

Tom glanced at Danny. He was looking at Al's gravestone. Tom wondered if it was true. Why would he talk to someone that was practically a stranger to him? He didn't like the way Peeta was talking. Like she knew Danny. She knew nothing.

"The kid hasn't had a feeling in months. You know he's not right in the head?" even when it came out of his mouth, he wanted to chase his words and shove them back down his throat.

She laughed mirthlessly. "Who isn't these days?"

He looked at her with narrowed eyes. "He thinks he's dead Peeta."

Danny interjected. "Ah I am dead." he looked between them both. "Can we be clear about that?"

Tom raised his eyebrows at Peeta and she rolled her eyes.

"Oh, so what? Get over yourself Tom. You've always been such a—just so *concerned* with what people think."

"Me? You're kidding right?"

She sniffed. "You might pretend you don't care, but I see you."

How did she know exactly what to say to piss him off? It was truly a talent. Tom looked around, hoping there was an empty grave he could push her in.

She smiled. "See? If you really didn't care what I thought, you wouldn't be so angry right now."

He opened his mouth and closed it stupidly. She smiled and hugged Danny as a way of goodbye, patting Tom on the arm as she passed him.

"Just try to let it go. Then you'll do better by Danny."

He wrenched his arm from under the clasp of her talons.

"Thanks for the advice, Oprah." he yelled after her as he watched her sashay down the aisle like it was a catwalk.

He would do anything to help Danny. Anything to make him better. Peet had no idea. He couldn't talk to *this* Danny. Every conversation they'd had in the last month had been... utterly bizarre. He didn't know *how* to talk to him anymore.

CHAPTER TWENTY-FIVE

Mary Mother of Joseph

"Well, that is truly one of the most terrifying things I've ever seen."

A woman was running, a look of pure terror etched upon her beautiful face as she gazed upon the horned beast clawing at her tattered dress. In the background, all manner of ghastly figures were cavorting about. Tom could see a wiry half-goat, half-man dancing upon a mound of human skulls. In the top left hand-corner, a young, handsome man was being quartered by a cackling group of black-winged fairies. Licks of red and orange wildfire spurted from mounds in the earthy ground. Tom supposed the scene was set in a cavernous chamber, deep within the Earth's core.

Danny had lost none of his artistic talent.

"Mary mother of Joseph." Georgia whispered.

Tom looked at his mother, her mouth hanging agape.

"It's a bit cliche, really. Like c'mon, of course it's gonna look like that right?"

Georgia said nothing, instead she snapped her jaw closed, burying her mouth in her hand.

"I thought he lost his paints." she said faintly.

Tom didn't look at her, his eyed stuck to the mural on the wall. "Well, looks like he found them."

Paint was dripping from Danny's bedroom wall, pooling softly in a puddle onto the floorboards.

If Tom thought about it, he had noticed the house had been extra quiet in the last day or so. He should have recognised it for what it was: the type of heavy quiet a dog owner experiences when said dog has found its way into the fridge.

Georgia began to pace about the room. After they'd begun to smell his room from the hallway, they'd coaxed Danny out and into the lounge room with the promise of snacks and TV. Tom assumed Danny had been giving them the silent treatment ever since his demand for a funeral had been refused. He'd hardly left his room in the last few days, although that was normal for him.

Tom craned his head out of the bedroom to make sure Danny was still there. Sure enough, Danny was shovelling potato chips into his mouth as if his life depended on it. How the boy could be convinced that he was dead was beyond him. He said he wasn't hungry, but in the last hour, Danny had consumed enough calories to feed a small army. Danny was on his knees on the floor, his eyes about three inches from the TV screen. Tom shook his head and turned back to Danny's bedroom, taking in the mess before him.

You know how growing up you would always have that one friend who was a disgusting pig, and you'd enter their room with a mixture of apprehension and curiosity? Towers of cups and plates would be stacked sky high on their bed-side table, little pools of furry, marshy green proliferating in the dregs. There'd be so many mountains of dirty clothes on the floor that you could only see specks of carpet. You'd have to tip-toe to sit on their unmade bed, and you'd precariously sit on the very end, worried that you might catch the plague if any part of your skin came into contact with the bedsheets.

Well, Danny's room looked like that, but the door had been closed for so long with the curtains drawn and window shut, that it was like the room itself had started to turn. Tom thought it might be worth simply demolishing the whole thing and starting again. It smelt like old socks made of cheese and bananas. He didn't know if it was the smell or the painting, but he felt slightly sick.

Georgia began to sweep up the pile of clothes, her little arms like forklifts, the first pile teetering as she swept past Tom to, he assumed, the laundry to either wash the clothes, or the kitchen to burn them in the oven. He stood motionless, listening to the blare of the TV from the living room and the bang, snip and hum as Georgia brought the washing machine to life. She averted his gaze as she re-entered

Danny's room, making a beeline for the dirty dishes.

"Did you check his pockets? The little grub always has something in there. Remember the time he left that pen in his shorts' pocket and blue ink went through all our clothes?"

She nodded her assent, piling plates into the crook of her arm.

"It's only a painting mum. It's like when little kids do drawings of weird stuff when they're in kindergarten. They don't know what they're drawing. They don't know what they've done is weird and disturbing. You just nod and tell them they did a good job."

She nodded again.

"Mum."

She rounded on him. "He's punishing us, Tom."

He looked at the painting and sighed.

"It's like he blames us. What are we doing Tom?"

He knew she would have thrown her hands up in the air if they hadn't been full of dishes. She raised her eyebrows, her dark eyes drilling into his. God, she was a little bit terrifying. Her face was saying everything her body couldn't. The frown lines on her forehead were like little speed humps.

"What are we doing? We don't even know what is happening." Tom let a little frustration colour his own voice. "Maybe Danny has a point. Maybe we aren't helping."

"Well, we've tried. We've tried to get him to exercise, to eat right…"

Tom knew, even to her ears, it sounded weak. Half-hearted.

Tom nodded at the painting. "Yeah, we've even *encouraged* him to take up some of his hobbies." he grimaced as his pinkie finger brushed up against some used tissues on Danny's drawer. "We could… go back to the doctor?" he said the words as if they were land mines and he could get himself blown to smithereens at any moment. It was like playing a real-life game of minesweeper.

"I am not taking him back there," she hissed.

Flecks of spit landed on Tom's forehead. Yep, land mine behind that box.

"We don't know what they'll do with him."

"Ma, it's not the 1800s anymore. They're not going to jam him in an asylum."

"But that's the thing—we don't know *where* they're going to jam him, or *what* they're going to jam him with."

He raised an eyebrow, "Well this is starting to sound like an episode of X files now. Like they're going to do alien prob—"

"Tom!"

"They'll probably just give him some Xanax and he'll be as happy as Larry! We can only do what we've been doing, or we can get help. They are only options."

"Pills didn't fix him in the past, they won't fix him now." she said flatly.

"Yeah… but—" he cut himself off, unsure of if he should finish his sentence. Clearly, she was upset, and if the past was any indication, he had a knack of not making her feel any better. For about the hundredth time, he wished he had more tact. Or maybe he had it. Maybe he just preferred honesty.

"Besides," she said, rounding on Tom, "You're assuming he will be accepting of our help."

Tom gave a mirthless laugh. "I don't give a rat's ass if he wants our help or not."

"Oh? So you'll do what? Threaten him? Force him? You try that, you lose his trust. And then maybe when you wake up in the morning, he's not there anymore. Can you imagine, him on the streets, alone the way he is right now? He's already upset with us."

She pushed past him and he heard the sounds of the dishwasher being forcefully opened. Hard. He heard the tinkling of breaking glass.

"Oh, for f—sake." she dropped her voice low when she swore.

He wondered what it would take for her to lose it, like *really* lose it. He'd never seen it. It was maddening, how she internalised everything. She'd be fighting with you, and you wouldn't even know it. It was all there though, if you knew to look. You could see it, the rage, spilling from her pores. She came back into the room, her hands on her head now, as if she'd just finished running a marathon.

"It's the 21st century. How can it be this hard? If we can't take Danny to a doctor, can't we just get a doctor to come to Danny?" he pleaded.

"And how is that any different? If he's not interested in going to see a doctor, he's not going to want one marching into his bedroom."

He could see her hands shaking, hear her voice shaking. She took a great, shuddering breath.

"We have no idea how Danny will react if we do that to him. What happens when the doctor leaves? Do you think he'll be magically fixed?"

He heard the derision in her voice.

"Ok! Ok! I get it! *Jesus.*"

She always knew best, didn't she? He could see it in her eyes. He was the child, still a newborn, incapable of thinking, of knowing how an adult should deal with adult problems.

"It's not that I don't want to help him, Tom."

Her voice ground against his ear drums. He couldn't take another word.

"Stop talking!" he yelled through gritted teeth. His brain was whirling, flicking madly through its directory, grasping for a solution. His brain could not, would not compute what she was saying and if she kept talking, it was likely to shut down altogether.

Thankfully, she obeyed. It looked like she wanted to say more, but maybe she could sense that Tom was close to a meltdown. Did he look now like he did when he was a toddler? Ready to throw his body down and beat his fists madly against the floor?

Slowly, she bent over to pick up empty chip packets from Danny's floor. She quickly recoiled, a small scream escaping from her throat.

A small, very dead mouse lay in front of her.

Tom did not move. Instead, he let a hard smile shadow his lips. When Georgia looked up at him, he let her see it.

It was far too late for them to be going for a leisurely stroll, but Tom had to get them out of the house. He had to try and talk to Danny at least.

"Danny."

It took him almost ten minutes just to force those words from his mouth. He wasn't even sure his brother was listening. Danny was looking at his feet as he dragged them, a step behind Tom. Really, Tom had no idea why his brother had agreed to come out with him, but it made him hopeful, gave him the courage he needed.

"Would you…be interested in seeing a doctor?"

For a moment, Tom didn't think he was going to get an answer.

Danny showed no indication he had heard him, but he spoke, so quietly Tom almost missed it.

"Why?"

Because you think you're dead.

"Because I think you might need some help?" Tom had no idea was he was saying. The words sounded wrong. They didn't sound like the words he wanted to say.

Danny stopped walking. "I don't need help," Danny said flatly. "I won't talk to a doctor." he began to shake his head furiously. "I won't, I won't, I won't."

Tom had never seen his eyes like that before. Wild with fear. Tom was reminded of what Georgia had said, about pushing him. He had a sudden image of Danny turning from him and running down the street, never to be seen again. It could happen so easily. Tom could lose him in the blink of an eye. He couldn't ever allow that to happen. He wasn't sure of much, but he knew losing Danny would break him into a million tiny pieces.

"Okay, Okay. It was just a thought."

Even though Danny was standing a foot behind him, it felt like football fields separated them. Tom began walking again. *Good one Tom. Where do you go from here, smart guy?* As he was contemplating what he would say next, it took Tom longer than he'd like to admit to realise that Danny wasn't trudging along beside him. Tom stopped in his tracks, ignoring the protest of a passer-by that narrowly avoiding cannoning into his back. Tom scanned the sidewalk behind him and sucked in a sigh of relief when he noticed Danny peering into a doorway. It was clear he was oblivious to the fact that Tom had almost lost him. And it was little wonder why. Men and women spilled from the doorway, laughing raucously, dressed in black leather and little else. One man sported a metal studded dog collar around his neck. Even from a distance, Tom could see Danny's eyes widen. He quickened his strides and caught the back of Danny's collar as he began to walk inside. The doorway was really an antechamber to a steep stairway that disappeared underground.

"Hey what—"

Danny's protests were drowned out by the street noise; the engines of passing cars competed with the calls and jeers of night-time revellers.

"You can't go in there." said Tom flatly, quickening his pace, half dragging Danny behind him.

"Why not?"

"Well, firstly, because you're not eighteen and secondly, because—it's not—it's a place of *ill repute*."

Tom was painfully aware that he sounded like the narrator of a made-for-TV period drama.

"Ill repute?"

Tom sighed. "It's not a normal nightclub."

"I'm eighteen next week."

Tom was surprised that Danny remembered his own birthday. "What do you want to do for your birthday?" he asked brightly.

"I want to go to a place of ill repute." Danny said, ogling a woman standing by the doorway. She was wearing a red latex bodysuit. "They seem like my type of people."

"Trust me, it's not for you."

Tom yanked on Danny's collar again before he could get any more ideas. Danny looked wistfully at the doorway, but allowed himself to be dragged away. But Tom didn't really know what *was* for Danny anymore. His brother was a stranger.

CHAPTER TWENTY-SIX

Groundhog Day

His brother and mother seemed like strangers these days. They didn't even talk to him anymore. Danny saw the looks they gave him, the way they dodged him in the hallways. When they did try to talk to him, they wanted something. They wanted him to stay inside, to leave his room, not to talk to strangers, to talk to a doctor he didn't know. It didn't make sense to him. He didn't understand how they could think it made sense. There was only one person he trusted now, and he'd returned most nights to the graveyard to find her again.

"Peet!" he said as he spotted her skipping up the row towards him.

She beamed at him. "I had no idea I was so memorable."

She smoothed her skirt over her buttocks as she plonked down next to him, as if they were both enjoying a picnic in a sunny meadow.

"So, what's news? Still dead?"

"'Fraid so."

"And how's that going for you?"

He frowned at her. "It's not *going* anywhere. Things can't change when you're dead."

"How poetic." she murmured. "I know what you mean. Nothing ever changes, does it? I get those movies. Like Groundhog Day and stuff. Really, they were written for people like *us*. People who don't feel the change. That is, if things ever really do change. Do you get me?"

He nodded, as he watched the moon reflect in her big shiny eyes. The truth was, she'd lost him at 'Groundhog Day', but he liked the way she said things. He liked the way she made him feel like he was somewhere, anchored to something.

"I like you Peet."

She smiled at him. "I like you Dead. I like how you don't pretend to be anything other than what you are. It rare to meet someone else like that. Everyone is always so worried about what other people *think.* It turns them into mindless zombies. You're so... alive."

"Am not."

"You get what I mean."

He nodded, but he really didn't.

"I'm eighteen next week." he said.

She didn't balk at his change of subject.

"Is that a birthday or a death day?"

"Birthday."

"What do you want to do for your birthday? Got any ideas?" she asked brightly.

He smiled at her. "I do actually."

CHAPTER TWENTY-SEVEN

Sid Vicious

It took Tom a moment to realise where he was when he woke that night. In his bed. He was in his bed, where he should be.

"Tom, wake up."

And his mother was in his room.

"Why?" he asked groggily. He checked his phone. It was two in the morning.

"Because your brother is not home Tom." he'd never got up faster in his life. There was that one time when he was twelve when he sat on a pencil, but still, this was faster.

"Mum no, no, no. Tell me you're kidding."

"I'm not joking Tom, why would I joke about this?" her voice was an octave higher than normal.

"Do you have any idea where he would have gone? Did he mention anything to you?"

He could tell she was near hysterical.

He'd never gotten dressed faster in his life, except for maybe the time he'd almost slept with—no, now was not the time to think about that.

"Yeah, sure, he came up to me earlier tonight and asked me what the weather was going to be like later because he wanted to go for a moonlight sail across the bay." he said.

"Your sarcasm is really helpful."

He threw his hands up, now that had managed to dress himself.

"Well, it was a stupid question. I have no idea. As far as I was aware, he had no interest in anything these days." Tom paused for a moment, one leg in his jeans. "He has interest in *some* things." he swore under his breath.

"What. Out with it. Where is he?"

"I don't know for sure, but he saw a ... *club* the other day that caught his attention." Tom stopped, hoping this was enough information for his mother.

"A nightclub?"

"Yeahhhh, kind of."

She looked at him expectedly, until it clicked. She brought her hands to her mouth.

"Oh my god. A sex club? My baby boy. At a sex club."

"Calm down. It wasn't a sex club. I'm not even sure if that's legal? It's just a nightclub. But they do like theme nights a lot— I think." he added hastily.

She looked at him, her eyes narrowed. "But he's not eighteen!"

Tom looked at her grimly, holding up his phone so the time flashed at her. "He is as of two hours ago."

They had planned a quiet celebration for him at home. There was a chocolate cake sitting in the fridge.

"You know, he could have been into that kind of thing before he was sick mum. I'm sure I've seen a pair of leather chaps in his wardrobe."

"Shut up. Why do you think he wanted to go there?"

Tom shrugged, swiping his hand across his chest of drawers to find his car keys. God, his room was starting to look like Danny's.

"He probably saw the people dressed up and thought that they were like him."

"Dead you mean?"

"Yeah."

She sighed. "Okay Sherlock, if this is what you reckon. Let's go. Where are we going?"

"Not sure exactly, but I know it was in the CBD. Google search 'sex clubs Melbourne CBD Friday nights' and then clear your search history from that government department issued phone of yours."

He saw the look on her face.

"I'm joking. I *swear* it's not a sex club."

The dashboard clock flashed 2:30 am. as they parked on King Street, a row of dark, narrow buildings looming over them. Tom could hear the faint sounds of a deep, repetitive beat humming from the walls of the club.

"Which one is it?"

"Probably that one."

Tom pointed midway down the street, where a bouncer stood watch in front of an innocuous doorway. He always liked that about the city: how you had no idea what was lurking beyond the doorways, unless they wanted to reveal their secrets to you.

Georgia took a deep breath. "Alright, let's go."

After the warmth of the car, the night air was surprisingly cold, considering how hot the day had been. Tom hadn't thought to bring a jacket. The bouncer stared at them as they approached, sucking on a cigarette. He was thin for a bouncer, but there was something in his air that warned Tom that he'd won a few fights in his time. Georgia marched up to him, and Tom had to admit he was impressed with her moxie.

"Excuse me, my son might be in here and we just wanted to make sure he's okay."

"Yeah ok. No need for excuses here." he laughed, and a puff of smoke whirled into the night.

"No really, we do. This is my other son. Can we just come in and have a look for him?"

The bouncer looked them both up and down. "Head right on in." he said, in a tone that suggested he'd tired of their conversation. He gestured lazily to the door, which was ajar. A dim yellow light beckoned from inside. Georgia inched a hand forward, looked at Tom and then gave the door a gentle push to reveal the dark antechamber. Two velvet chairs were arranged under a large mirror opposite an ornate countertop. Lush green ferns, reeds and hanging plants seemed to sprout from the walls themselves. Tom imagined that it looked something like what the Garden of Eden would have looked like right after Adam and Eve ate the apples and the world found sex and debauchery.

"What a sexy couple! Are we having a good night? Up for a bit of fun?"

A pair of long, black boots introduced an equally excellent pair of thighs clad in minuscule leather shorts. A blonde woman was smiling at them. The lanyard on her neck introduced her as 'The Dungeon Master'.

"Not exactly."

Noticing Georgia's tone, a group entering the club looked back at them curiously. The men in the group were dressed similarly to one another, in the sense that they were all shirtless and sporting leather collars.

Tom listened as his mother explained their predicament.

"Oh no! What a naughty boy!" the Dungeon Master gave a tinkering laugh.

Georgia ignored her. "So do you think we can come inside and look for him then?" she pressed.

"Of course. It's just a $30 fee for tonight love. And I'm afraid you guys will have to... dress down a little." she winked one of her dark, heavily made-up eyes. "We wouldn't want to make our other patrons feel self-conscious." she whispered dramatically.

Georgia and Tom looked at each other, weighing up their options.

Tom finally spoke. "Mum, it's just too weird if we go in there together. I'm okay with living in a horror movie, but not a Greek tragedy. Just let me go."

Georgia looked between her son and the smiling woman. She sighed in defeat.

"Just find him Tom." she went to walk outside.

"Sweetheart!" the Dungeon Master called after her. "I think you should leave your leather jacket for him." she smiled wickedly.

"I don't want to know," said Georgia as she threw her jacket at Tom and left the passageway.

Tom slipped it on and looked at the Dungeon Master hopefully. The woman shook her head slowly and looked pointedly at his t-shirt and then at the sign behind her which read: "No Effort, No Play". Tom grimaced and pulled it off. He looked down at his pasty, reedy chest.

"Now, put that jacket on."

"It's a bit tight."

"Even better then!" she stood back to admire her work. "My, doesn't he look like Sid Vicious!"

"Just like him." purred a woman from behind him. Tom wasn't aware he had an audience.

"Alright, is this good enough then?" Tom noticed that his voice came out deeper, like it could save his pride if he spoke an octave lower.

The Dungeon Master looked pointedly at his black jeans.

"No come on, not my jeans. You just said I looked good! Trust me, I am *not* going to look sexy in my undies. They're far from my best pair. I think they've got holes in them to be honest."

She put a comforting hand on Tom's shoulder and laughed. "As intrigued as I am to see such a vision, I was joking. You look fantastic pet. Now, go in and enjoy yourself. There's a fine line between embarrassment and liberation. Own it, and you'll feel more alive than you ever have."

"I hope you gave that little speech to my brother," he said to himself.

Every part of him cursed Danny. He wanted to turn and bolt out the doors. The Dungeon Master had shaken him. Even as he walked slowly down the spiral staircase, he could feel his cheeks burning. He was hyper aware of his mother's jacket, stretched tight across his shoulders. He felt completely, utterly ridiculous.

The theme of the entrance continued with the main rooms, although Tom didn't know if it was the black walls or the lotus patterned carpet, but it felt more decadent. Loud, techno music rang in his ears as he scanned the crowd before him. Tom's first thought was that a lot of cows must have died to dress the occupants of this nightclub. Leather pants, shorts, tops, bras and even a few bodysuits. And it wasn't just leather. Feathers, nylon and velvet were popular as well. Several men were seated at the bar in sundresses, chatting to one another animatedly.

Strangely, it all seemed kind of … normal. There was music, drinks and conversation, just like any other club. But Tom didn't belong. His skin itched. He had to find Danny and get out.

"In and out." he muttered to himself, "In and out."

"Are you trying to dirty talk me?" a man wearing fishnet stockings grinned toothily at Tom as he brushed past. Tom looked at him in horror and muttered something about talking to himself before he

193

backtracked. The dance floor was packed. He had no idea how he was supposed to—

"Oh. My. God."

His eyes locked on a girl. Her hair was short and yellow now. It looked like she'd cut it herself with gardening shears. She wore a leather corset, her breasts plumped up to her chin. Sweat poured down her face as she danced animatedly, her hands linked with—

"Danny!"

He strode up to the pair, pushing through groups of dancers, throwing his elbows into their backs to get past. He heard protests, even felt a few shove him back.

He didn't even care.

He stood speechless before them. Danny was wearing a short sleeve, black shirt, unbuttoned, and black jeans like Tom's. He was also sporting a pair of cat ears. When they saw Tom, Danny beamed at him. The smile dropped from Peet's face.

"Tom?" she asked, like she was unsure of who he was.

"Yeah, that's right." he said viciously, not even knowing where his thoughts were. It was so loud—he couldn't think, couldn't process anything.

"What are you doing here? This isn't really your *scene*." she smirked when she said that, and Tom felt his blood hiss and spit.

"No, it isn't. And it's not Danny's either."

The rage threatened to throttle him. She wasn't getting it. Didn't she know how messed up Danny was? He didn't care, didn't want answers now. He just wanted to get Danny out.

"How could you bring him here!" he hissed, despite himself.

Peet looked surprised at the venom in his voice. "I didn't. It's his birthday. He wanted to go out."

Tom looked at her with all the hatred he could muster. She just sneered at him.

"Why am I even explaining myself to you?" she made to turn away from him.

"Can't you see how messed up he is? Why don't you get that!" he said, raising his voice.

She whirled around, looking between Danny and Tom. Danny was quiet, his eyes fixed on the clubbers around him. He'd stopped dancing.

She moved towards Tom, their noses almost touching. "You're the one that's *messed up*. He's not hurting anyone, Tom. He's harmless. In fact, we were actually having fun before you showed up."

He felt something pang in his chest and the heat inside him dimmed. "I just—I have to get him home Peet."

She looked at him like he'd asked her to kiss his feet. "Why? Why does he need to come home?"

"Because—" he stopped, looking for the right words.

She moved towards him, smirking again. He wished he could slap it off her face.

"You think you can have everything your way, on your terms. But you can't always be in control Tom."

"I have to be!" he screamed the words at her, but the music sucked them up. He couldn't even control that, couldn't even make the world feel his anger.

"You don't," she said softly. "You can't control what is happening with Danny. You can't make him act like you want, in the way you think is normal, acceptable."

"Oh yeah?"

He knew he must have had some control over himself, because in that moment, he lost it completely. His hand snaked out, grasping Danny's wrist. "You're coming home. I don't care if you don't like it, I'm your brother and it's *my* job to look after you."

Tom vaguely registered that a few club goers were looking at him, muttering. He didn't care. How would they know? How could they possibly have any idea of what his family was going through?

Danny looked at him, his face contorting. Tom hated that he was the cause of that look.

"Let go of him Tom. I know you're upset, but you have to let go of him." Peet was looking at him so steadily, her voice so calm; it made him want to roar. He wished he wasn't human. The human voice was to civilised for what he was feeling.

He hung on.

Rough hands pulled his hand from Danny's, pushing him hard in the chest, and he stumbled backwards. A small group of men in sundresses had surrounded him, and Tom knew one of them had intervened.

"Leave them alone, man."

He had no idea who spoke, so Tom launched forward, grabbing, punching and kicking at whatever he could find— men's shirts, faces, kneecaps—it was all the same. Is that how Eddie had felt? Like throwing his fists out was the only way he could bring himself some relief? He got it now. But Tom had never been a fighter. Recent history could attest to that, so it wasn't long before he was flat on his back, getting lifted by the scruff of his neck by Mister *Champion Fighter* Bouncer. Tom watched, heaving for air, as Danny and Peet melted into the thick of the dance floor, swallowed up in a mass of black leather, as the bouncer promptly threw Tom out of the club.

In the alleyway outside, Tom stood by himself, every part of him burning and shaking. How could he be so useless? It was the 21st century. How could it be this hard to help someone you loved? It was so unfair. The rage cemented in his throat, and he blinked back tears with the effort of keeping it there.

He refused to accept it. He would turn the tides; he would put Danny back on course.

Whatever it took.

He would do it.

CHAPTER TWENTY-EIGHT

Born Again

"What's up with you?" Georgia finally said.

Tom knew she had sensed his mood. He'd been waiting all morning for her to say something.

"Nothing." he paused. "How's Danny today?"

He hadn't seen his brother all morning. But he'd come home at five in the morning. Tom and Georgia had slept in the lounge room, waiting all night to hear the jiggle of keys in the front door. But it was the sound of Danny's bedroom window scraping open that had woken Tom up. When Danny's light switched on, Tom's terror switched off. Danny was safe. That's all he needed. It didn't matter how angry he'd been last night. He just needed Danny safe.

Georgia let out a sigh. It was funny, how he knew what each of one of her sighs meant. Some signalled exhaustion, others defeat. This one was short and sharp—as if she had no time for exhaling, let alone him. She'd been in a mood, rightly so, ever since Tom had returned to the car last night, battered, bruised and Dannyless. She'd said nothing about his appearance, and he knew she was angry with him. She had no right to be. It wasn't his fault. But he'd still failed, and they both knew it.

It was always dangerous when the two of them entered each other's orbits like this. It was one thing he'd definitely inherited from her, that's for sure. Danny was like Simon, even before the sickness. Cool, calm, *impenetrable*. But Georgia and him were both hot-headed.

They felt everything. And they'd both spent their lives trying to pretend they didn't.

She was folding sheets with sharp, expert flicks of her wrists. He was thankful that she hadn't asked him to help. He didn't want to help her.

"He's in his room again." Tom said.

"Good spot." she stared at him. "What do you want me to do about it?"

It was the first time he'd heard her like that. Flat. Like a rock that had sat on the shoreline for years, beaten and battered relentlessly by the wind until it was smooth and blunted. He realised then that it wasn't just Danny's fight—it was everyone's. They were weathering that same storm. And they were both starting to crack.

Hadn't they had this conversation before? What was he expecting from her now? For her to swoop in and fix it all. That's what she was supposed to do. She was the parent.

"It's not fair," her voice dropped to a whisper, "I'm his mother. I should be able to do *something*." she cradled the tea towel now in her hands to her chest like it was a security blanket.

He pushed aside the voice that agreed with her and gently, he lifted the towel from her grasp and enveloped her into his long arms. It should feel better than this, he thought. Everything should be in this hug. It should heal and melt and fill them both with warmth. But they were two chips of granite coming up against each other, cold and grating.

"I'm his brother," he sighed, "*I* should be able to do something. I *have* to do something."

He *had* to find a way to shake Danny back into motion, to get him to grab the wheel again and spin it away from disaster. He had promised himself. It was the only way to heal what he had broken: his brother. In the back seat. His head swelling like a balloon.

Don't look, Tom.

But how? How to convince a dead man that he was alive?

The idea slammed into him like a steel anvil, crashing into the waters of his consciousness. How, how could he not have thought of this earlier? It was so simple. Simple, but utterly bonkers. But it made a strange kind of sense, to fight insanity with insanity.

"Tom?"

He realised he'd been standing there, staring into the laundry basket. By the look on Georgia's face, it must have been a while. Mustering a smile, he patted her on the shoulder, and retreated to his room. He would not accept defeat. He would rage against the world before he gave up on Danny.

Hours passed as he waited for her to leave, ticking over the plan in his head. There really wasn't much to it, so he just kept going back and forth, trying to drag up all the possible outcomes. He saw them play out in his head. Many were dark, ugly apparitions, and he shook his head to clear them from behind his eyes. Jail. Death. Serious injury. All were very possible outcomes. But to continue living as they were—it was a slow death, for all of them.

In some ways, Tom and Georgia had never been closer, but the cracks were there, under the surface, splintering more and more each day. There would come a time soon he knew, when it would all crumble around them. Their family would implode, completely this time, and Tom would be left with no one. It was necessary then, to take this risk. And if he was calculated, it might just work. Maybe.

He inched a toe from his room, twisting his head both ways as if he was about to cross a busy road. Damn their squeaking floorboards. Danny's head popped through the kitchen door the second he planted his feet in the hallway.

"Hi." said Tom plainly, testing to see if Danny was angry with him. They hadn't spoken since the night before. Again, he heard his mother's words. *If you do that, if you threaten him, you'll lose his trust.* But she didn't know what it would take to tear them apart. She didn't really know how strong their bond was. But Tom knew. And he was counting on it now.

"Hi." Danny's voice was flat, but it was enough. Enough to tell him he was forgiven or forgotten. He didn't much care at this point. He had more important things to think about right now.

"Is mum around?" Tom whispered, although if anything, his hushed tone carried his voice further.

Danny shook his head. "She's out."

"Good," Tom said, and marched down the hall to the back door they rarely ever used. He kicked the mess of boots and old bike parts from the door in a hurry—the last thing he wanted right now, was to run into Georgia. Danny watched him run outside, his face blank and slack.

Tom tried to recall the last time someone had entered the shed. By the look of it, it had been a while. Webs of spider's silk hung thick like silvery rope from the tops of the walls. He shuddered as he slithered inside, trying not to think about the creatures that had created them. Unfortunately, as he turned, he walked headlong into a sticky trail. Spluttering and twirling, he stumbled, nearly decapitated himself on a row of sharp metal shelves. He was saved from the fall by grabbing the corner of a heavy box, one in a tower of many. The boxes barely moved under his weight—what was even in there? Rocks? He breathed a sigh of relief, reassembling his broken nerves. He tucked his arms and head as close to his body as he could, looking like a turtle that had learned to walk on its hind legs. *Get what you need and get out.*

He eyed the contents of the shed, scanning over the assortment of gardening tools, old boxes and years of hoarded crap. There was an old trampoline, rescued from their youth, in pieces in the far corner. Canvases from Danny's early years were piled high in another, an old sheet wrapped loosely about them.

His eyes finally locked on the tools and camping gear piled on the shelf behind him. Nestled amongst the spanners and used gas cannisters was a bundle of rope. It was thin, but springy, the kind you might use to strap down a heavy load to a trailer. It looked new. He wondered if Georgia had purchased it, and if she had, what on earth she had intended to use it for. In fact, there was a lot of new looking tools in here. She was not the fix-it type. She'd just call a handyman and be done with it. They must be Simon's. There were hundreds of dollars' worth of stuff amongst all this crap. God, he must have been desperate to leave them if he hadn't bothered to sell his stuff. With a pang, he spotted Simon's golf clubs—the same ones he'd cracked his own head open on when Danny pushed him down the stairs. He hadn't even taken those with him. Were they really that horrible? Was he so desperate to escape them?

He shook his head. That was an old chapter of their lives. He wouldn't waste his time thinking about that old asshole. It was Danny that needed him now. Gingerly, he poked the rope with his index finger. If a spider was going to crawl out from underneath the bundle, then at least it could only eat one of his fingers. He prayed to the gods as seconds hung in the air and no big fat hairy body scurried from it. He breathed a sigh of relief as his fingers remained untouched. It was a testament really, to how much he loved his stupid brother that he was willing to have his extremities fondled by creepy crawlies.

Like a sleeping serpent, the rope lay coiled on his bedspread. He stared at it, willing it to form into the shape he required. But no, it lay there like a plateful of silky spaghetti. Thank God for the internet. He punched what he needed to know into his phone, his heart jumping wildly as he waited for the page to load. The first hit was a link to Lifeline. He almost laughed. Well, he can't say he was surprised about that. What would happen if he clicked on it? Would they send out a little van, with a flashing light on top, to come and rescue him? Didn't that negate the whole point of it all? Like if he wanted to be saved, he wouldn't be in trouble in the first place.

Two hours and a flurry of curse words later, he'd done it. He thought he had anyway. It kinda looked like one. But how to know if it would work? There was only one way, really. Carefully, like it was a diamond encrusted necklace, he slipped the noose over his neck.

Slowly, he pulled the longer end away from his body. The rope collar tightened. He was almost proud of his handiwork. Aside from Year Eight woodwork, he'd never made anything in his life. Even then, it was a pretty crappy square alarm clock he'd made. If you ever went to touch it, you'd come back with a splinter the size of a nail lodged in your finger.

"What are you doing?"

Tom whirled around, and saw Danny standing in the doorway, his jaw slack, his voice soft and high. Tom stuttered a laugh and hurried to get the thing off his neck, accidentally yanking it tighter in his haste. He yelped like a pup and Danny darted forward. With fingers gentler than Tom expected, Danny worked the noose loose and lifted it over Tom's head. He kept a soft hand on his brother's collarbone.

"I had no idea." Danny breathed.

"What?"

Danny began to stroke Tom's collarbone in long, soft strokes. "I had no idea that you were struggling."

Tom paused for a moment before it finally clicked. "Oh—no, no, it's not like—"

"It's okay. I understand. I really do."

Tom turned and took a step back, away from Danny, shaking his head. He saw Danny's eyes were open wide, his hands outstretched towards him as if he were a tiger that needed taming. This was going terribly. This wasn't supposed to be about him. He needed to find a way to turn the tables.

"Danny I—"

"I told you. It's okay. You don't have to explain anything." he moved closer, and Tom found himself trapped in those big, round eyes. "I am here for you."

The eyes. The hands. The pure, simple earnestness. It made what he had to say so much harder.

"It's not for me Danny."

His brother's forehead creased in confusion.

"It's for you."

Danny's eyes widened as he backed away from Tom, his eyes on Tom's hands, probably imagining the fingers clasping snugly around his neck. Tom looked at them too. They'd always been thin and spindly, the fingers long, the palms smooth like glass. They were hands made for delicate work. Hands for making music, art, love. He could never be a tradesman. They'd buckle and shred like tissue paper the second he picked up a brick. They weren't murderer's hands.

"I'm not going to hurt you, Danny. Please. Trust me."

Not surprisingly, Danny looked unconvinced. But he stopped. Tom edged towards him, dodging the edge of his bed. "Just hear me out, okay? I want to give you a funeral. I really do."

Danny paused. "So, then do it."

"It's not that simple."

"Yes, it is. Send out some invitations. Put on a black suit."

Tom shook his head. He was dimly aware that the noose was still in his hands. He kept running his hands over it, tightening then loosening it. To Danny, it must have looked threatening, but really, Tom was just trying to buy time.

"First, I have to be sure."

"Sure, of what?" Danny asked incredulously.

Tom looked him in the eyes. "Sure that you're really dead."

Danny looked offended. "But I've told you that I am."

"Yes," Tom said slowly, "And as much as that is *damning* evidence, I thought we could gather some more *tangible* proof."

Danny's eyes narrowed. "Like what?" he asked, but by the way his eyes darted to the noose, Tom could guess that he'd already put it together.

Tom held up the noose gently, as if it were an offering. Which it kind of was.

"If you're dead, then this is harmless, isn't it?"

Danny's mouth opened and closed.

Tom tried not to smile.

He'd won. That is, if convincing your brother to hang himself was really winning.

Sweat poured from every orifice of Tom's body. What was he thinking? Even by his standards, this was insane. As he wrapped the rope around the woodwork above the hallway, he tried to quell his nerves. There was no way that Danny could *actually* be hurt. Tom would be holding him the whole time, ready to cut him down the second he showed any signs of well, dying. In the shed, he'd also found a large pair of gardening shears. He had them open and ready to snip, but he was sure he wouldn't even need them. He'd be holding onto Danny the whole time.

It was completely insane. But it was the only thing that made sense. The only thing Dan had actually agreed to. Making him see a doctor was a terrible betrayal, but asking him to hang himself was acceptable. Go figure. But Tom had to do it. He had to save his family. Danny needed to be shocked back to life. The way forward was never clear. Sometimes you had to do bad things. Terrible things. Split your soul to save it, or he'd spend the rest of his life wondering what he could have done, should have done, to save his brother. We always have to live with our guilt, Tom thought. But sometimes we get to choose what we feel guilty for.

"Okay, are you ready?" asked Tom.

Danny nodded, the rope bobbing along with him obediently.

"Now, remember, I'm going to be holding onto you the whole time. So nothing can happen to you, okay?"

Tom thought he heard Danny sigh impatiently.

"It's fine. Like you said, I'm dead anyway. What can happen?"

"Yes… of course."

As Danny stood on the chair and Tom beneath him, Tom envisioned Georgia coming home and opening the door. It was like he was a young boy again, caught doing something outrageously bad. But unlike those times, this couldn't be excused by age. She'd have her own son locked up. And he'd deserve it. He was an accessory to— whatever crime this was.

But it wasn't real. It was only pretend. This was nothing like the real thing.

"Ready?" Tom asked again.

"Yes, yes, let's get this over with so we can start planning. I think I know what kind of casket I'd like to have."

With shaking hands, Tom gently lifted Danny from the chair. He barely loosened his hold on Danny's weight.

"Oh Tom, this feels strange."

Swallowing, Tom silenced the chorus of voices screaming at him to stop, to cut Danny down.

He loosened his grip.

"Tom, I'm finding it quite difficult to breathe."

Tom gritted his teeth. "And breathing is important because…?"

Danny didn't answer. Something broke inside Tom. Every ounce of his body stiffened with determination. This would work. It had to work.

Tom let go altogether.

Almost immediately, Danny started to make terrible sounds. Tom forced himself to look up. The expression on Danny's face almost would have been comical if the situation was different. Almost. Funny how those two things so often nearly overlapped. His eyes were bulging. He looked down at Tom, and Tom saw in his eyes what he had been looking for.

Fear.

Almost spear tackling him, Tom grabbed Danny's legs, lifting him back to the chair. Something between a grunt and a sob escaped from Tom as he slashed through the rope for good measure. Before he even knew what was happening, Tom was on the floor, his hands shaking uncontrollably, his back to Danny. He couldn't look at him, couldn't believe what he'd just talked him into doing. He'd asked Danny to trust him, and he'd betrayed him. Bribed him. Risked his life to save it. It was abominable.

It hissed and leaked out of Tom like a fork had been jabbed into his sides. All of a sudden, he was deflating, collapsing like a souffle, the tears gathering in his eyes, spit bubbling from his lips. He was howling. Never in his life, had he cried like this. Vividly, he could recall the time when he was eight and he fell off his bike and gouged a hole in his knee. Oh, how he'd cried. Great, huffy howls into the street. Just like then, he could not be calmed. His whole body shook and shuddered. The more he tried to quell them, the more they racked his body. Danny said nothing, but after a while Tom felt hands touch his back.

The hands pulled him in, closer and closer with each gasp, until Tom was practically wearing Danny like a coat. Danny's grip around him didn't loosen, not even for a moment.

"It's ok. I've got you."

Through shuddering breaths, Tom realised it was the most human moment they'd shared in months. To have his brother here with him, holding him. It was almost normal.

"I'm so sorry Danny, I'm so sorry." he kept saying it, over and over again.

"Why are you sorry? You were right Tom. I can die."

Tom turned at the expression in Danny's voice, his face wet. There was something in it and it wasn't fear.

"I can die. And I can be *resurrected*."

"W-what?" Tom rasped.

Danny looked at Tom. "Well think about it. I died. And then must have come back to life at some point, because I just died again then. I am— like *Jesus*." he said the last word with soft reverence.

Tom didn't know whether to cry or feel relieved. His insane plan had failed. Danny was as deluded as ever. It had all been for nothing. Would they always end up here? Was there nothing that he could do to fix his brother?

Maybe there was still something he could do. Maybe Danny had been trying to tell them from the beginning what they needed to do to help him.

"Do you still want that funeral Danny?" Tom asked quietly.

His brother beamed at him in reply. Tom smiled grimly.

If he were honest with himself, he knew why he was offering it to Danny. His brother might not see that he'd done anything wrong, but Tom knew the truth. He would never forgive himself for it.

He would take the memory to his grave.

He didn't want anyone to know what he had done. All he could do was to hope that no one would ever find out. If it remained a secret, then maybe he could forget it had ever happened. That's how it worked right? Guilt without an audience just melts backstage, doesn't it? The curtains close and the show is over?

The curtains hadn't closed on the accident. He saw every part play out under bright lights. That's how it would be with this too, he knew it. He'd catch the matinee show every day. Critique his own villainous performance until the day he died.

"Your capacity for self-pity is endless."

He looked up to see Mickey watching him with a knowing eye. He'd had to get out. If he didn't escape from his thoughts, he was going to be swallowed by them. But they were still there, throwing him images of the day before, of the noose… of Danny…

Don't. Just don't look Tom.

He'd messaged the only person he could even stomach looking at. Now he wished he'd stayed inside.

"Excuse me?" Tom said, stopping in his tracks. He'd met Mickey by a walking track that hugged the river, the sun glistening across the water. The sight felt wrong to him.

"I've never known you to be so…"

She raised an eyebrow at him, waiting. He wanted to back away, to shrink into a corner.

"Honest? Unapologetic? Brutal?" she smirked, looking away from him. "I've always been like that."

"No you haven't." he mumbled.

"Maybe I haven't with *you*. But I don't know, things changed."

He looked at her, waiting as they began to walk again.

"I guess I don't— have you up on a pedestal anymore."

"Why not?" he blurted out.

"Because I see you now."

"What?"

"Look it doesn't matter. Anyway, you need to stop feeling sorry for yourself."

He hardly heard her. She didn't like him anymore. Well, that made two of them. He didn't like himself much these days.

"Easier said than done." he broke off a stick from a bush and threw it in the river. He threw it hard. It was meant to rip into the water, split it into two, but they both watched as it plopped gently onto the surface and floated away.

"You don't know what's going on." he said quietly. He meant to add *you don't know what I've done,* but he couldn't bear the thought of telling her. God, when did he become such a pathetic weasel?

"I know. All I'm saying is to look outside your little bubble. Look what's happening to other people Tom. My friend, she's a social worker, she tells me the most heartbreaking stories. She works with a 6-year-old girl whose dad is a heroin addict. She doesn't understand why she can't see her daddy anymore. It's horrible. Remember Year 12 Lit? Remember when we studied King Lear? There was that quote. Something about when the worst happens, you'll know because you'll be utterly speechless. You'll be a shell of a human being."

Was her story supposed to make him feel better? Why do people do that? Put your problems on an emotional barometer? She seemed to sense his thoughts.

"I'm not telling you this to make you feel bad. What's happening to your family is terrible Tom. Whatever it is that's happening. I know it's bad. I can see how much it's hurting you. But just—it could always be worse. Don't lose sight of that."

He nodded, and they walked in silence for a while. He really didn't know how he felt about what she'd said. It was honest. And he liked when people told their truths. And it hurt. He liked that. He didn't deserve pity.

"Mum, I've been thinking." he said eagerly. He reached out and grabbed her hand across the kitchen table. "We need to try something new to help Danny."

He expected her face to perk up, but she looked at him sadly.

"I think maybe the only person who can help Danny is Danny."

He reeled back, breaking the thin webbing of their weakly linked arms. "Surely you can't think that?"

She looked at him then, the same look he got all those years ago when she was there, watching him, monitoring him, when he found out Santa Claus was a fraud.

"At some point, it's up to Danny, isn't it? Like, he's got to want our help. What really are our options if he doesn't think there's a problem?"

"No." he said, a little too simply and a little too forcefully. Tom couldn't believe it, wouldn't believe it. "We haven't tried everything, there's got to be more we can do."

"Like what? I guess maybe we should call the hospital. Try and get a hold of his *actual* physician. He'll want to keep Danny there, do tests. Maybe it's time…" Georgia had almost started talking to herself. "Of course, he won't go, so we'll have to call the police. And they'll… they take him."

Tom couldn't listen. He would not do that to Danny. He'd do a lot of things, clearly, but he wouldn't do that. "What if we do give him a funeral?" Tom cut in.

She began to shake her head.

"Hear me out. What if the funeral isn't really about having a funeral? What if it's about closure."

"Sorry, I didn't know Cliff's Chicken shop gave out degrees in psychology."

He ignored the jibe. "It could fix everything."

"What does he even need closure for?"

Tom hadn't even considered that. "I—I don't know. Maybe dad leaving?" her eyes flared at that, so he continued quickly. "But it fits, doesn't it? He needs to close the book on that chapter, so to speak."

His mother's silence was assent enough.

"It would cost us nothing."

"Just our pride." she sniffed.

He looked at her for a long moment. "I think I'm ready to pay it."

She looked at him for a long time. Slowly, she nodded her head.

CHAPTER TWENTY-NINE

Teats of an Old Dog

Georgia shivered. It was exactly how she thought it would be. Despite the large windows, the whole building was dark, as if the sun knew it was not welcome here. Large waxy candles glowed from iron stands by the cold fireplace and strange assortments of flowers emitted a sickly, almost rotten perfume. The walls were an old-fashioned pale pink with heavy wooden panelling. For all the displays in the room, it seemed bare.

She could not believe she was here. Tom was the one that thought this would work, so why was she the one visiting a funeral parlour? But Tom convinced her that it should be her, that no one would take two teenage boys seriously. *But you're not a teenager* she'd hissed as she made the call. She'd had no strategy when she'd opened her mouth and told the receptionist that her dearly beloved mother had suddenly passed away. *The family was in shock. I am the one that was supposed to pick up the pieces,* she'd said. The lie had come so naturally, she wondered what it really said about her relationship with her mother. God, she was starting to sound like Tom, the self-proclaimed psychology major.

The pale-faced director had been waiting for her when she'd arrived the next day, a small, sad smile plastered to his thin lips. His face was flaccid and bloated, his cheeks sagged like the teats of an old dog. She wondered if it was just a coincidence, or if over time the place had morphed him to look this way. Places could do that. She was sure people sucked in the energy of a place. Or maybe places sucked in the energy of people.

"They're beautiful." breathed Danny, his eyes raking over the coffins.

"Whatever we choose, it will need to be over six feet long." she pretended to peruse a springy pine coffin nearby.

The director raised his eyebrows slightly.

"My mother, she was a tall woman." Georgia explained.

She smiled widely at the director and he smiled back, delicately placing a hand on her arm. It was icy cold. The touch sent a current up her back that made her spine curl. From the corner of her eye, she saw Danny run his nose along the edge of a casket, inhaling the rich smell of the wood. Thankfully, the director was oblivious, his eyes focused on making a sale out of her.

"When can we, ah, be expecting the arrival of you mother? It wasn't clear on the phone where she'd be coming from. Is she currently housed at another local parlour?" he said, looking at her expectedly.

"I can't just... buy a coffin?"

He chortled, holding his belly. "And do what with it my dear?" he put a hand on her shoulder. She really wished he would stop touching her. The effect was anything but comforting. "Don't worry, we will manage everything for you, once your mother arrives."

He gave her a solemn smile, and it dawned on her that perhaps you couldn't simply walk into a funeral parlour and buy a coffin. That's it, there was no alternative: she was going to have to produce a dead body. She'd left herself no other way. Did she know anyone that was actually dying? But then if she used their coffin for Danny, what would they go in? Dear God. She'd dug a hole so deep, she was in danger of burying herself.

"So, you just need—you need to see..."

She burst into tears. The tears spring freely, like they'd been there, building up, just waiting for her command. She idly wondered if she'd become a sociopath, lying and crying on queue.

"Oh no, don't cry, please don't cry Mrs Carter, it's okay. These things are hard to talk about, I know."

Even with the tears bubbling from her eyes, she felt an urge to bark at him to call her Georgia. She didn't like being called a *missus*. With a quick flip of his hand, he expertly produced a neat little packet of tissues from the folds of his suit jacket and pressed them into her palm. He led her out of the display room and back to reception.

"Why don't you take a moment, Mrs Carter. Collect your thoughts, have a seat, find comfort in your son." he nodded towards Danny who had thankfully followed them. She couldn't imagine having to try to coax him away from the coffins. She waited for the soft heels of the director's dress shoes to clip across the floor before she rounded on her son.

"Get up, get up, get up. Oh, Jesus Christ we need to leave." she hissed.

"But I like it here."

"Of course you do," she breathed to herself. "You *promised*. You promised if I took you with me, you wouldn't do what you did in the cemetery. You'd come home. No arguments." she hissed.

He sighed and nodded. He was surprisingly fair for a walking corpse.

She heard the clopping of shoes on tiled floor. "Quick, he's coming back!" Georgia yanked Danny to his feet, nearly breaking her neck trying to skate to the doors in her heels. The receptionist looked up as they hurried out, but Georgia didn't stop—she doubted she even could.

CHAPTER THIRTY

Rats and Mice

By the sounds of his mother's harrowing ordeal, securing a coffin for his very much alive brother's funeral was a much harder task than they had anticipated. Tom had thought about building one himself, but a quick YouTube search had showed him it was close to impossible. As soon as the guy in the clip pulled out a saw, he knew he was out of his depth.

"Where do you find a coffin?" Georgia asked as she flicked through a catalogue.

"Oh, hang on, I'm good at riddles. In a graveyard?" In a hearse?" In the ground?"

She shushed him. "Oh my God." she stabbed a finger at page in the catalogue, shoving it under Tom's nose.

"Oh my God." he echoed. There, right in front of him, was a glossy page from a Costco catalogue advertising everything from meat platters to— "They sell coffins at Costco!"

She nodded eagerly, sipping on her tea like they were talking about bulk-buying toilet paper.

"I'm not doing it," they both said in unison.

"But I went to the funeral parlour!"

"Yeah, but if we buy a coffin, I can't carry it out by myself."

"Surely, they'll deliver."

"Mum, I'm sure my taste in coffins is just as bad as my taste in clothes." he yanked on his over-sized ripped t-shirt. "Do you really want to put me in charge of this?"

Georgia sighed. "We'll both go."

It was exactly as Tom imagined. He'd never been to Costco, but he'd seen it in films: the giant warehouse, the crates of oversized teddy bears, tinned goods and wine bottles. He felt like he'd been shrunk to pocket-sized and no one had told him.

He picked up a block of cheese the size of his head. "Look at this! When would I ever need a block of cheese this big?"

"Maybe if you were trying to catch a really big mouse?" Georgia offered.

"A rat you mean," he said.

"Rats and mice aren't the same thing." she said absentmindedly as she craned her neck in all directions. "I have no idea where to start looking."

"Mum. Mum please. You're embarrassing yourself."

She sighed. "How do you not know this? It's very common knowledge. A rat and a mouse are not the same."

"I bet you this block of cheese they're the same thing," he said, trying to cross his arms, which was difficult on account of the cheese block in his hands.

"I have failed you as a parent. I don't even like cheese that much *and* I'm lactose intolerant, but I will sit and eat that whole block in front of your face just to teach you a lesson."

They shook hands just as a young clerk passed by. Tom flagged her down.

"Excuse me, two things."

The girl nodded politely.

"One: can you settle an argument for my mum and I?"

Georgia shook her head in embarrassment and feinted interest in a display of dog beds a few feet away.

"Are rat and mice the same? *She* seems to think they aren't."

The clerk blinked but took it in her stride. "No. They're definitely different species. In fact, rats are known to eat mice."

"For someone who works at Costco you seem to know far too much about the predatory habits of rodents." Tom said, his eyes narrowing.

The clerk smiled. "I'm studying a Bio major."

Tom looked impressed. "Okay and two: where are the coffins?"

The girl looked as though she didn't know whether to be amused or alarmed, so she raised her eyebrows, smiled and pointed to the other side of the store.

"These are hella fancy." said Tom, running his hands over the polished black surface of the nearest coffin.

A surprising number of caskets were on display. A few lay on the cement floor, others were propped up on stands, decorated with ornamental flowers. Georgia, hummed in agreement. Tom could see her mind ticking over.

"How will we know if it'll fit him?" she asked.

Tom looked furtively around before he casually walked over and slung a leg into the nearest one.

"What are you doing!"

"Relax. No one's around. We're being practical. Gotta try before you buy."

Lowering himself carefully inside, he wiggled into position.

"This feels odd. I am surprisingly comfortable."

The soft velvety lining cradled his head. He felt as though he was a little boy again, and had been tucked into bed for a long, good night's sleep.

"How many people can say they've laid in a coffin? This is cool." he let out a long, low groan. "I feel like Snow White. I do not understand why she ever got up when the prince kissed her because this is ridiculously comfortable. Now I know why we've never been invaded by zombies. They're all too comfortable in their coffins to get up and start eating our brains."

She ignored him. "Do you reckon it'll fit Dan?"

Tom wriggled his toes, stretching them out to see if he could reach the end of the casket. "Look. I can't touch the end, but if he can, we'll just fold his legs up like a towel."

"Tom."

"What? He's dead, isn't he? It won't hurt him."

"I know you're enjoying yourself there, but can you get out please," she tapped the side of the casket. "Particularly now that I've checked the price."

He scrambled out and looked at it for himself. "They didn't advertise *that* in the catalogue, did they? With that much money, we could actually pay someone to kill Dan and just get rid of his body all together for us," he gave her a sidelong glance, "Would save us a hell a' lot of money."

"No. And can you stop talking like a street urchin." she sighed and rested upon a nearby crate.

"What the hell a' we gonna do?"

"What's gotten into you? One second you're moping about the house, the next you buzzing about."

He shrugged, losing his energy. Why did she have to do that? Why couldn't she just let him forget about it all just for a moment.

"I guess it's finally nice to feel useful." he said softly.

She sighed. It was a surprise that there was anything left of her, with all the exhaling she did. If you cracked open your parents, is that all you would find? Hot air?

"I am not paying that much for a fake coffin." she finally said.

"Well, it's a real coffin. It's just the funeral that's fake." he corrected. "Look. Don't worry about it. Leave it up to me. I can sort this out. I come across heaps of cheap coffins in my line of work."

"At a chicken store?"

He waved a hand into the air dismissively. "It's just an expression. The point is, I can handle this. Trust me. I'll come up with the goods."

"Ok," she led the way back towards the exit, "And speaking of 'coming up with the goods'— you owe me that block of cheese."

It was a Tuesday evening when it finally arrived. Tom stood in the living room assessing his purchase.

"Oh my God. Is that what I think it is?" said Georgia as she walked into the room. She took his silence as confirmation. "It looks like a toy box."

"No, don't be silly. It's a wooden outdoor storage unit."

"It does not look like a coffin."

"Mum, you're not using your imagination. A few pillows, a nice little white satin sheet—it'll be perrrrfect."

She looked it over for a long moment, pacing around it and peering inside. "Do you think Danny will go for it?"

"Well see here's my thinking around that: Danny's dead."

She flinched a little.

"Sorry—Danny's 'dead', and when someone d—passes away, they unfortunately, do not get a say in their funeral proceedings. So, if that diii—dingus—" he gestured in the direction of Danny's room, "Tries to complain about it, then I'll just remind him of the fact that he no longer possesses the ability to complain."

"What's all this?"

Tom raised a hand to his heart. "Bloody hell. Say his name three times and he'll appear."

Danny slunk around the door frame, his tartan pyjama pants slipping down his hips. He looked at the storage box.

"What's that?"

"A storage box."

"Why do you have a storage box?"

"To store something in."

"What are you storing?" Danny looked at Georgia.

Her eyes bulged in panic. "It's just something that we don't really... know what to do with." she said.

A smile of old times past flickered across Danny's face. "It sounds like you killed someone. Are you trying to hide the body? I hope that's not the case, because we've spoken about this. You've got to get rid of the body guys. Trying to hide it is madness. Someone is going to notice the smell. Dogs are going to come sniffing around and then—"

"Technically we aren't trying to *hide* a dead body. We want to use the box to *display* it." said Tom.

Danny looked at him blankly.

"You're going in the box dude. We couldn't get a proper coffin."

"Oh." Danny's brow knitted. "It doesn't look very big."

"Well, it's not a permanent solution, is it? But it'll do the trick."

"I really don't think I'll fit in there."

"Well, I think that you're out of options. And I think that if you really truly are dead, then you wouldn't be complaining about your funeral arrangements."

Dan paused for a moment to consider his brother's logic, and then gave a little shrug and lifted his feet, one at a time, gingerly climbing into the box. He lay down, his legs tucked up so that his heels were digging into the back of his thighs.

Georgia let out a spurt of laughter. "Oh my God. It looks like you're about to give birth."

Tom shot a warning glance at her. "Don't listen to her. It's fine. We'll just throw a blanket over your bottom half, and no one will know. It will be very dignified. Trust me. I can make this fancy. I have excellent creative vision."

After Danny had slunk back to his room, satisfied with his makeshift coffin, Tom and Georgia sat down to negotiate the other particulars of the funeral. He felt like he was in a board meeting except it was late at night and they were both in their pyjamas.

"I absolutely will not." Georgia folded her arms as if the gesture made her refusal more final.

Tom threw up his hands. "Well, then I don't know what to do. We are at an impaste."

"An impaste?"

"Yeah. It's like a metaphorical roadblock where two opposing opinions—"

She rolled her eyes, cutting him off. "I know what an *impasse* is. I don't want to invite people, Tom. It's insane."

"So what if it is? Everyone has crazy shit going on in their lives." he didn't know why he was fighting so hard for it. He didn't want an audience either. But he knew it would feel wrong if they didn't. Like they weren't taking it seriously.

She laughed mirthlessly. "Not like this."

"Maybe not like this." he conceded. "But it's not like it used to be. Everyone is airing their dirty laundry these days. You won't believe what I found out the other day about—"

She shook her head, cutting him off. "I—can't. I can't bear it."

"Just like you couldn't bear to tell anyone about dad leaving right?"

He saw her face beginning to cloud up like a thunderstorm and knew he only had moments to get a few more punches in before he had to run away, lest he be caught in the downpour.

"We can't bury it all forever. People are going to find out eventually."

Run, run, run away now.

He stood up, his back straight and stiff and looked at her one last time before he turned and walked quickly from the room. As he hurried down the hall, he heard her voice clear as day.

"Since when did I raise such a know it all! I'm your mother! How dare you—"

He felt half relieved, half guilty when he reached his bedroom and snipped the door closed. Doors. What a beautiful invention.

CHAPTER THIRTY-ONE

He Aint Heavy

The sun pierced through the sky, the air already thick and warm despite the early hour. Tom knew gum leaves would litter the path that wound through the park, as they did all throughout the year, but the heat would make them shrivel and crackle under foot. The park was small—barely the size of an ordinary house block, but with its little duck pond and fruitful garden beds, it was a quaint little spot for a funeral.

Tom had hoped that the public would be deterred from visiting the little park because of its size and the early hour. Ideally, they would have had the funeral in their backyard—except they didn't really have one. It seemed the universe was bent on making this a spectacle.

He couldn't stop pacing the halls of their house. The procession was to begin in an hour. The clock continued its steady beat, no matter how hard he stared at it. He could think of a million things he would rather be doing. In fact, he would rather:

- Hold a spider in his bare hands
- Take an 8-hour maths lecture
- Eat dog poo (just a little bit)

To his surprise, his mother had come around to the idea of inviting people to the funeral.

Kind of.

"Peet and Julie are coming." she had sniffed when she had walked into the kitchen a week earlier.

Tom had dribbled his cereal down his shirt. He didn't know if he could stomach seeing Peet again. Every time he saw her, she just seemed to bring out the worst in him. That look she'd given him when he'd tried to get Danny out of the club… he shuddered.

"Peet called me. I can't even remember the last time I saw her. Asked if there was anything she could do to help. I don't know how they found out. But I guess everyone knows now. I said she might as well invite everyone else."

Tom had a pretty good idea how she'd found out. But he wasn't about to tell his mother that Peet was Danny's graveyard girlfriend.

It wasn't quite the change in perspective he'd wished for, but it was good enough. He understood her reluctance though, even more so when he had to tell people about it himself. With a shudder, his mind went back to some of the conversations he'd had in the past week. He'd blurted it out to Cliff when the old man had called him to check in.

"Hey so we are having like this event for my brother next week. It would be really great if you could come." he could imagine the expression on Cliff's face.

"Of course." Cliff had said, mild surprise colouring his tone.

Tom knew he was waiting for more. "It's kind of hard to explain. But since the accident… he's not been well. He's having delusions. So anyway, we are having a funeral for him." there was no good way to say that.

"Open or closed casket?" Cliff had finally said.

Tom had smiled into the phone, a wave of relief rushing over him.

"I tried to convince him to have a closed casket, you know, on account of his ugliness, but the stubborn bastard refused."

There was a moment of silence. "So, your brother thinks he's dead or something?"

Tom paused. "Something like that."

"I'll be there." Cliff said gruffly.

How, how could a person just take that in their stride? If their positions were reversed, Tom didn't even want to think about how he would react. Shame settled deep in his chest. Cliff knew when to speak and when to shut up. Tom was beginning to see how that could be a favourable quality in another human being. One he wished he had. One he wished some of the other people he'd spoken to had.

* * *

"And what is the event exactly?"

"It's kind of like a fake… funeral."

"A funeral?"

"Yes."

"Why?"

Tom had cleared his throat. "Well, he's not doing very well, and it's kind of the only thing he really wants at the moment."

"A funeral?"

Tom could hear the derision, the disbelief packed into those two words.

"Yes."

They paused. "What's wrong with him?"

How much time do you have?

"Well, he's a little bit… he's not himself lately."

Another pause. "Have you tried medication? Have you seen a doctor?"

What a great idea! Why didn't we think of that!

"Look it's complicated."

"How's your mum going? How come I haven't heard anything from her?"

Literally everything you've said has been a question.

"She's…"

It was the first question to really stump him. He didn't really know what to say. How was he's mum doing?

Bad. It was the first word that came into his head.

"She's okay."

Feet pattered across the floor and Tom looked up. As much as he didn't want to admit it, Danny looked good. He was dressed in a classic black two piece, the jacket outlining the broadness of his shoulders, even though they lacked meat or muscle. He looked like a man. He looked like a young, spindly James Bond. Except in James Bond's hands he usually held a gun or a woman. In Danny's hands, he held a woman's small compact. Wordlessly, he extended it to Tom.

"What are you doing with this?"

"I want to eat it," Danny rolled his eyes, "Obviously I want you to put it on me."

"Your skin looks fine mate."

"Oh, I know. I asked mum to buy this. It's white makeup. I want to look the part today."

Tom was at his breaking point. He was right there, ready to pack it all in, but he pushed the rising tide down when he saw the light gleaming in his brother's eyes. Jesus Christ. If putting a little bit of foundation on his brother was what he had to do to see him even remotely happy he'd do it. If Danny wanted Tom to dance around in a tutu, he would do it in a heartbeat—anything to stop the kid from walking around like a zombie. Anything to bring him back to even a speck of what he was before the accident. Tom had to remind himself of that today—why he was doing this. He did not care, not even a little bit, what anyone thought about him or his family. A layer of cement hardened his down his spine. He would not break today. That sounded like a lyric from a Britney Spears song. But, if so, he got it. The woman knew what it was all about.

When he was done, Danny looked like a ken doll that was suffering from vampirism and iron deficiency. Like a toddler, he had kept demanding *more, more, more,* and Tom obliged, making the foundation so thick that Tom was sure he could scratch his own name into it.

"Good enough?"

Danny peered into the bathroom mirror, turning to both sides and angling his cheeks. He scanned his face one last time. "Yes. I am ready now. I am ready for my funeral."

"I'd almost forgotten about that."

Dan took his elbow and led him out of the bathroom. "Tom it's ok. Funerals are really a celebration. You'll see that today." he patted Tom's arm and trotted out towards the front door before Tom could give him a reply.

Getting him into the van was painful. Literally.

As it turned out, Danny did have some friends, although Tom had never seen or heard of them before. Idly, he wondered if Danny was an international teenage spy, sworn under oath to keep his private life a secret.

The boys, Leeroy, Ali and Grant, were next to Tom, helping him lift the coffin, but Tom still felt his spine twist and bend like an accordion. Tom greeted the boys with a smile. Only Leeroy returned it. He sighed inwardly. Really, he was surprised to get even a lukewarm welcome from one of them. He couldn't imagine what they thought of today.

"Bend with your knees, Tom. You don't want to hurt your back." Danny was sitting in the coffin like he was tanning himself on a sun lounge.

"Aren't corpses supposed to be still? And quiet?" Tom snapped.

"Sometimes we try to help the living. Haven't you seen a *Christmas Carol*? Those ghosts tried their best to help old scrooge," Danny laughed to himself, "Scrooge. I might call you that from now on."

"And I might just call you Edward."

The boys, including Danny, frowned at Tom.

"Who's Edward?" Ali asked.

"Edward, the dude from Twilight," Tom looked at their blank faces, "You know, because he's a vampire and old mate over here looks like one."

They looked only mildly satiated.

"My back hurts, I'm not on my game." Tom took his wounded spine and pride to the driver's seat.

Surely, the little prick was messing with him. For the processional music, he had chosen The Hollies' "*He ain't heavy, he's my brother.*" Frowning, Tom looked down at his little brother, lying with his eyes closed in the coffin, a look of utter serenity on his face. But as Tom heard the lyrics, he looked toward the cloudless blue sky, blinking back tears.

The road is long
With many a winding turn
That leads us to who knows where
Who knows where
But I'm strong
Strong enough to carry him
He ain't heavy, he's my brother

He hadn't listened to the song before today. He'd just assumed Danny was having a laugh. But surely, he'd chosen it on purpose. Did he know then, what Tom would do for him? That he would carry him to the ends of the Earth if he had to? Regardless of where they ended up?

Tom watched as Danny, in a manner that he must have thought subtle, craned his head out of the coffin to get a good look at exactly how many mourners he had. He poked a finger out and did a thorough head count.

"It's not a huge crowd," he said in a carrying whisper to Tom. "But I understand the absences. It must be so hard to say goodbye to a close friend. I meant so much to so many." he nodded solemnly and nestled back into his box.

With a final swell of music, the song faded, and the group sat down on flimsy plastic chairs Tom had borrowed from the chicken store. His eyes rested on Cliff for a moment, his grave face as expressionless as always.

Danny solemnly waved to a few mourners as Tom stepped away from the coffin and faced the crowd. It was time for him to give the eulogy. God, he hated public speaking. He looked over the crowd again, trying not to see the individual faces. He didn't want to see the confusion or derision or pity. He just needed to get through what he had to say. He didn't know if he could. The song had shaken him. There was a thick, traitorous lump in his throat.

Tom spoke slowly, taking a slow, deep breath. "Thank you to you all for coming to this... *event*. We know that it is a little— unorthodox. I want to thank you all for coming today and supporting our family."

Danny lifted his hands from the coffin, pedalling them together in a 'wrap it up' motion. Tom ignored him as a few people in the crowd tittered.

"And before I begin, I just want to say that I hope you understand. Obviously, because you're here you support us, but I hope you understand that this is not a joke. It mortifies me to think that some might believe what we are doing here today is some sort of prank. No, in my eyes, today is instead about what a family will do in order to save each other."

He swallowed, the lump cutting into his throat. His voice felt raspy, too thick and dry to speak. Tom gazed out into the small crowd, his eyes a few feet above their faces. He wished words captured it better. Or that he knew the words that would. He wished he could make people see what their life had become. The constant worry. The anger. The fear. If they could feel all of that all at once like he did, then they would understand.

The noose.

The gasping breath.

He would do *anything*. As much as it haunted him, he'd do it again if he thought it had a chance of fixing Danny. And he'd happily carry that burden for eternity.

"I couldn't live with myself if I didn't do everything I possibly could to make my brother better." he said finally, his voice breaking, his teeth gritted. "I hope that helps you make sense of all of this."

He paused and saw people in the crowd dabbing at their eyes. Danny gave him a thumbs up.

"I read King Lear when I was in high school. I can't say I took much away from it, but this one bit stuck with me:

'And worse I may be yet.

The worst is not

So long as we can say

This is the worst.'"

Tom's eyes locked with Mickey's. He felt like he was standing in front of her naked in the middle of a snowstorm. It was exhilarating, but he wished he had something to cover himself up with. The best he could do was to look away. He fixed his eyes on a eucalyptus sapling to his left, its little green leaves reaching towards the sun.

"Ever since I read that, or should I say—since I have been reminded of it, I have hoped to God that day would never come. The day when I am in such agony, faced with such grief, that I do not have the presence of mind to acknowledge it. As bad as any day might be, I know the day my brother dies would be the worst. It would be the day when words would fail me completely. I would give up and never get up again."

He glanced at Danny, but the boy was so exalted by his surroundings, he hadn't noticed Tom's slip to future tense. Neither did he see the tears that now flowed freely down Tom's face. Tom looked at his mother. She was crying, smiling up at him.

Tom continued, "So much grief of course, is equal to the amount of love you have for someone. So, I am glad this hurts so much right now.

I want to feel this pain. This anger. This complete, all-consuming fucking *sadness*. Because I know it's really just love."

Were you supposed to swear in eulogies? Tom didn't care. He looked towards the coffin and gave it something of a salute. Dan saluted him back.

"Dan—you're the man, and I'll love you for a lifespan."

Tom drifted away from the front of the crowd to take a seat in the front row, his mind completely blank for maybe the first time in his life. He felt like Danny had died. He felt like someone had poured salt on the soil of his soul and nothing would ever grow again. He could not stop the tears from pouring down his cheeks. He didn't try to.

As the service continued, Tom felt as if he were in a dream. It was hauntingly beautiful to hear Leeroy give a tribute and his mother read the closing poem. He had never expected it to feel real. But he had meant every word of what he said, and it was clear that everyone else had too. He didn't want to know what it meant—the grief that had eaten away his insides. He stared at his brother, lying deadly still for the final viewings, sometimes lifting a hand to shake the hand of the mourner paying their respects to him. Tom prayed. He prayed that this had been enough for him. That things would start to go back to normal now.

He just wanted his brother back.

He kept his eyes averted as he approached Mickey. He couldn't look at her. She'd seen it all now.

"So on a scale of one to ten, how weird was that?"

She smiled, "Well I once walked in on a community meeting for middle aged men where they were sitting in a circle naked, so this probably only rates a seven."

"I'm not going to ask."

She laughed. "Well, that was pretty much the whole story, anyway. I got the hell out of there pretty quickly."

"Yeah, Danny wanted us all to do the service naked, but I talked him out of it."

"Shame. He could have gone out of this world the way he came into it. Would have been poetic. Speaking of which – nice eulogy," she looked up at him covertly.

Naked. He felt so, so naked.

"Thanks." every syllable tripped out of his mouth.

"I was selfish today." she said.

He looked at her then, his face contorted. "What? Why's that?"

"I think I just wanted to be around people who knew what it was like."

"What it's like to have a brother think he's dead?" Tom regretted saying it, even before he saw the look of disappointment in her eyes. He knew what she meant.

"No." she said simply. "To have someone so far down the chasm that you don't know if you can get them back."

"Who—"

She shook her head and began to walk away. "Another time."

Chasm. What a strange word. He always wanted to pronounce the H, even though he knew it was wrong. He was rolling the word around in his mouth, repeating in his head.

Chasm. Chasm. Chasm.

"Why isn't anyone crying?"

Dan's breath blew over Tom like a burst hose. Why did he smell like off milk when he'd been drinking beers for the last few hours? The smell brought sharp tears to Tom's eyes.

"Oh, that's better. You are crying."

Danny towered over them. The group was huddled in a cramped booth in the back corner of the bar. If he didn't think about the events of the day, he could almost convince himself that he was on a regular night out, having a few casual drinks at their local.

Tom stood up. "I think all you need to do mate, is to sit down and talk to some people. That's all you'll need to get them to start crying."

Tom smiled and walked away as Mickey glared at him. With a laugh he looked back to see Danny squeeze into the booth, his shoulders rubbing against Mickey's. *So bad.* He couldn't remember a time he'd ever smelt breath so bad.

Tom walked into the beer garden, only to find himself walking in on a conversation not meant for his ears.

"It's not right man."

Tom recognised the voice as Ali's. He peered around the corner to see him and Leeroy standing together, the glow of their cigarettes casting their faces in long shadows.

"It's a joke."

Leeroy inhaled before responding. "I don't think it's like that." he said softly.

"It is. It's a fucking mockery."

The venom in Ali's voice made Tom shiver.

"He's not right man." said Leeroy.

"So? It doesn't make this okay. Doesn't mean we should pretend this isn't completely messed up."

Leeroy sighed. "That's true. But there's no easy answer."

Ali laughed. "Yeah, there is. Get the kid some help! Take him to a doctor."

"Ali." Leeroy said, but even Tom knew the rebuke was a weak one.

"They're just going along with it all! They're enabling the madness."

Tom felt like he'd been slapped. He felt a tidal wave rising over him. The two boys were quiet, puffing furiously on the end of their cigarettes.

"Yeah maybe." Leeroy said. He stamped on his butt. "Anyway, it's done now."

"Thank God. Well, I've done my bit."

Leeroy nodded and Tom quickly retraced his steps, blindly walking through the dimly lit corridors. He could think of nothing, the sound of Ali's derision playing in his head, over and over again. Tom knew Ali was right. It was completely messed up. But it was for something. It had to have meant something.

He walked straight into a woman. It took him a moment to take in the skirt, the cropped hair.

Peet.

He'd managed to avoid her all day. He did not need this right now.

"Tom?"

Why was she always surprised to see him? Like she'd forgotten he existed.

"What do you want?" even he knew how childish he sounded.

"Well, to go to the bathroom. But now that you're here—" she looked at him. Not with sympathy or anger or contempt. She just looked. "I know today was hard for you."

Before he knew what he was saying, he was telling her about what he did. About what he'd made Danny do. The hallway. The noose. He couldn't keep the secret anymore. He was done with that. He'd made a vow to tell the truth. It was time he started honouring it.

"That's really fucked up." was all she finally said when Tom had finished.

"I know."

She nodded, almost to herself, and then sidestepped him. He watched her round a corner and disappear, his breathing starting to slow. Maybe she was right about him. Maybe he did care too much about what other people thought. But he didn't have to let it consume him. He didn't have to buy into what Ali has said. He could just see it for what it was. A hard day. A shit time. A weight he had to carry. It was heavy, but it was Danny. He could bear it.

CHAPTER THIRTY-TWO

Chunks of Carrot

It ran down the sidewalk in little rivets, racing towards the drain faster than Tom thought it could ever move.

"That's alright mate, get it all out."

Dan heaved, and it sounded like a scene from the exorcist. It was as if his soul was shooting out of his mouth and down the drainpipe.

"I think I'm dying," he choked out between heaves.

"I thought you were already dead," Tom muttered to himself. "Yeah, it feels that way, hey. C'mon, we're nearly home. Not too much further."

They were standing on the cobbled footpath at the opening of their darkly lit street, but they might as well have been in Antarctica: Tom had a feeling that moving Danny the last 100 meters was going to be like towing a small car with his teeth. Although, there was something almost satisfying about seeing someone else in an utter state—like you were some sort of got-it-together person. Like your life was a perfect circle and they were a pathetic oblong.

"What's wrong with me? Why have I done this to myself?"

"If we knew the answer to that, we wouldn't do it to begin with."

Danny stumbled, teetering on the balls of his feet for a few moments before he came crashing down into a neighbour's hedge. A light inside flicked on. Tom squared up. He thought of all the times when he was a kid when he'd do something stupid and would have to deal with the wrath of a neighbour, or a parent or a teacher, and terror would shoot through his heart and the end of his life would be visible in front of his hands. He laughed at that little boy now. If only he knew what was coming. A blurry face peered out from behind the window at him and he could hear their shouts from the street.

"Yes okay, I can hear you! I would move him if I could! Please, feel free to come out here and lend a hand—or don't. Call the cops. At least then I might have some help to get him home."

For good measure, he flipped them off, just because he didn't really have a reason not to. It felt good, pushing his finger out as far as he could, almost like it would detach from his body.

He couldn't see the neighbour's face, but he imagined the shock that was plastered to them right now. *Look at this little delinquent. Look at what the youth of today is coming to.*

Tom groaned inwardly as he saw a silhouette emerge from the front door. For a moment, just one tiny little moment, he considered running away and leaving Danny in the bushes.

"Tom?"

Tom squinted into the darkness. "Oh my God. Cliff?"

The figure hobbled down the front veranda in the dark and Tom saw that it was indeed his boss.

"What are you doing here?"

Cliff raised his eyebrows. "I thought that would have been obvious."

"You live here?"

Cliff nodded.

"But we're practically neighbours!"

Cliff nodded again, as if Tom had suddenly become very simple.

"I'm sorry, but I'm shocked. I had no idea. You never said anything."

Cliff moved to the hedge to assess Danny's condition. "Well, I'm not usually in the habit of exchanging addresses with my younger employees."

Tom nodded, looking away. Cliff seemed to read his thoughts.

"Look, it never came up, okay? It's not a big deal."

Tom leaned around Cliff, trying to peer into his front window. "Who's in there with you? Your wife?"

"Let's get your brother out of this hedge."

"Your hedge." Tom said.

Cliff rolled his eyes.

"I didn't think you were married. I thought you had a thing for my mum." Tom watched his face carefully. "Are you going to be my new daddy Cliff?"

"Jesus Christ!" Cliff said, amongst a string of other profanities: Danny had vomited all over his feet. Although Tom swore the old man looked almost thankful for the vomit on his—

"You're wearing slippers!" Tom didn't know what he was more shocked by: the fact that Cliff lived in the same street as him, or that the toughest bloke he knew wore slippers after 8 pm.

Cliff ignored him. "I'll bring the car around."

"We're just down the street!"

Cliff looked between the two brothers, his eyes settling on Danny's crumpled, hulking form.

"I am not carrying *that* down the street."

Unceremoniously, they bundled Danny up like a pile of twigs and got him in the back of the car. When Tom was seated in the passenger seat, he looked at Cliff and found him giving him one of those looks. One of those knowing looks. Tom braced himself. Good thing he had his seatbelt on.

"You okay?"

No.

I don't know.

Tom looked at Danny, a little bit of vomit dripping onto the back seat.

"Better than him."

Cliff grunted at him. "Sometimes it's okay to say it like it is."

"That's rich, coming from you."

Tom noticed Cliff carefully check his blind spot and turn his indicator on, even though it was the dead of the night. In this part of town, no one would be on the streets past 10 pm. No one other than them.

"You need to stop acting like you know everything there is to know about a person."

The rebuke was unexpected, and Tom felt his cheeks burn. He didn't know why, but it was all the worse coming from Cliff.

"Everyone's human. You need to forgive them for it."

"I—I don't think—" Tom trailed off feebly. "How did we even get here?"

"Because I said it how it was."

"Hey, I'm always one to tell the truth. Didn't you tell me not that long ago that I had to learn how to shut my mouth?"

"Oh, you're very good at talking about things that don't matter. Or about *other* people."

Tom heard the implication in his voice and knew he was right.

"I feel like nothing will ever be right in my world again. That's how I feel. Like someone has died. Like maybe I've died and woken up in Hell."

Danny made a groan that sounded as if it had come from an animal that had been fatally shot. Tom saw Cliff's eyes flash to the back seat.

"If he throws up on the leather you are cleaning it."

Tom almost hoped he did vomit, so he didn't have to think about what he had said to Cliff.

"It was my daughter, by the way." Cliff said, breaking the silence.

"What?"

Cliff cleared his throat. "Inside. It was my daughter. Not my wife. I'm not married."

Tom looked at him in amazement. Cliff was right. Tom was completely clueless. He had no idea what was going on in people's heads or in their homes. Did any of us really though? Could we ever know what it was like to step through the threshold of someone else's door, and see their whole life, exactly as they saw it?

"How old?"

"About your age. Bit younger."

Tom opened his mouth, "Is she h—"

"It's Saraya, you dolt."

"From the chicken store?" he said dumbly, thinking of the quiet, pimply teen.

Cliff didn't reply. Tom sat back in his seat, gobsmacked.

When they arrived at the house, Tom wasn't in the least bit surprised to see a light on in the lounge room. He was amazed Georgia had even let them go out after the funeral. Not that she really had any control over either of them anymore. Was that all it took to escape the clasps of parental authority? Just have a complete and total family crisis? Wrapped in her thin dressing gown, she looked small, like a child, but she hastened down the porch steps like a security guard, ready to escort Danny safely inside.

"Easy now." said Cliff as him and Tom maneuvered Danny out of the car. "Where are we putting him?" he asked gruffly, taking the full weight of Danny's melon head and chest as Tom let Danny's legs dangle uselessly on the ground.

"This— this way." Georgia said, jumping ahead of them.

It occurred to Tom that she probably had no idea who the stranger was that she was letting into their home. She'd only met Cliff once when Tom got his nose shattered, well, anyway, she wasn't about to start asking questions, even though Tom could tell she was close to jumping out of her skin. Even after all this time, they were still uncomfortable with having people in the house. They were whatever the opposite of agoraphobics is.

Once Danny was put to bed, Georgia turned to Cliff.

"I'm so sorry. Thank you so much for helping Tom. My youngest son, he's—"

Cliff put up a hand, cutting her off. "Don't worry about it. I know."

She looked at him blankly.

"I work with your son— we spoke on the phone once—you came into the store—"

"Oh, that's right! Cliff!" she said, laying her hand on Cliff's bicep.

Both Tom and Cliff looked at the hand.

Cliff cleared his throat. "I live around the corner, actually. And I saw the boys from my window walking home." *Walking*. They were just as likely to have been able to have flown home, with Danny in his current state.

"We really appreciate it."

Tom could hear the emotion in her voice. It made him want to bury his head in his armpit. Cliff didn't do emotion.

"Lately it's just been so—" she began to cry and Cliff pulled her into a hug.

What was happening here?

Tom expected Georgia to collect herself, to laugh and extricate her body from Cliff's, but instead she sank into his arms. They looked like a book cover for *Romancing the Elderly*. Tom cleared his throat loudly, and the two separated. He almost felt bad, but he knew that if it went for a second longer, he was going to have to gouge out his eyes.

"Well, I will leave you to it." Cliff's eyes turned to Tom. "Tom, make sure you give your mother my number." he looked back to Georgia. "I'm here for a chat anytime, love. Everyone needs someone to talk to."

As he walked back to his car, Tom could have sworn the wily old bastard winked at him. Tom waited until Cliff was in his car before turning to Georgia.

"You're not seriously going to—" he trailed off as she shrugged, her cheeks a peachy pink.

He spluttered to himself. Sure, he *joked* about it. But Cliff was so *old*. And his mother... well. There are some things a boy can't say about their own mother, but she was... well she wasn't *unattractive*. And Cliff owned a chicken store. He wasn't sure she'd ever even eaten fried chicken in her life. What could he possibly have to offer her?

Sensing his unspoken question, she shrugged again. "I don't know. It might be nice. To have some company." She walked slowly back into the house and Tom watched her go, her bony shoulders pressing through her silk wrap. He'd never really thought of her as frail, but she looked it then. Even her back looked sad.

Tom realised she might have more in common with Cliff than he thought.

If Danny looked white at the funeral yesterday, then he was practically transparent now. It was two o'clock in the afternoon when Tom finally heard noises from his room. All day, Tom had been creeping up to Danny's door to check for signs of life. Partly to make sure he was still alive, but also to see when he might be lucid enough for Tom to talk to him. Not that he could ever be considered 'lucid' these days. But finally, Tom had hope.

Tom poked his head in and found Danny sprawled across his bed, cradling a bucket. The room smelt like death. He was mildly impressed that Danny had the presence of mind to get up and get himself a bucket from the laundry.

"You right mate?"

Danny groaned like a sword had been poked deep into his innards.

"Yep. That good, hey."

Danny gasped. "I'm dying."

"Yeah, you've been saying that for a while."

"No living man could possibly feel this sick and still be alive."

Tom nodded. "Well, I can't really help you there. Got to let it run its course. Aside from the hangover, how are you feeling?"

He had to wait a few minutes while Danny retched into the bucket. There's nothing quite like the sound.

"What did you drink last night?" Tom said, after Danny had finally spluttered to a stop, his breathing fast and heavy.

"Everything." he curled into a ball, and his eyes fluttered closed.

"Danny." Tom said, holding his breath as Danny did the opposite, letting out a painful exhale. "Do you... feel better after the funeral?"

Danny gave a gargle that Tom thought might have been a laugh.

"You know what I mean. Are you... satisfied with what we did for you yesterday?"

Danny looked at him with genuine confusion etched onto his face. "How can a person be satisfied with death?"

The tone. The look on Danny's face. It all told him the same thing: nothing had changed. He was still... whatever he was these days. Not Danny.

"Isn't death supposed to bring peace?" Tom asked him quietly.

"Do I look at peace to you?"

A thread of saliva hung from Danny's mouth, latching to the bucket. Tom thought about picking up the bucket and upturning it on Danny's head.

"You're so *selfish*." the words hissed from his mouth before he even knew what he was saying. "I have done everything, *everything* I can for you." his throat was ripping into pieces. "And nothing is good enough."

Tom was breathing heavily. His brain felt like their linen cupboard —he could barely close the doors and keep the mess inside contained.

"So, what next? What do I have to do next?" he tried to keep the anger from his voice, but he heard it there anyway.

Danny was quiet, his mouth tight. Tom sensed something had unravelled in him.

"Can you please empty the bucket? The smell is making everything worse." he said finally, pulling the bed covers tight over his head as he turned his back to Tom.

Despite himself, despite everything he felt, Tom picked up the stupid bucket. He looked inside, instantly regretting his decision. Why was it that vomit, no matter what you'd eaten the night before, always had chunks of carrot in it?

CHAPTER THIRTY-THREE

But Danny Wasn't — He Was Just —

Tom didn't think it was possible for the boy to spend any more time in his room, but he hadn't seen Danny leave it for days. Part of Tom was relieved, the part that had seemed to whisper to him louder and louder these days, as if it had grown fat and greedy from his thoughts.

It's easier this way.

At least he's safe.

As long as he's in there, then everything is fine.

But Tom knew, Danny was not fine. And it was Tom's fault. If only he'd been able to keep it in. If only he hadn't shouted at Danny. For so long, he'd been able to squash it all down. Maybe he'd finally reached capacity. He had no emotional vacancy left.

He had a feeling his mother felt the same way. At first, he hadn't noticed it, but she was starting to look more and more like Danny. Aren't children supposed to grow up and look like their parents? The change wasn't quite physical, although she did look thin and pale now that he thought about it. But it was more her... air. It was the same thing that hung around Danny's door. It was wafting from her pores.

"Why are you staring at me?"

Quickly, he averted his gaze, fixing his eyes on the dining table instead. Yeah, great plan. Look away now. That helps.

"I'm sorry about the funeral." he didn't really know what was going to come out of his mouth, but that was unexpected.

Georgia also looked taken aback. "Why?" she said as she clanged about the kitchen.

"Because it didn't work."

She laughed mirthlessly. "It was never going to work."

He blinked. "Then why did you let me do it?"

"Because you were so... eager. So determined. I had to let you try."

She was talking like he was a seven-year-old again, when she'd let him sell tomatoes from their backyard to their neighbours. She hadn't encouraged him, but she'd let him do it. He only sold one bag, and a great big dog had chased him up the street. Any time he tried to do something, he failed. Then, now. It was no different. Danny was another one of his train wrecks. And Georgia was content to sit back and watch it all derail.

"What made you so sure?" he said, eyes narrowing.

She stopped packing dishes and looked at him like he was stupid. "Tom, he thinks he's *dead*. That's not something that's just going to go away."

Don't. Don't ask. We don't look remember?

"Mum."

He swallowed the barb in his throat. It seemed to be a permanent addition to his anatomy these days. "Will he ever get better?"

Her look was answer enough. He nodded to himself, tears beginning to rack his body. He knew. He'd already buried Danny. And as he felt his mother's arms wrapped around him, felt her own tears take hold of her body, he knew she'd done the same. He didn't know how long they held each other like that, but he knew he wasn't done. He couldn't accept this warmth. God, he was a masochist.

He had to ask. "Mum? What really happened to Dad?" he asked, because he'd always known the truth.

"Oh Tom." her eyes looked so sad. It was for him, he knew. She had never looked at him like that before. It scared him.

"I don't know," she said simply, "I think he was ... struggling."

He was shocked. He hadn't expected her to answer.

"And you just... let him go? Off on his own? God knows where."

"Yes."

"You should have stopped him!"

"And how am I supposed to do that? You act like I'm superhuman Tom. But I'm not. I couldn't have stopped him from leaving."

"But he could be in trouble!"

Her eyes shifted, and he knew then, that he'd never had the full story.

"I've been getting emails from him. Since he left. He's fine."

He felt like he'd been slapped in the face. "All this time? You never said anything. You never told us."

"Did you really want to know? That he didn't want to see you? Didn't want to see anyone?"

"Yes."

No.

I don't know.

"Well, you can read them now if you like. The emails. A warning though. They're pretty… *full on.*"

His brain could not compute the fact that they existed, let alone reading something so personal from a man he thought incapable of feeling. Maybe it was the opposite. Maybe he felt so much that it had just deadened him inside.

Moments ago, Tom had thought he was at his limit. He'd imploded. But instead of it bringing bliss, he just kept falling and falling, explosions rocketing his insides. Would it never stop? He wanted to rage. He wanted to run away. But he was passed that now. He couldn't even be angry at her.

"Let me— let me finish those."

He felt her stare follow him as he stood by the sink full of dishes, and he understood. It was the first time in his life he'd ever voluntarily done a chore. He wished it was gallantry. Or empathy. But it was self-preservation. His hands needed to be busier than his brain. Finally, he understood something about his mother. Housework was medicine. Housework was oblivion.

He must be losing it. Like absolutely losing it. Something must have possessed him. He could think of no other reason as to why he'd actually invite Peet into their home. But there she was, standing on the porch, peering into the house behind him.

"Are you going to let me in or —?"

His feet were glued to the welcome mat.

"We haven't cleaned."

The house was spotless.

"Do you think I care?"

"I've got no biscuits. Can't even make you a cup of tea."

"I didn't come here for earl grey and scotch fingers." she levelled a look at him. "Why did you invite me, Tom?"

He sighed, and stepped to the side. She pushed passed him and then stopped a few feet down the hallway.

"What?" he asked.

"I don't actually know where I'm going."

He almost laughed, but instead gestured for her to enter the lounge room. Out of habit, he glanced uneasily at Danny's bedroom door, even though that was the reason he'd asked Peet over. He didn't know what to expect, but it had felt like the right thing to do. Her eyes followed his.

"Is that—?"

Tom nodded. Even though she'd just sat down, she jumped back up.

"What are you doing?" Tom hissed, even though her intentions were clear. "We haven't even discussed—"

"Oh relax. I'm just going to talk to him. Is that so scary?"

"Yes."

She stopped and looked at him.

"I was joking." he said.

"I don't think you were. He's still your brother Tom. He's still a person."

Tom closed his eyes for a moment. At some point, he had stopped thinking of Danny as his brother. He thought back to his interactions with Danny since the accident. In every single one, he'd called him a—

Ghost.

Fruitloop.

Vampire.

Weirdo.

Monster.

He didn't think he'd said that last one out loud, but he'd definitely thought it. He was thinking it now. Don't wake the monster.

Peet rapped on the bedroom door. As usual, there was no answer. She waited a few moments before she knocked again.

"Danny."

There was no question to her call. It was a demand. Open your door or I'll blow your house down.

"You're good at this." Tom said quietly.

She shrugged, her eyes fixed on the door. "It's not my first rodeo."

He looked at her, waiting for her to say more.

"Al." was all she said.

Al? Peet herself had said at his funeral that he'd been—But Danny wasn't—he was just—the kid thought he was *dead*. That wasn't like what Al had. It was nothing like *that*. But it suddenly dawned on Tom that he had no idea what *it* was. What *it* looked like. Sure, he'd heard about *it*. But he'd never seen *it* himself. This whole time, was that something Danny was struggling with? Was the whole delusion thing just some sort of subconscious coping mechanism? If so, how hadn't he seen it?

"Al used to do the same thing." Peet said, oblivious to Tom's thoughts. "Hide in his room. Avoid us. We couldn't be sad about it, because that would just make him feel worse. I got very good at pretending that everything was fine, that I was happy and oblivious."

"*How.*"

She shrugged. "Because I had to. It was the only thing that worked. It made him feel better. Well, it didn't make him feel worse. Danny, we are coming in now."

Tom looked at her. Peeta, the big bad wolf. He'd never known. He'd always thought of her as a bitch in black clothing. But now... ugh what was that feeling? Was that... admiration? But he'd sworn to hate her for eternity.

Gently, Peet pushed Danny's door open. As always, Tom was shocked by how dark it was inside. It was the middle of summer; how could he possibly get it this dark? Looking at the windows, Tom had his answer. Danny had hung what looked like several thick blankets across his window. When did he even get them? Tom shuddered to think about him creeping about the house while they were sleeping.

"Hey Danny." said Peet, completely ignoring the fact that he hadn't moved an inch and his face was still buried in his pillow. Tom couldn't even see a speck of his skin. The doona was pulled high over his head.

"What are you doing?" Peet had grabbed Tom's arm. He hadn't

even realised it, but he had started to back out of the room.

He shook his head, trying to fill it with something to say.

"How are you feeling today?" she asked Danny, sitting on the edge of his bed. She looked completely at ease, as if it were her own bed, her own room. Tom felt like he was in a museum. He was too scared to move in case he touched something and destroyed everything.

Danny didn't answer her, but it didn't seem to bother Peet.

"A bad day today? That's okay."

And she just sat there, patting Danny's side in smooth strokes. She looked at Tom and gave him a strange look. It took him a moment to figure out what it was, because he'd never seen it on her face before.

Sympathy.

There was some validation in that look. Lately, he'd started to feel like the worst person on the planet. But that look at least told him he had a reason to be.

Soon, Peet's visits became normal. And any kind of normal in their lives was refreshing. She'd stroll in, pushing past Tom when he opened the door and she would simply let herself into Danny's room. Sometimes, she convinced Danny to sit on the couch. Sometimes, she got him talking. Danny was right about her. She was an angel.

Tom could barely listen to it, when she got Danny talking. Hearing Danny talk about the accident made him see things again. Hear things again.

The squealing tires.

The tail of that kangaroo whipping up into the headlights.

Danny's final gasp of air before the impact.

It was almost more than Tom could bear. He had sworn he wouldn't. He'd put the lid on those memories and promised himself he'd never open it.

Georgia joined them sometimes. But she never stayed with them for long. She would busy herself with making tea and coffee. Tom knew, it wasn't because she was uncomfortable. Although, they both felt uncomfortable. It was because she knew there were just some things you can't say around a parent. He wondered how she felt about that. No matter how hard she might try, she could never be Danny's confidant. Tom could be. There was no reason why he shouldn't be able to fill that role. There had been no one in the world closer to Danny than he. So why hadn't he? Why had it fallen to Peet, an almost stranger? Like usual, he had failed. The irony was, he had failed in something he was actually good at. *Talking*.

"I swear to god, if you don't stop moping about this house—"

Peet had left and Danny had returned to his room. Georgia was shaking her head at Tom as he got up from the couch. She could talk. Which was clearly a metaphor, because neither of them were talking. When had they both become mutes? He wanted to yell and curse at her for being so unsympathetic. But instead, he simply looked at her.

"Why can Peet talk to Danny and I can't?"

She sighed, her frustration escaping with her exhale. She sat down, pulling him back down. He almost resisted. The last thing he felt like was more talking, even though he had only been listening to Peet and Danny.

"She doesn't love Danny like you do. The closer you are, the harder it is to help someone I think."

"Why? It doesn't make sense."

She nodded. "The more you love someone, the easier it is to be angry and disappointed with them. Anger is just rejected love."

"I'm not—" he stopped himself.

They both knew it was true.

She squeezed his shoulders. "I'm angry with him too. And I know it's not fair, and it's selfish. And I'm a terrible mother. But this hurts us too."

He'd accused Danny of being selfish, but really, he was the selfish one. He saw that now. How he'd practically demanded Danny get better. It wasn't for Danny's sake, but his own. So he could be normal, so Tom could still love him like he used to.

"It's terrible. I want to be able to talk with him. But it just seems— impossible. I *can't*."

The lump was back in his throat. He wished he could forget it all, wipe his brain clean. It would be the only way he could find peace again.

"I don't think there's anything more difficult than seeing, really seeing, how much pain someone you love is feeling. And letting them see how much pain you're in."

He went to open his mouth, to tell her that he was fine, that he wasn't hurting, that Danny could never hurt him, but she cut him off.

"Just let yourself feel it. *All* of it. Then you won't feel sorry for yourself. The guilt will eat you alive Tom." she waved her hands over her own evaporating body. "I'm a testimony to that."

"How do you know I feel guilty?" he asked, letting the tears spring to his eyes, hoping they would dissolve the barb in his throat, the pain clutching his chest.

"How could we not?"

CHAPTER THIRTY-FOUR

Look

Don't. Don't look.

"Shut up." he said, looking around to see if anyone else had noticed him talking to himself. But he knew that Danny was in his room and he couldn't see Georgia from his doorway. He steeled himself, marching the whole 10 metres to Danny's door before he could change his mind. Following Peet's example, he rapped once, before pushing the door open. Was it really that easy? Yes, that's literally how doors work.

"Danny?"

He didn't know why he said it as a question. It was clearly Danny sitting at his desk. Tom took that as a good sign. At least he wasn't in bed. Danny said nothing, only turning his chair as a way of acknowledging Tom's presence.

"I... was hoping I could talk to you."

Danny swivelled back around. "I'm pretty tired."

So it wasn't all in Tom's head. "Why don't you want to talk to me?"

He expected Danny to ignore him, for that to be the end of it, but he swivelled back. He would get nauseous soon.

"Because I'm like this!"

"It's okay." God, could he sound any less convincing.

Danny laughed, but it was more like a wheeze. "No, it's not. And I can't take it. I can't take the look on your face."

Why? Why did his face have to mirror every single thought and emotion he had? Tom moved closer, sitting on the edge of the bed with a soft thunk.

"What was it, Danny? Was it the accident? I'm sorry—I didn't mean to crash—" great big fat tears dribbled from his eyes. His whole body shook and shuddered, trying to reject the tears, expelling them from his eye sockets. It felt horrible. It didn't feel cathartic. It felt like torture.

"It was... everything."

"D-dad leaving? Al dying? School?"

Tom still didn't know why Al's death had bothered Danny so much. The guy was a toolbag. A mean, grumpy old depressed—

Ah.

They were all right. Cliff, Mickey, his mum. Tom really had *no* idea. His whole life, he thought he knew his brother inside out. He thought he knew everything about everyone. But how well can you really know a person? You can't know their secrets, their wants or their fears. His whole life, Danny had been hiding things from them. Tom saw it now. The addiction. The pain. His school grades. Tom didn't blame him. Even when people are honest with you, half the time they don't know what they're saying. He was a testament to that himself. Half the stuff that came out his own mouth was a traitorous lie. It couldn't ever do justice to how he felt.

His heart ached for Danny. Tom just wanted to know what had caused all of *this*. Even after all this time, he was still trying to make sense of it. Find the origin. If he could find that then maybe he could—

Danny was shaking his head. "It was *everything*. And it was nothing. I just couldn't—I can't make sense of anything anymore." he whispered.

Tom vividly remembered then, sitting in their kitchen, before the accident, complaining of his bad luck, telling Danny his own fears about how there was something ready to claim him, completely unaware that it already had its claws deep in Danny. He was a complete idiot for thinking he knew what even a slither of that felt like.

"I'm sorry Danny. I'm sorry for everything."

Tom was surprised when Danny nodded. He didn't think he would be able to hear him through his garbled sobs. Tom had nothing more to say. He didn't know what he had expected from Danny. But he was cold and reserved. Had he expected that? He didn't know. Their talk wasn't everything he wanted it to be. There were no revelations. No miracles. But as he shakily snipped Danny's door behind him, Tom felt... *lighter*. Not absolved. He still had so much to learn. But he broke through the barrier. That counted for something.

"So, why don't you like me?"

Tom hadn't been able to let it go. Mickey had become another regular visitor to the house, now that he had stopped ignoring her messages. He still didn't know why she'd persisted.

Where Peet pushed past him, Mickey waited patiently on the front doorstep to be let in. But he stood in her way, arms crossed, demanding an answer.

"It's because of that!" she burst out.

"Because of what?" he asked, finally allowing her through now she'd decided to bite.

"Because of your incessant need to know everything. To fix everything. No one's allowed to have a problem, especially with you. Everything has to be perfect."

Georgia poked her head out of the laundry at that moment, raising her eyebrows.

"Hi, Mickey." she said with a self-satisfied smile. Mickey waved at her down the hallway and Georgia's head disappeared.

Tom rounded on Mickey as she followed him into the lounge room.

"So, you don't like me anymore because I'm perfect?"

"Perfectly *insecure*. Sorry." Mickey added, after seeing the look on his face.

Was he? He'd never thought of himself that way. When he thought of insecure, he thought of pimply, body-conscious teenagers. He wasn't one of them. He was confident. Surely everyone saw that.

Mickey laughed to herself. "You're thinking about it now, aren't you?"

"No." he allowed a small smile to show on his face.

"You can't be perfect Tom. No one can. You can't control everything."

"I can control if you ever come back inside this house." he'd meant it as a joke, but she didn't laugh. Her face was flat. "I'm sorry." he said. Usually, he had to think about that. They weren't words he usually said in a hurry. But he'd been saying them a lot lately.

"I'm sorry I shut you out."

She nodded. Part of him was hoping she'd laugh his apology away, tell him it was unnecessary, but she simply nodded. "It hurt. I only wanted to help you."

He realised then, what he'd done. Without knowing, he'd hurt her.

"I'm sorry."

He knew then, that in some way, he'd lost her. He would never regain what she had taken back. And that was okay, because he knew he didn't deserve it anyway. It was his punishment for being a bad friend and an even worse human.

"Hey," he said, suddenly remembering what she'd said at the funeral. "Who in your family has—" he saw her face clam up. "I'm sorry, I didn't mean to pry. I just thought you might like to—or maybe one day, you'd like to talk about it."

"It was my sister." she said softly.

He'd never even known she'd had a sister. God, he was evil. Pure evil.

"You know Eddie?" she said.

His nose gave an uncomfortable twitch. "Yeah," he said slowly. *His fist and my nose are intimately acquainted.*

"She was his girlfriend. They dated for years before..." she shook her head. "Anyway, that's why I'm always trying to get him out. I know he wants to forget, to stay angry at the world, but I don't think she'd want that. I think it'd make her feel worse, you know? If we couldn't forgive her."

Tom swallowed, Eddie's cold eyes dancing before him. "Maybe he doesn't want to forgive her."

She looked at him for a long moment. "He should. It wasn't her fault."

"I'm so angry at him Mickey. I'm so angry at Danny."

It felt good to say it out loud. All this time, he'd pushed it down, refusing to see it was there, to see what it meant. He loved Danny with his whole heart. How could he blame him, hate him even, when he loved him? It wasn't Danny's fault. He knew it wasn't fair. He knew that, and yet... the anger was there. Danny, the one person he felt like he really truly loved, was stolen away—by Danny.

"You can be angry at Danny. But you have to be able to forgive him too. He needs to know you still love him."

His vision blurred as he looked at her. "Was it—like Danny? Your sister?"

She nodded slowly. "In... a way. It's always different. Even when it's similar."

"What is wrong with the world? Does it have to come after all of us? Danny? Your sister, Al..." another name whispered into his brain.

Dad.

It was obvious now. Like Mickey said. It was different with him. But surely, it was the same thing.

She smiled at him sadly. "Who knows? That's the scary thing isn't it. We don't know if or when it's coming. What it looks like. Or what we can even do about it."

Tom knew that if it came for him, it would chew him up and spit him out like wasted chicken bones. Before he could say anything else, his nose caught wind of something. Something funky.

Eggs.

Rotten eggs.

"Jesus Tom, if I didn't like you before, that'll sure do it." Mickey was pinching her nose.

"That wasn't—" something clicked.

Gas leaks smell like rotten eggs.

Except for the time he'd come down with an unexpected bout of gastro as he walked home from school, he could not recall a time he'd moved faster. He launched himself from the hall, almost toppling over as he found his feet. Wasting no time, he ran to the kitchen, following his nose. Danny looked up as he burst in, Tom's eyes wild as they took in the stove top, almost as if he expected to see it shaking, spitting fumes of thick nauseous gas into the air.

"How long has the gas been on?"

Tom stormed to the saucepan and quickly turned the dial off, pushing Danny out of the kitchen and opening the window, almost in the same movement. Georgia and Mickey arrived at the same time. They both stopped and watched the two brothers from the doorway, as if they somehow knew that they were not supposed to interrupt.

Danny looked nonplussed. "Like ten minutes?" he looked down at his bare feet. "I was cooking eggs." he said quietly.

No gas. Just actual rotten eggs. Tom put a hand to his racing heart.

"I thought you were—it doesn't matter."

"Sorry."

Tom reached a hand out, cupping his shoulder. "It's okay. Just… let's use the *fresh* eggs."

As he stuck his head in the fridge, he froze. It had seemed so natural; he hadn't even noticed it at first.

Danny was cooking.

He hadn't done that since before the accident. A thrill ran through Tom, but he kept his voice calm.

"So, what are we making? Eggs?"

No part of him wanted eggs. The smell in the kitchen was eye watering. He imagined it would take days to get it out of the house.

"Yes."

"Just eggs?"

A frown creased on Danny's forehead. "And… some toast?" he offered.

"Sounds good."

Tom opened the cupboard and pulled out a loaf of bread.

"And… do we have bacon?" asked Danny.

There was more to his voice now. It was thicker.

Tom fought to keep his face expressionless. "I'll check." he stuck his head in the fridge again. "Yep."

"Get the bacon out please."

Never in his life had Tom been excited to have been given an order. Not at work, where that was literally all he was given, and certainly not by his mum. But for Danny—he'd do somersaults on command. That would never change. It didn't matter how angry he was, or what it cost him. If Danny called, he'd always come running. Tom kept a tight rope around his body, forcing his limbs to move as they usually would. No celebrations. He moved slowly and deliberately about the kitchen, allowing himself to be guided by Danny's commands.

Chop this. Fry that.

Yes sir. Yes sir.

At some point, Tom became aware that Mickey had slipped out. Again, he had neglected her. But he couldn't feel bad about it. This was a moment he had been waiting for since— he couldn't even remember anymore. "Danny, we've made enough for mum as well don't you think?"

"Probably not. I'm pretty hungry."

He was hungry? Georgia's eyes bulged out of her head.

Tom ignored Danny. "Take a seat mum. There's plenty."

Tom had done everything he could to fill the kitchen with words, talking to Danny, to Georgia and himself in a non-stop torrent of light, filler conversation, but as they sat down to eat, a silence fell over the three of them.

"I can't remember the last time we all sat here together." Georgia said before Tom could think of anything to fill the silence.

He shot her a look, then eyed Danny from his peripherals. He was shovelling eggs into his mouth at a rate that might have broken the sound barrier. Was Tom hearing him swallow seconds after he'd already done it? He pulled his eyes away from the spectacle, and fixed them on Georgia, confident his brother was paying them no heed.

"Me either. Danny—" he said suddenly, watching his brother lick his plate clean. Not metaphorical. He was actually licking the plate clean. "When was the last time you had a migraine?"

Danny stopped mid lick and then lowered his plate. "I haven't had a migraine since…"

"Before the accident?" Georgia offered.

Danny nodded.

"Well, that's something isn't it?" Georgia looked at Tom. No, she didn't just look at him. She beamed at him. Like a delighted child. In the big scheme of things, it was huge. But they both knew it was a little win. Because Danny didn't have migraines anymore. Just crippling depression and a delusional disorder.

Woo.

But like Georgia said, a little win was *something*. No, it was *everything*. That's all life was, Tom realised. Little wins. You had to take them, had to acknowledge them. Because if Tom waited until life was perfect to be happy, then he'd be waiting until he was dead.

"I think—I think I should go away for a while," Tom said.

Georgia stopped chewing. "That sounds very Bilbo Baggins-esque."

Tom rolled his eyes. "I'm not running away, nothing like that, but I think it would be good for me. For all of us. I'll travel. Clear my head."

"You're restless."

He nodded. "I am. My head... it's all over the place."

"You'd miss us."

"I know. And I think that's why I should go. I'm never going to appreciate what I have until I've properly missed it."

She nodded slowly. "Sounds almost masochistic."

"It is. But it'll bury me, if I don't."

She looked at him for a long time. "Sounds like a plan," she finally said.

"But if I come back, and I find out that Cliff has moved in, and he's claimed the couch as his own... I won't be happy."

She laughed. "Yessir."

Tom nodded slowly and fixed his eyes on his plate. "Speaking of masochistic, I was wondering if I could have the email address? The one you've been using to talk to Dad?"

Georgia looked at him like he was running a high fever.

He cleared his throat. "I don't really want to, but I think I should make sure he's okay. And to make sure he knows that we still love him." he looked at Georgia and knew his eyes looked ridiculously child-like. "Because I do. I know I still do. And Dan—"

Danny looked up at him, almost as if he were surprised they knew he was at the table.

"Love you, Tom." he said quickly, getting in first.

Always the overachiever. He was still putting Tom to shame. Still showing up his big brother. Tom was okay with that.

He'd always been okay with that.

Acknowledgments

When you've been writing a book for more than a decade, there ends up being a lot of people who have shaped the story in some way.

Firstly, thank you to my friends for letting me borrow some of our stories— those little moments were always the ones that meant the most to me.

To my dear friend Trelawney who diligently completed my final line edit. You have no idea how grateful I am that you caught all those stupid mistakes before I sent the book to print.

My sister-in-law Kirsty, your ability to see the essence of a story is unparalleled. Your input made Somewhere In Between a more engaging and complex story. I'm so excited to have you be the first to read my fantasy novel!

A big thank you to the bookstagram community and my ARC readers, especially those that have shared this story. I have always found the community to be such a safe and supportive place and for that I am eternally grateful.

To my very first beta reader, Christina Yother, who was so kind and gentle with her feedback. It filled me with a confidence that I still carry.

To Luke, who carved a path for me in the self publishing world. Without your guidance I'm sure I would have shed many tears of frustration (what is a whole sale discount, I still don't really know).

And finally, to my pup Gem. She was my emotional crutch and my writing buddy, whether she knew it or not.

CPSIA information can be obtained
at www.ICGtesting.com
Printed in the USA
LVHW110842230822
726590LV00006B/239

9 780645 513707